"Exactly what is it you want?"

"I want your help."

"Doing what?"

With a shiver, Shanna folded her arms across her chest. "To keep me alive long enough to make Channing pay."

"You want me to protect you from him."

"Yes."

He could do that, Rory thought grimly. The U.S. Army had spent a fortune training him to do just that—to provide unbreachable security for a person. But he couldn't—*wouldn't*—protect her from himself. "And what do I get," he asked, his voice low and mocking, "in return for my considerable skills?"

"You tell me." Her voice was weak and breathy. "What do you want?"

He slid his fingers down her cheek to her jaw. He faced her, too close but not touching, too dangerous but not threatening. He answered her simply. "You. I want you."

Dear Reader,

When two people fall in love, the world is suddenly new and exciting, and it's that same excitement we bring to you in Silhouette Intimate Moments. These are stories with scope and grandeur. The characters lead lives we all dream of, and everything they do reflects the wonder of being in love.

Longer and more sensuous than most romances, Silhouette Intimate Moments novels take you away from everyday life and let you share the magic of love. Adventure, glamour, drama, even suspense— these are the passwords that let you into a world where love has a power beyond the ordinary, where the best authors in the field today create stories of love and commitment that will stay with you always.

In coming months look for novels by your favorite authors: Nora Roberts, Heather Graham Pozzessere, Emilie Richards and Kathleen Eagle, to name just a few. And whenever you buy books, look for all the Silhouette Intimate Moments, love stories *for* today's woman *by* today's woman.

Leslie J. Wainger
Senior Editor and Editorial Coordinator

MARILYN PAPPANO

A Dangerous Man

SILHOUETTE·INTIMATE·MOMENTS®

Published by Silhouette Books New York

America's Publisher of Contemporary Romance

SILHOUETTE BOOKS
300 East 42nd St., New York, N.Y. 10017

A DANGEROUS MAN

ISBN: 0-373-07381-X

First Silhouette Books printing May 1991

Printed in the U.S.A.

Books by Marilyn Pappano

Silhouette Intimate Moments

Within Reach #182
The Lights of Home #214
Guilt by Association #233
Cody Daniels' Return #258
Room at the Inn #268
Something of Heaven #294
Somebody's Baby #310
Not Without Honor #338
Safe Haven #363
A Dangerous Man #381

Silhouette Books

Silhouette Christmas Stories 1989
"The Greatest Gift"

MARILYN PAPPANO

has been writing as long as she can remember, just for the fun of it, but a few years ago, she decided to take her lifelong hobby seriously. She was encouraging a friend to write a romance novel and ended up writing one herself. It was accepted, and she plans to continue as an author for a long time. When she's not involved in writing, she enjoys camping, quilting, sewing and, most of all, reading. Not surprisingly, her favorite books are romance novels.

Her husband is in the navy, and in the course of her marriage, she has lived all over the U.S. Currently, she lives in Georgia with her husband and son.

Chapter 1

The sound of her own soft helpless cries woke Shanna Cassidy from a restless sleep. She rolled onto her side to look at the clock—three-seventeen, right on time—then got up, peeling her damp gown over her head as she walked to the window.

The dreams came about the same time most nights, when she was deeply asleep, all her defenses relaxed. That made them even more frightening, more draining, she thought, parting the sheer curtain with one hand, because they were so unexpected.

The street below was quiet. Other than the scorched marks left on the pavement from the intense heat of the fire and the blackened grass near the curb, there was no sign of the explosion that had happened there a week ago. No sign that her father had died there when his truck went up in flames. If she closed her eyes, though, she could still picture the scene—the bright morning sun, the chill in the spring air, the tangy smoke from a neighbor's chimney, the birds chirping in the trees.

Then the bomb. She had just come out of the house, almost ready for work, wearing her suit without the jacket and fluffy slippers on her feet. She'd kissed her father goodbye only moments earlier, then had followed him outside, calling his name; then her calls had turned to screams as the truck exploded, pieces of metal ripped apart and flying through the air, glass shattering, hot smoky flames engulfing the truck. The stench of burning gasoline and rubber had filled the air, along with the screams. *Her* screams.

She shivered in the coolness of the bedroom, let the curtain fall back and turned away. In the dim light she could make out the furnishings in the room—the big bed she'd slept in since she was a child, the rocker where her mother had read bedtime stories to her, the glass box on the dresser that held her most treasured gifts from her father: diamond earrings to mark her graduation from high school, a matching bracelet for college graduation and a diamond pendant to celebrate her graduation from law school. He had been so pleased that she had chosen to follow in his footsteps and become a lawyer. He had often told her that when he settled the Channing case, he would resign from his position as district attorney and they could go into practice together. Cassidy and Daughter, she had replied with a laugh, and he had gently corrected her. No, Cassidy and Father. Now it would never happen.

She blinked back the tears that burned her eyes and made her way to the closet, pulling a heavy terry-cloth robe from a hook on the back of the door. She wrapped it around her, tied the belt tightly and left the bedroom.

The house was so quiet. For the first few days after the explosion, her family had returned home—her mother from Dallas, her brother Jody from Austin, their younger brother Alex from Oklahoma City. They had stayed for the funeral, had shared their grief and offered each other support, then they had returned to their homes, leaving Shanna alone in the house she had shared with their father. Alone with her sorrow.

She went down the stairs, pausing in front of the door on the landing. The room was her father's office, its walls lined floor to ceiling with bookshelves, the shelves filled with law books. Since the nearest law library was hours away, Joseph Cassidy had stocked his own personal library well, and he'd given Shanna free access. She hadn't been in there since his death.

Continuing down the stairs, she went into the kitchen, looking for the bottle of expensive Scotch a grateful client had once given her. For months it had been uncapped only when her father wanted a drink to help him relax from a hard week's work, but the past few nights, she'd been helping herself. It made sleep easier after the nightmares.

Tomorrow she would go back to work for the first time since the explosion, but not until she'd cleaned out her father's office in the courthouse. She wanted to sort through his papers, wanted to find everything he'd gathered on the Channing investigation.

Grimly she filled her glass from the bottle, emptied it and filled it again. Tomorrow she would find out why Lawrence Channing had murdered her father.

Sandy Spring was a small town that had flourished in the barrenness of West Texas. It had been settled a hundred years ago by pioneers of the sturdiest stock, Shanna's family among them. They had carved a town out of the desert, and they had prospered. It was a pleasant little town, a good place to raise your children, an oasis of comfortable life thriving in a harsh environment.

At least, it *had* been.

Shanna sat behind the cluttered desk in her office, staring sightlessly across the room. She had spent the morning in her father's office two blocks away, sorting through his desk and the file cabinets, packing personal items, leaving official documents for the man who would take his place. For Lawrence Channing's man.

She shuddered. That made Channing's power complete. He owned the sheriff and the deputies, the town council, the judge. Now he owned the district attorney, too.

She had known that her father was investigating Channing; he'd made no secret of it to her or anyone else in town. He'd grown tired of the two sets of standards that were applied to the people of Sandy Spring—the law as written for the average citizen, and the looser, look-the-other-way attitude for Channing and his people. She had known that Bert Webster, one of the only two other lawyers in town, earned an impressive living working strictly for Channing. She had known that most people in town were suspicious of Channing's activities and wary of the man himself.

She had even known Channing was willing to kill to protect his business. But God help her, she hadn't expected him to kill her father. She had foolishly, naively thought Joseph would somehow be safe from Channing's power. She had thought the law, God and right would protect him. But she had been wrong. Tragically wrong.

Leaning back, she raised her hands to her head, massaging her temples. She had a headache—she usually did these days. It came from the restless nights, she told herself, not from the nearly-full fifth of Scotch she'd drunk over the past few days. She just needed time to deal with her father's death and with the dreams.

There was a tap at the door, then her secretary stepped inside. "Are you okay?" Susan asked softly, bringing a cup of coffee to the desk and clearing a place for it. As soon as she set it down, she pulled an aspirin bottle from her pocket and laid it beside the coffee.

Shanna smiled wanly and reached for the ceramic mug and the bottle. "Thanks, Susan." She swallowed two tablets, then settled back again.

"Did you get Joseph's office cleaned out?"

Shanna nodded.

"Tough, wasn't it?" Susan sat on the arm of the chair across the desk and drew a handful of small pink papers from another pocket. "You got these calls while you were out the past week. Most of them are about your father. Also, Janet Rosenthal rescheduled her appointment for next week, and Greg Black canceled his; he and Trudy are going to try the marriage again."

Shanna nodded, although she wasn't really paying attention. Susan noticed and stood up, smiling uneasily. "I'll take care of things, okay?"

Susan's departure barely registered in Shanna's mind. She swiveled her chair around and stared down at the small box she'd brought with her from Joseph's office. It held plaques for awards he'd received, his college and law school degrees, photographs of his family and a few files marked Personal. She had already thumbed through those. They contained letters, a few newspaper clippings, a belated birthday card—nothing that could help her.

The box also held his appointment calendar. Leaning forward, she fished it out and for a long moment simply held it. It was small, bound in leather, and engraved in gold across the front was his name. It had been a Christmas present from her mother, a tradition that Judith had begun with his graduation from law school and one that had continued even after their divorce. Shanna had an identical one in her right-hand drawer.

When she opened it and saw her father's familiar, cramped handwriting that filled the pages, tears burned her eyes. It was so hard to believe he was dead, to accept that she would never see him again, would never ask for his advice or receive his help or feel his love again.

Blinking back the tears, she turned to the week beginning February twenty-fifth. He'd had a full schedule planned—interviews with defendants and witnesses, an appointment in his office with an attorney from Odessa, jury selection for an armed robbery trial that had now been postponed indefinitely. Every hour of every day contained a memorandum about one meeting or another except that first day. Monday afternoon. The entire afternoon had been left free and was marked with only one notation.

See Rory Hawkes about L.C.

She stared at the name, reading it again and again. Rory Hawkes was the last person she'd expected to find listed in her father's appointment book. As far as she knew, Joseph hadn't seen him in years, and he'd spoken of him only a few times, his remarks never complimentary. Yet he had set aside an entire afternoon from his busy schedule to meet with Rory about Lawrence Channing. Why?

She shifted in her chair, trying to ease the discomfort curling through her, trying to ignore the flush of guilt that had crept across her face. She could never think of Rory without remembering the last time she'd been with him, the last words she'd spoken to him. There were very few things in her past that shamed her, but after more than twenty years, Rory Hawkes—and her treatment of him—was one of them.

She forced the memory of the boy to the back of her mind and concentrated on what she knew about the man. Older than her by three years, he was the only son of Mary Kay and Joe Hawkes. Mary Kay had worked for years as Grandmother Cassidy's housekeeper, but Joe—"crazy Joe," everyone had called him—had never held a job, making the Hawkes family the poorest of the poor in a town where money counted for everything. With money you had power, respect, acceptance. Without it you were nothing.

After an adolescence filled with rejection and derision and marked, not surprisingly, by numerous arrests that her father had prosecuted, Rory had left town to join the Army when he was barely eighteen. Shanna assumed that he had come back for his mother's funeral some ten years ago and again for his father's a few years later, but she hadn't seen nor heard anything about him until he'd returned once more nearly two months ago.

He'd gotten out of the Army—retired, some people said; booted out, others claimed—and had holed up in the house five miles out of town that his mother's parents had abandoned after her death. Aside from trips to get his mail and to buy groceries, no one in town ever saw him. They preferred it that way, and so, it seemed, did he.

To say he was unsociable was a mastery of understatement. He was a loner, a misfit and, according to rumor, probably more than a little unbalanced. Some said that he was wilder than ever—quite a feat, Shanna thought grimly, for someone who had always been the wildest of the wild kids in Sandy Spring. Still others said bluntly that he was as crazy as his old man, who had drifted through life hopelessly lost in a world of his own creation.

There was only one thing that everyone in Sandy Spring agreed on: Rory Hawkes was a dangerous man. When the news that he was back in town had reached her father, Joseph had done some checking into the more than twenty years he'd spent away, and he hadn't liked what he'd found. Rory Hawkes, he'd warned Shanna, was the coldest, meanest and deadliest man she was likely ever to meet. More recently he'd told her that, more than anyone else in town, Rory could deal with a man like Lawrence Channing.

Had Joseph gone to him for help? she wondered, tapping one rounded fingernail against the entry in the calendar. Twenty-one years ago he'd been convinced of Rory's absolute worthlessness. He had been unswerving in his belief back then that Rory was as bad as his father was crazy and that each time they met in court was simply one more step on the way to a life in prison.

But time had proven him wrong. Rory hadn't gone to prison. And Joseph had been frustrated by his inability to tie any of the crimes he knew Channing was responsible for to the man himself. He had been concerned by the sudden unwillingness of his witnesses to talk to him anymore. He had been frightened. And he had apparently believed that Rory could help.

Yes, she admitted, to save his town, to restore peace and security to its residents, he would have asked Rory Hawkes for help. And what had Rory's response been? Vindication that a man he must dislike intensely had come to him asking favors? Anger, after eighteen years of shabby living and shabbier treatment in Sandy Spring, that he was expected to solve their problems for them? Bitterness that, after all those years when the acceptance so important and necessary to teenagers had been denied him, now he was wanted, needed?

She would find out when she went to see him.

For a long moment, she sat motionless as the appointment book slid unnoticed from her fingers and landed on its side in the box at her feet. Go see Rory Hawkes? Was that what she was planning? She gave a disbelieving shake of her head. If remembering him was difficult, how much worse would seeing him be? And what if the rumors were true? What if he *was* as dangerous as her father had claimed?

But life was full of danger. Sandy Spring was filled with danger—hadn't Joseph's death proven that? And if she was going to retrace her father's footsteps, if she was going to find the evidence he'd had against Lawrence Channing and see that he was punished for his crimes, she was going to have to deal with the danger—starting with Rory Hawkes. Joseph had refused to discuss his investigation with her—hadn't wanted her involved—but if he'd asked Rory for help, he would have had to have given him details, facts, proof. Somehow she had to convince him to share it with her. That was all she wanted: information. Answers. A place to start.

She knew even as she reached for the phone that Rory wouldn't have a telephone—anyone who chose to isolate himself as completely as he did would have little use for it—and the directory assistance operator confirmed it for her. Determinedly she got her purse from the bottom desk drawer, dropped it in with her father's belongings, picked up the box and left the office.

Susan looked up from her computer. "Going out?"

"For a while, Susan. I—I need to take care of some things." She knew her secretary would assume that she was going home, that she wasn't quite recovered enough from her father's death to return to work, and she didn't set her straight. If she told her that she was going to see Rory Hawkes, Susan would be upset, would believe that Shanna's grief had robbed her of common sense and would do her best to talk her out of it. "I'll probably be back in a couple of hours, but if it takes longer, don't worry."

"Are you okay, Shanna?" the secretary asked for the second time.

"I'm fine." She smiled to reassure her, but knew the gesture simply looked sad. "Turn on the answering machine and go to lunch whenever you want. I'll see you later." Before the secretary could say anything else, Shanna left the small office, stepping outside into the bright spring day.

She got into her car, setting the box on the floor in back, and for a moment just sat there, hands trembling, unable to fit the key into the ignition. The sheriff had told her that the bomb in her father's truck had been wired to either the ignition or the brake pedal; either way, the electrical contact had triggered the explosion. This morning had been the first time she'd driven since then, and she almost hadn't found the courage. She was still afraid now as she slid the key into the slot and turned it.

The engine roared to life, but she didn't relax until she'd placed her foot on the brake, activating the brake lights. *Then* she gave a sigh of relief.

The house where Mary Kay Hawkes had grown up was five miles north of town. The first three miles were on a paved county road and passed more quickly than Shanna would have liked. The remaining two were dirt, rutted by the occasional hard rains and baked by the sun. She maneuvered her car carefully over the bumps, trying to straddle the deepest ruts, wincing each time the bottom of the car scraped over rock-hard dirt. Briefly she wished she had her father's truck—

Grimly she pressed her lips together, gripped the steering wheel tighter and concentrated on the road. When it ended at a makeshift gate of barbed wire and wooden posts, she got out of the car—still feeling the jolting of the road in her legs—opened the gate, drove through, stopped again and closed it behind her.

The house was another half mile from the gate, with only a faint trail visible on the sun-baked ground. When she reached it, she shut off the engine and sat there for a moment, looking for any sign of life.

The house was shabby. If it had ever been painted, it didn't show now. The boards were weathered to a smoky gray, and the porch sagged in the middle, where two stacks of concrete blocks now supported it. The screens over the windows were nailed directly to the wall and were badly rusted and gapped wide in places. But, as dilapidated as the house was, it was a vast improvement, Shanna admitted, over the tiny place in town that the Hawkes family had called home.

With a shiver of apprehension, she got out, climbed the wobbly steps to the porch and knocked. The door had once been painted white, but only flecks of color remained. It reminded her of an old-fashioned back door, with a large window of four separate panes. One pane was broken, the jagged edges braced within the frame by a piece of cardboard on the other side.

A curtain of dingy yellow covered the window, obscuring the room behind it. She hesitated, then knocked again. She wiped her damp palms on her skirt, adjusted her jacket, combed her fingers through her hair. She needed every ounce of professionalism she could dredge up to get her through this meeting. While Rory wouldn't be happy to see anyone from town on his front porch, she was afraid he would be even less happy to see *her* there.

After her third knock, she waited only a moment, then left the porch and walked around the house. In back was a grassless yard, a chicken coop that had finally collapsed, a shed in similar condition and a barn that didn't look much better. Pieces of long-discarded farm equipment, rusty and ancient, were scattered as if dropped from the sky. There were two vehicles parked near the barn—a pickup with no wheels and a car, a '56 Chevy, blue and white, windows broken out, tires flat and rotting, trunk rusted in the open position.

Shanna looked around, her hands in her pockets. There was no sign of Rory Hawkes or the black truck he drove now. Had he coincidentally picked today for one of his rare treks off the property and into civilization?

She was starting to turn away when a noise in the barn caught her attention. It could have been the light wind, she told herself, or even rodents. Still, she made her way to the barn to check. The big double doors stood open a few feet, wide enough for her to slip inside. She was just being nosy, she assured herself, not breaking in. After all, the door was open, and she wasn't going to disturb anything.

She stopped just inside the doorway, letting her eyes adjust to the darkness. It was cooler inside, musty smelling, dark except for the shafts of sunlight seeping through the cracks in the roof and the ill-fitting boards of the walls and the door behind her.

She focused on the truck parked in the center of the space at the same time she felt the gun against her temple. She froze, completely motionless, afraid to look, to shift her eyes, to even breathe. She knew it was Rory Hawkes holding the gun, but that knowledge didn't reassure her. What if he *was* as crazy as his father had been, even wilder than he'd been as a kid? What if his desire for privacy that kept him out here away from everyone else had become an obsession that he would protect at all costs?

"What do you want?"

The voice that came from the darkness behind her was as rusty and unused as the machinery outside. It was a low, vicious growl that would have made her shiver if she hadn't been too terrified to move. "I—I want to talk to you."

There was a moment of long tense silence; then the gun was pulled back, the safety clicked on. "I don't want to talk. Get the hell off my property."

She turned then, wanting to put a face with the angry voice, to plead for just a few minutes of his time, but no one was there. Frantically she looked around, searching the cluttered room for some sign of him. She'd heard nothing, seen nothing, and now he was gone. *How?*

"Wait, please . . . I need to talk to you."

As her words faded, she stood still, holding her breath, listening so hard that she heard echoes of sounds that weren't there, then a sound that was—the scratch of a match on a rough surface. She smelled the sulfur, then tobacco, at the same time she saw the flame, shadowed by cupped hands, in the far corner.

He was seated on an old worktable built into the wall, a cigarette resting between two fingers, its tip glowing in the dark. She approached him cautiously, picking her way around piles of junk. Finally she stopped, less than a dozen feet away, clasped her hands together, breathed deeply and opened her mouth.

Before any words made it out, he was speaking again. "Whatever you want, the answer is no."

"How can you turn me down before you hear what I have to say?" she protested.

"Because I don't care what you have to say. The answer is still no."

She took a step closer. She could see from here that he wore jeans, boots and nothing else, but his face was in shadow, obscuring his expression. "Listen—" Breaking off, she watched the glowing cigarette move to his mouth, smelled his smoky exhalation, then forced herself to say his name, to begin again. "Rory, I just want to ask you a few questions."

The cigarette moved again to his mouth, then down. When he said nothing, she moved a step closer and continued. "Do you remember me? I'm Shanna Cassidy, and I want—"

"Of course I remember you," he said derisively. "That's the only reason I didn't blow your brains out at the door." The table creaked as he got to his feet. He tossed the cigarette to the dirt floor in a shower of tiny sparks, then ground it out and came closer, so close that she had to tilt her head back to see his face. "Now get the hell off my property before I remove you."

He thought he had her intimidated, Shanna thought, with his gun, his hostility, his greater size, his threats, but she wasn't leaving so easily. She had come here to ask him about her father, and she wasn't leaving until she'd done so. "No."

For an instant she could actually feel the anger humming through him before he controlled it, and she panicked. What was she doing? she wondered wildly. She was all alone out here with a man who had only moments ago pulled a gun on her, and now she was defying him? He could easily kill her and never be suspected. No one had known she was coming here. They would never look for her here.

Then she gave herself a mental shake. This was *Rory*, for God's sake. Twenty-one years ago, for a brief time, he'd been her friend. He had given her her first kiss and, in spite of his reputation as a wild kid, as a bad kid, he'd done so gently, with the care he'd always shown her. Even though she had repaid his gentleness with insults and had destroyed his caution with derision, she didn't believe he would hurt her now. He was simply trying to frighten her, and she had too much at stake to be frightened.

Drawing courage from that, she focused in the dim light on the dark face above her. "My father came to see you last week, didn't he?" She tried to sound confident, as if she already knew the answer. He offered no response. "He told you about the problems in town."

Still he said nothing.

"And he asked for your help."

She was still guessing, but his response told her she was right. He took a step back, and she felt his gaze, cold and contemptuous, moving over her. "I'll tell you the same thing I told him: my price is high. More than he—or you—could pay." He stood motionless for a moment, then turned away.

"Let me decide that."

He glanced at her over his shoulder. She had the uncanny feeling that he could see her in the gloom much better than she could see him. Then he looked away from her again.

He wasn't going to answer her. She closed the distance between them and touched her hand to his shoulder. He slid away as if he found her touch distasteful. "Get out of here," he ordered, his voice soft, almost conversational. She knew instinctively—from the tiny little shivers running down her spine and the rapid thud of her heart and the sudden dryness of her mouth—that, like a rattler preparing to strike, he was most dangerous when he was quiet. But still she persisted.

"Rory—" She touched him again, grasping his bent arm just below his elbow, and he reacted swiftly, shoving her away, then using the momentum to pull his arm free. Caught off guard, Shanna stumbled back and fell against a shelf nailed to the wall. It came tumbling down, dropping a rusted collection of nails, nuts and bolts to the floor around her.

By the time she'd regained her balance, he was gone again, and this time she let him go. Now she had a better idea of his response to her father's visit, she thought ruefully as she rubbed her shoulder where it had connected with the shelf. Joseph hadn't found any help here, and neither had she, but it didn't matter. Somehow she would finish what Joseph had started, would find the proof to send Lawrence Channing to prison, and she would do it without Rory Hawkes.

When her legs were steady enough to support her, she wound her way back to the patch of light at the doors. She crossed the backyard, circled around the house to her car and left without a backward glance.

Long after she'd driven through the gate, stopping conscientiously to close it behind her, Rory stood at the single window in the hayloft and watched. When her small blue car disappeared from sight, he finally turned away.

A lifetime ago he would have sold his soul to have Shanna Cassidy approach him, wanting something—anything— from him. But then, he thought with a bitter smile, considering what his attraction to her had cost him, maybe he *had*.

He climbed halfway down the ladder, then jumped the remaining distance to the ground. He switched on the overhead light, then pushed open the double doors that he'd barely closed upon hearing the approaching car. The hood of the truck was raised, and he returned now to the job Shanna had interrupted, but changing the spark plugs wasn't demanding enough to keep his mind occupied.

And naturally when it wandered, it wandered to her.

Shanna Cassidy. She had always been a symbol to him— of all the things he'd wanted to have but couldn't, of all the things he'd wanted to be but wasn't. Their lives had been as different as rich and poor, good and bad, worthy and worthless. She'd been the princess, the only daughter of the district attorney, granddaughter of the town's mayor, niece of the bank president, and he'd been nothing. Nobody. The son of the village idiot. The wild kid who'd been arrested a half dozen times before he was fifteen, who would never amount to anything, who would be dead or in prison before he was twenty.

But they'd been wrong. He'd never gone to prison, had never been arrested again once he'd left Sandy Spring, and he *had* amounted to something. He was a Master Sergeant, United States Army, Retired—the next-to-the-highest rank an enlisted man could achieve. If he'd been willing to stay in longer than the nearly twenty-one years he'd served, there was no doubt he would have made sergeant major, but he'd wanted to get out. He had wanted to come back here, to the place where he'd spent his miserable first eighteen years, and—

And do what? he wondered as he wiped his hands on a worn towel. Drown himself in bitterness and anger? Lock himself away from all human contact and wallow in self-pity?

No, he'd wanted to come here and be left alone. He hadn't wanted to see anyone, deal with anyone. He hadn't wanted to face the world any longer. After years in a job that had required the most of him both physically and mentally, he'd wanted to unwind, to simply relax and enjoy a few weeks, maybe even a few months, of freedom, of no demands, no intensive training, no crises.

And so he had come here, knowing that he would find the solitude he craved, that the good people of Sandy Spring would leave him alone, would want nothing to do with him. He had slept, puttered around the house, worked on his truck and thought about the future—about selling this house and the ten acres that surrounded it, about breaking his last ties with this town, about where he would go, what he would do and how he would live.

And for the first time in his life, for long hours at a time, he had done nothing. He had simply rested his mind and his body.

Then Joseph Cassidy had come to see him, and now Shanna Cassidy. The two people who had influenced so much of his life. The two people who had brought home to him, each in their own way, the hard reality of who and what he was: inferior. Worthless. No good. Those had been Joseph's words, and Shanna's had merely been a variation. *Not good enough.*

He smiled, but it was icy and empty of pleasure. After years of tolerating Joseph's scorn, after enduring the public humiliation Shanna's cruel little game had caused him, it was satisfying to know that finally he *was* worth something to them. At last—in one sense, at least—he was good enough for them.

Her father's visit last week had lasted only a few minutes longer than Shanna's, and Joseph hadn't said much—just that there were problems in town. He had tentatively sounded out Rory about helping him solve them. He had somehow gotten hold of enough of Rory's military records to know that Rory Hawkes had the experience, the skill and the training to go up against anyone in this part of the state—and destroy them.

But Rory had turned him down. He wasn't in the helpgiving business anymore, he'd told him, and as far as he was concerned, Joseph Cassidy and the entire town of Sandy Spring could go straight to hell.

Now Joseph had brought out the big guns: he'd sent Shanna to speak for him—Shanna with her silky black hair and soft brown eyes and low, sweet voice. But his plan wasn't going to work. Rory wasn't young enough, dazzled enough, hungry enough or foolish enough to let himself be enticed into playing Joseph's game.

He slammed the hood shut, wiped the greasy marks his fingers had left, then closed the barn doors. He crossed the barren yard and entered the house through the back door, which led straight into the kitchen. There were no halls or passageways in the house, just four small rooms connected one to the other, with a long narrow bathroom squeezed between the two bedrooms. It had begun as a single room, the walls added later as his great-grandfather who'd built it had been able to afford them.

He had never been inside the house while his grandparents lived there. They had adamantly opposed his mother's marriage to crazy Joe Hawkes, and they had never welcomed him or his son into their house. He could remember sitting on the rickety steps out front, listening to his mother plead with them to see him just once, to acknowledge their only grandson just once, but they had refused. For a time he'd hated them—not because they didn't want him, but

because they'd hurt his mother. So many people had hurt
her, but she'd never lost faith in their inherent goodness. She
had never lost hope.

He grinned bitterly. *He* had never had any to lose.

After washing his hands, he removed the holster clipped
onto the waistband of his jeans in back and laid it and the
gun it held on the table. He had used the pistol many times,
but he'd drawn it in the barn for the sole purpose of frightening Shanna. The moment she'd rounded the corner of the
house, he'd known who she was, had known he would never
hurt her. He had expected her to rush away, terrified, the
moment he pulled the pistol away from her temple, but
she'd stood her ground. She'd been foolish, but he had admired her. He'd never expected courage from a pampered
little girl like her.

Little girl. He smiled faintly. Shanna Cassidy was definitely no little girl. She had fulfilled the promise of beauty
he'd seen in her fifteen-year-old face. The only flaws were
temporary ones—an abrasion across her cheek, a bruise that
darkened the length of her jaw, a laceration, shallow and
healing, on her throat. He wondered what had happened,
the muscles in his jaw tightening in rebellion against the
thought of her hurt.

Picking up the gun, he went into the bathroom, where he
tucked it between two towels on the wall shelf. He tugged off
his boots, stripped off his jeans and briefs, and stepped into
the bathtub, pulling the shower curtain shut with one hand
while turning on the water with the other.

It would be satisfying to offer Joseph Cassidy his help, he
thought as the cool water rushed over him—to name his
price, to exact a payment dear to the man who had cost *him*
dearly. But not money—Cassidy had too much of it to miss
whatever amount he might ask for. And not gratitude—it
was meaningless. Or respect—meaningless, too, after years
of derision.

What could he ask for? What price could crazy Joe
Hawkes's son name that would cost Joseph Cassidy almost

more than he could bear? he wondered, closing his eyes and lifting his face to the spray. And the answer formed in his mind, delicate and beautiful. Shanna. That was what he would want in exchange for helping Joseph.

It was too much. Joseph Cassidy would never barter away his precious daughter, no matter how desperate his situation. He would say no, but Rory would walk away with the satisfaction of knowing that once, just once, the tables had been turned. Just once, the wants and needs of the almighty Cassidys had been thwarted by a Hawkes.

And what if Joseph said yes? What if he was anxious enough, frightened enough, to sacrifice Shanna in order to accomplish his goals?

He smiled bitterly. If Joseph agreed—and Shanna, too—then they would use him, as Cassidys always did, and in the long run he would lose, as Hawkeses always did. But this time they would lose, too. This time Shanna would lose.

Shanna had gone back to the office after her meeting with Rory, but shortly after four, unable to concentrate on work, she'd given up and started home. She was disappointed by Rory's refusal to talk to her, although she knew she shouldn't be. After the way the townspeople had treated him—after the way *she* had treated him—it had been foolish to think that he would cooperate with her. Still, she had hoped. Anything he could have told her about her father might have helped, might have told her where to start in her investigation.

With a weary sigh, she parked her car in the narrow driveway beside the house and shut off the engine, taking care to lock the doors as she got out. Juggling her briefcase and purse, she walked to the back door and wiggled the key into the old lock. It turned with a creak of protest, and she swung the door open, shutting it with her hip once she was inside.

She walked through the small utility room to the kitchen, where she nudged the light switch next to the door with her

elbow. She set her briefcase and handbag on the table, then
started down the darkened hallway to the stairs.

When she reached the living room, she stopped short.
Furniture had been moved, cushions thrown on the floor,
tables overturned, drawers dumped haphazardly. She stared
at the scene for a moment, then slowly shifted her gaze toward the stairs, toward her father's office. Dreading what
she would find, she rushed up the short flight of stairs and
pushed the door open.

Even in the dim light coming through the window, she
could see that this room had received the same treatment.
All of her father's precious law books had been taken from
the shelves, searched and dropped to the floor, and his desk
was piled high with the contents of its drawers. The files
from the two oak cabinets behind the desk were also on the
floor, thousands of pages carelessly discarded.

A quick tour of the house revealed that all the rooms had
been searched. Even the kitchen, she saw when she returned, had been given a quick examination; there just
weren't as many hiding places as in the other rooms, so they
hadn't made such an effort there.

Numbly she went to the phone on the wall, dialing the
number for the sheriff's office from memory. Reporting the
break-in wasn't going to accomplish much, not when Lawrence Channing was involved, but she had to go through the
motions.

A half hour later a deputy arrived to take her report, followed a few minutes later by Sheriff Hart himself and two
more deputies. They made a cursory inspection, not bothering to dust for fingerprints, to find out where the intruder had gained entry or to question her neighbors. When
she suggested that they do these things, Hart laughed, patted her arm and condescendingly advised that she leave the
police work to them.

Swearing below her breath, she locked the door behind
them, then went upstairs to change from her business suit
into sweatpants and a T-shirt. She pulled her hair out of the

way into a ponytail, then set about restoring order, first to the least affected rooms, the dining room and the kitchen.

After that, she took a break and put a frozen dinner in the microwave, ate it at the cramped kitchen table and drank a glass of tea. She was thinking morosely about the mess that waited her in the living room and longingly about the bottle of Scotch in the cabinet that would make dealing with this easier when she suddenly realized that she wasn't alone. Wondering fearfully if the culprits had returned, if she was in danger here, she slowly turned toward the doorway between the kitchen and the utility room and the dark, lean figure standing there.

Rory Hawkes. She hadn't gotten a clear look at him this morning in his barn, but she recognized him, recognized the air of danger about him. Oddly it made her feel safer. Rising to her feet, she laid her silverware on the kitchen counter and dropped the plastic tray in the wastebasket, then turned to him. "If you'd knocked, I would have let you in."

"I did knock." His gaze swept around the room, taking note of the single microwave tray she'd just thrown away, the lone fork and spoon on the counter, the one glass of tea. Either Cassidy wasn't home or he and his daughter were eating separately these days.

Shanna shifted from one bare foot to the other, trying to summon her experienced-attorney persona. It wasn't easy in these clothes, in this setting, with this man. "Are you ready to talk?"

His eyes came back to her. They were blue, cool and mysterious and revealing nothing of his thoughts or feelings. "Tell your father I have an offer for him."

Tell her father— She swallowed hard. He didn't know about Joseph's death. She had just assumed, because everyone in town knew every detail, that he would know, too, but of course she'd been wrong. Unless he'd made a trip in to town the last few days, how could he know what had happened last week?

She sat down rather hard in the chair behind her and linked her fingers together to stop them from trembling. But nothing could stop the quaver in her voice. "You'll have to deal with me."

"I'll make the arrangements with him." He trusted Shanna to do only one thing: lie. She would promise everything—and deliver nothing. But if her father made the deal, if he agreed to Rory's outrageous demand, she would follow through. Everything she'd done in her life—from making straight A's to being Homecoming Queen to dating only the right boys to attending the same college and choosing the same career—had all been done for her dear father. This would be no different. "Get him."

"I can't."

With a grim shake of his head, he turned to leave. Quickly Shanna jumped to her feet and started toward him. "Please, Rory—don't go. My father..." She squeezed her eyes shut, swallowed, then looked at him again. "My father is dead. He was killed last week."

He stared at her for a long time, the expression in his eyes briefly open and unguarded. He was surprised, she saw. Not sorry—just surprised. Then, as she watched, the openness disappeared, and the dark glassy look was back. "When did it happen?"

"Two days after he went to see you."

"Where?"

"Out front."

"In front of the house?"

Shanna led the way to the living room, using the hall light to make her way across the chaos in the room to the big picture window. She pushed one half of the drapes back and gestured to the street outside. "There."

Rory glanced around the room, his expression growing hard, then stopped at the window directly behind her. He could smell her cologne and shampoo as he looked over her shoulder to the street. In the dim light of the street lamp, he could see the all-too-familiar pattern of scorching, blackest near the curb and radiating out to include most of the width of the street and a large portion of the Cassidy yard.

For a moment he had difficulty breathing. He'd thought he had left this scene behind, had thought he would never have to see it again. He'd spent half his lifetime dealing with death and violence and brutality, and he had thought he was free of it now.

But he'd been wrong.

"A bomb." He didn't realize he had spoken aloud until she looked over her shoulder at him. He could see from the thoughtful look in her soft brown eyes that she was wondering how he could tell by simply looking at the marks left behind what had caused them, but he had no desire to tell her.

He turned away and surveyed the damage in the room once more. "When did this happen?"

"Sometime today."

"Was anything stolen?"

"I don't know. I don't think so."

"Did you call the sheriff?"

"Yes. He and his men spent about five minutes here. When I suggested that they do more than simply look, he patted me on the head like I was a silly little girl," she snidely exaggerated, "and told me to mind my own business."

He looked at her for a long moment, then bent to pick up a broken glass figurine. It had once been a ballerina, delicate and graceful. He knew Shanna, like all little princesses, had studied ballet. He could remember the big fuss her grandmother had made over every recital, the formal dinners and parties that had usually required his mother to work long past quitting time without extra pay. He could remember waiting at the older Mrs. Cassidy's house for his mother to get off work and watching Shanna play after dance class, still wearing the pink leotard and white tights that clung tightly to her developing young girl's body. He could remember, several years later, catching her, unsteady and laughing, after a series of dizzying twirls had spun her right into his arms. He had laughed, too, and then they had both grown serious, and he had kissed her....

Angrily he brushed the memory away. It had all been part of her game. She had amused herself at his expense—had made him fall for her, then had openly, publicly made a fool of him. She had made him hate her. By the time he left here tonight, the situation would be reversed. *She* would hate *him*.

He set a table straight and laid what was left of the dancer on it, then set the lamp in place and clicked it on. In its bright, shadeless light, the room looked even worse. "You think this has something to do with your father's death."

It wasn't a question, just a cool, emotionless statement of fact, but she nodded anyway, then sank onto the sofa without even noticing the missing cushions. "What did he tell you when he came to see you?"

Rory gestured for her to get up, and he replaced the seat cushions on the couch and the two armchairs. She sat back down, but he continued to prowl around the room, occasionally picking up some item, studying it, then setting it down again on the nearest surface.

Had he always been so intense? Shanna wondered, rubbing the ache in her temples as she watched him. It wasn't just that he was in constant motion; after their brief encounter in the barn this morning, she knew the tension was there even when he wasn't moving a muscle. It radiated from inside him, from some deep angry place where she suspected he stored the bitterness, the cynicism, the hatred that darkened his eyes and colored his voice and shadowed his face.

At last he answered the question she'd nearly forgotten asking. "He said there was trouble in town." He picked up a photograph, its frame bent, the glass smashed. He easily identified Joseph and Shanna. He knew the others were Joseph's ex-wife and their two sons, but he didn't care. The rest of Shanna's family had never mattered to him.

"Did he give you any details?"

"No, and I didn't ask."

"Because he was Joseph Cassidy?"

He glanced back at her. "Because I don't give a damn about this town or the people in it."

The flat, empty tone of his voice was more convincing than anger could have been. Even though his response made sense—after all, no one in Sandy Spring besides his parents had ever given a damn about him, so why should he care now what happened to the town? She dropped her gaze to her clenched hands to hide her disappointment.

He set another table up and laid the photograph face-down on it. "What did your father have that was worth dying for?"

His blunt question made her shudder. "I don't know."

He gave her a long, judging look over his shoulder that clearly said he didn't believe her.

"Honestly, I don't know. Dad didn't tell me anything. He didn't want me involved."

That he believed. Joseph Cassidy had always shielded his little princess from the seamier aspects of life—had, on at least one occasion, misused his authority to protect her from *him*. If, in fact, something bad was going on in town, it was in character for him to keep it hidden from her, to keep it from touching her. But this time he hadn't succeeded. This time it had damn sure touched her when that bomb had exploded out front.

He stopped in front of the window again, but this time his attention was on the window itself, not the scene outside. He drew his finger over the putty that held the glass in place. It had been applied recently, meaning the concussion from the blast had shattered the original window. Then he looked back at Shanna, still sitting on the couch. Her back was to him, but he could recall the injuries she'd suffered simply by closing his eyes—the abrasion, the bruise, the laceration. She'd been nearby when the bomb had detonated—not too close, or she would be as dead as her father, but close enough to feel the blast. It had probably knocked her down, explaining the abrasion and the bruise, and shattering glass could have caused the laceration.

He completed his circle around the room, coming to stand a few feet in front of her. "Who killed your father?"

"Lawrence Channing."

"Who is he?"

"A..." She searched for the right word, but each one she tried seemed so inadequate. "A businessman," she said at last. "He's involved in everything legal and practically everything illegal. He owns half the county—including the mayor, the council, the sheriff..."

"And the new district attorney."

She nodded.

"Do you have proof?"

"No. But I think my father did. I think that's why Channing killed him—because my dad was getting too close."

His only response was a noncommittal shrug as he looked around the room at the malicious destruction once more. Joseph Cassidy's death meant that the problems in Sandy Spring went beyond serious. It meant that Lawrence Channing, whoever he was, would go to any lengths to protect himself and his business. This break-in meant that Channing didn't believe the threat to him had died with Cassidy. And *that* meant—

"You're not going to take the sheriff's advice, are you?" he asked, and he knew her answer before she gave it: no, she wouldn't mind her own business. She wouldn't forget that her father had been murdered. She wouldn't let them get away with it.

And *that* meant she was in danger.

He shouldn't care. It shouldn't make one bit of difference to him if she got blown to bits in the next explosion or if today's intruder returned at night and murdered her in her bed or if a random shooting just happened to claim her as victim.

But he did care.

He turned away from her, bending to pick up a single coral rose from the hearth where the crystal vase that had held it lay shattered. The outer petals were soft and limp, and even as he cradled it in his palm, one fell off and floated to the floor, vivid against the tan carpet.

Shanna watched him, her gaze locked on his hand and the gentle way he held the flower. "Look, I don't know what my father knew about you that made him think you could help him stop Channing. I don't know what evidence he had gathered against Channing, or where it is now or if they destroyed it when they blew up his truck or if they found it when they searched the house. All I know is I can't forget it. I just can't let it go."

"If Lawrence Channing is what you say he is, he'll kill you, too." He closed his hand, the one with the flower, into a fist and crushed the delicate petals, then let them fall.

"You said when you came here that you had an offer for my father. What kind of offer?"

His smile was cool. "An expensive one."

"For your help?" She didn't need to see his nod. "Exactly what is it you can do?"

He turned the question back on her. "Exactly what is it you want?"

She considered that for a moment. "Justice."

"Justice? Not revenge?"

"I want Channing to pay for what he did."

"You want me to kill him."

She was shocked—not so much by what he'd said as the way he'd said it, as if killing were something that came easily to him. Something routine. Something normal. "Of course not! I want him to spend the rest of his life in prison for what he's done to my father and to countless others in this town!" She stood up and paced to the doorway and back again. "I want your help."

"Doing what?"

With a shiver, Shanna hugged her arms across her chest. "I don't know. To do whatever my father would have asked

you to do. To make sure this doesn't happen again. To keep
me alive long enough to make Channing pay.''

"You want me to protect you from him.''

"Yes.''

He could do that, Rory thought grimly. The U.S. Army
had spent a fortune in taxpayer money training him to do
just that—to take control of a situation, to provide unbreachable security for a person or a place, to kill quietly
and efficiently to protect that person or place. It was only
fair to put those skills to work for someone who had helped
pay for them.

But he couldn't—*wouldn't*—protect her from himself.

He closed the distance between them, raised his hand and
touched her cheek. It was a tentative gesture, a test, and with
her sudden flinch, she failed. In spite of her plea for help,
she was afraid of him—afraid of what he would ask for,
afraid of what he would do, most of all afraid of what he
would take from her.

Deliberately he caressed her cheek, making his touch as
tender as he knew how. He watched her lips part, saw her
shiver, felt her skin grow warm. She felt like… He could say
satin or silk or velvet, but it wouldn't be true, because he'd
never touched satin or silk or velvet. She felt as soft as old
faded denim. As soft as lamb's wool.

"And what do I get,'' he asked, his voice low and mocking, "in return for the use of my considerable skills?''

"You tell me.'' Her voice was weak and breathy. "What
do you want in exchange for helping me?''

He slid his fingers down her cheek to her jaw, followed the
bruise there to the center of her chin, then pulled away. He
faced her, too close but not touching, too dangerous but not
threatening. Leaning closer, face-to-face, noses almost
touching, close enough to feel the warmth of her breath, he
answered her simply.

"You. I want you.''

Chapter 2

Shanna's first foolish thought was that she hadn't heard him correctly. What could Rory Hawkes possibly want with *her?* Then she heard the echo of their earlier conversation in her mind: justice. Revenge. Growing up in Sandy Spring had given him reason to dislike practically everyone in town, but he had particularly good reasons to hate the Cassidys— her grandmother who had treated Mary Kay Hawkes not as a person, but merely a servant, with no respect, no regard for her feelings; her father who had prosecuted Rory in court, who could have taken steps to help the troubled boy but instead had been intent on seeing him in prison for his youthful crimes; and Shanna herself. She winced at the memory of what *she* had done to deserve his hatred.

"You'll help me," she said, trying to sound as unemotional as he had, "and in return, I . . . sleep with you." She wanted to be sure of what he was asking, wanted to know that he wouldn't expect anything more.

His agreement was no more than a blink of long lashes.

"Once? Twice? Regularly? For how long?" She swallowed hard upon hearing her own words. Dear God, was she really considering having an affair with Rory Hawkes?

"Whenever. For as long as I'm working with you."

And when their work ended, he would have no further use for her. Yes, she thought bleakly, justice and revenge were his motives. After years of being looked down on by the Cassidys, after being told coldly, brutally, that he wasn't good enough for the only daughter of Joseph Cassidy, now he had the chance for revenge. Now he could have an affair with that same daughter, could let everyone in town know that crazy Joe Hawkes's boy was sleeping with Joseph Cassidy's daughter. And when it was all over, when Channing had been punished, he could reject her as openly, as shamefully, as she had once rejected him.

And she would let him do it, no matter how difficult or painful it was, because it couldn't be worse than the horror of the scene she'd witnessed a week ago. It couldn't be worse than the dreams that haunted her night after night. It couldn't be worse than letting Lawrence Channing win.

"All right."

Rory felt no pleasure, no satisfaction. He knew what that answer, whispered and bleak, had cost her—almost as much as asking had cost him. He was simply better at keeping the pain, the sorrow and the shame out of his eyes, his face and his voice. He fought the urge to tell her never mind, he would help her for free, would protect her because he couldn't bear to let anything happen to her. After all, regardless of his feelings for her now, she had been his dream when he was young enough and foolish enough to believe in dreams.

But he kept the words inside, burying them under years of rejection, under the crippling feelings of worthlessness that she and her family and others like them had nurtured and fed. With the look on his face darker and steelier than ever, he turned his attention to more important matters. "I'll move in here—"

"Here?" she echoed in dismay. "You can't—"

He silenced her protest with a look. "I can't protect you if I'm not with you. Tomorrow I'll get my things from the house. Everyone will assume that we've been having an affair, that we kept it secret because of your father's feelings toward me. Let them believe it."

Shanna nodded numbly.

"Also tomorrow I'll change the locks on all the doors. It took me less than two minutes to pick the lock on your back door."

"Do you make a habit of that?" It was a meaningless question, the only kind, he suspected, that she was capable of coming up with right now. She looked and sounded stunned, as if she'd suffered too big a blow to absorb all at once.

"I make a habit of being safe." He walked into the hallway, looking for a moment at the front door. Its lock was identical to the one in the back. Cassidy should have known better, he thought derisively. If he hadn't worried about his own safety—and apparently he hadn't—he should at least have been concerned about his daughter's. He should have known that going after Channing would put her in danger if for no other reason than that she lived in this house.

He started up the stairs, then paused to look back at her. She still stood in the middle of the room. "I'll put an alarm on your car tomorrow, too. Don't drive it until I do."

"Why do I need an alarm?"

"If someone touches the car, it will go off."

"Great. So every time someone bumps my car or the kids in the neighborhood get too close while they're playing, an alarm goes off."

"Yeah." He scowled at her. "And if someone tries to wire a bomb to the ignition, an alarm will go off then, too. So warn the parents of the kids in the neighborhood to keep them the hell away from here."

Shanna sank onto the sofa, her face in her hands. Still holding tight to his self-control, Rory took one last look at her, then climbed the stairs to the landing.

The door there stood open a few inches. He slowly pushed it wider, then turned on the lights. Joseph's office. There was a wide window in the opposite wall and built-in bookcases practically everywhere else. What little wall space that was bare was papered in dark green to match the drapes at the window and the pillows in the leather easy chairs.

The disorder in the living room was repeated here. Dozens of books had been thrown to the floor, some pages ripped out, spines broken. The cushions of all three chairs had been slashed, the stuffing spilling onto the carpet. The desk drawers had been emptied, then shattered, only the polished oak fronts remaining intact, and the contents of the file cabinets were tossed carelessly over everything. The monitor to the desktop computer lay on its side against one wall, its screen kicked in, and the rest of the system was in similar condition. Even the carpet—some type of Persian rug, he guessed, probably old and valuable—had been pulled up where possible and cut apart where the heavy desk anchored it.

"When was your father's funeral?"

Shanna grimaced at his lean back. She would have sworn her bare feet had made no noise as she'd climbed the stairs, but he had known she was there anyway. Maybe he had a sixth sense—or more likely, she admitted, he was simply so much more in tune with the other five than most people. "Saturday afternoon."

"When did you go back to work?"

"Today."

"Who knew this would be your first day back?"

She leaned against the side door opposite him. "Sandy Spring is still a small town," she reminded him with a weary sigh. "Everyone knows everyone else's business. My secretary, Susan, knew, and everyone I'd had appointments with last week and this week, my friends . . ."

"So anyone who wanted to know could have found out."
She nodded.

He turned from the room and started up the stairs, his steps slowing as he neared the top. There were only bedrooms up here, he knew—the boys' rooms, Joseph's... and Shanna's. He paused in the long hallway, then turned into the room at the front of the house on the left. It was hers.

He wanted to back out, close the door and never go inside again, but he forced himself to walk to the center of the room and look around. The colors were peach and soft green, with an occasional splash of coral and white. The drawers in the dresser and the tall chest had been dumped onto the floor, spilling out bright-colored socks, hose and T-shirts and piles of lingerie—soft pastels, lacy, beribboned and bowed, erotic. He thought of her in the tailored business suit she'd worn this morning and the T-shirt and sweatpants she had on now and wondered if she wore these small, sexy scraps of ribbons and lace underneath them.

He had the right to find out.

The sly, whispered thought sent tension spiraling through him. He had asked for—no, had demanded—that right, and she had granted it. He could call her in here, could pull off the plain cotton shirt and strip the baggy sweatpants down her long legs and see exactly what she was wearing underneath. And whatever it was, he could strip that off, too, and claim his payment in her body. He could take her right here, right now, and tomorrow and every day and every night until their job was done, and she couldn't complain, because that was their agreement: her body for his help.

How desperate she must be, he thought bitterly, that she was willing to prostitute herself—and to that worthless Hawkes kid, no less. He was ashamed that he'd asked such a thing of her—and more ashamed that he wanted it enough to hold her to their agreement, even though it would make her hate him. Even though it would make him hate himself.

But not tonight. He wouldn't do it tonight, or tomorrow or the next day or the next. He wouldn't do it until she wanted it, until she wanted *him*. And if that day never came, as he suspected it wouldn't?

Then he would take her just once to end their arrangement, just once to know the pleasure of her body, just once to fill that empty place in his soul.

He walked to the window that faced the street and pushed the sheer white curtains aside. It was quiet outside, lights glowing in the windows of every house on the opposite side of the street. There was little traffic in this part of town. People who didn't belong here didn't come around—except him. He didn't belong, but he was here, and he was staying.

But not in this room.

He left and crossed the hall to the next bedroom. From the corner of his eye, he saw Shanna standing near the stairs, leaning against the railing there, waiting. He didn't blame her for not wanting to join him in the intimacy of her bedroom or anyone else's.

This room showed fewer signs of the search. Covers had been pulled from the bed and tossed in a heap on the floor, sheets emptied from the bottom of the dresser drawer, extra blankets dragged off the closet shelf, a half dozen trophies inscribed with Alex Cassidy's name tossed carelessly to the floor. The third room, down the hall and beside hers, was the same.

That meant the last room was Joseph's. He hesitated at the closed door, then twisted the knob and went inside, flipping the light switch as he passed it. He found himself in a suite bigger than the house he lived in now. A sitting area filled one large corner, a comfortable-looking sofa and chairs grouped around graceful tables, and the rest of the room was devoted to the bedroom. The wood furniture was mahogany, gleaming and very old and expensive. All the tables, including the nightstands, were topped with marble, and all the fabrics—the sheets, the comforter, the drapes, the skirts on two tables and the upholstery—matched. It was a beautiful room, but it lacked the warmth, the welcome, of Shanna's smaller room.

Welcome? he thought sardonically as he crossed the room to the door opposite the bed. Not for him. She would never welcome him.

The door opened into a dressing room that connected to the private bath and two large closets. One closet held Joseph's clothes; the other was empty but for a few boxes on the shelves. Like Shanna's room, like all the rooms downstairs, these were a mess.

When he came out of the dressing room, he saw her standing in the doorway. Afraid to leave him alone in her precious father's room? he wondered, his cynicism heavy and sharp. "I'll sleep in here," he said—not because he'd never in his life slept in so elegantly decorated a room, and not because he relished the idea of sleeping in Joseph Cassidy's bed while he was seducing Joseph Cassidy's daughter, but simply because he expected her to tell him no.

For an instant surprise darkened her eyes. "You're not— I thought—"

He watched the blush spread over her face. She'd thought he would be sharing her room, he realized. She had thought she would have to share the intimacy of going to bed beside him every night and waking up there every morning, and she had still agreed to his terms. She must be even more desperate than he'd thought. "When it's time to fulfill your end of our bargain," he said slowly, making his voice harsh and cold, "I'll let you know. Until then I want my own room."

She stayed where she was, still blushing, her body rigid with tension. "There are clean sheets in the closet on the second shelf." Then, without looking at him or anything else in the room, she gave a little shake of her head. "They're probably on the floor now. Towels, an extra toothbrush, a razor—whatever you need is in the bathroom under the sink."

She wasn't going to deny him the privilege of sleeping here, he thought, not sure whether he was pleased or disappointed, but she damn sure wasn't going to set foot inside to help him get settled. Because she didn't want to get too close to him? Or because she hadn't been inside her father's room since he died?

Impatiently he turned out the lights in the dressing room behind him. "Forget it. The room across from yours will be fine." At the door he waited for her to move, then followed her down the hall to Alex's room.

In the front bedroom, she made the bed with clean sheets while he picked up the few items that had been dumped during the search. This room was more his style, Rory thought as he replaced the last trophy. The walls were painted pale blue, the curtains and bedspread were dark blue, and the furniture was plain, simple, not elegant, not expensive, just functional.

Shanna finished with the bed, leaving the covers turned back, bending to smooth a wrinkle from the soft blue sheet. She stepped back and looked up at him, her dark eyes more than a little uneasy. "Have you had dinner? I could fix something...."

"I don't eat frozen dinners."

She smiled weakly at his warning. "Of course not. I usually don't, either. It's just easier than cooking for only..." Her voice broke, and she let the explanation trail off.

Easier than cooking for only herself, Rory thought, grimly struggling against the sympathy for her that was trying to build inside him. All her life she'd been extraordinarily close to her father, had gone off to his college, had chosen his career, then returned to his town and his home to share his life. But now he was dead, and she was alone. Alone with a man Joseph had hated, had always hated.

Maybe that was why she'd treated him so badly so long ago: her father had despised him, and so, mindlessly, like a good daughter, she had, too. But almost immediately he rejected that possibility. Joseph Cassidy had been a bastard, but he'd never been deliberately cruel. Everything Shanna had done—the long, secret talks, the gentle teasing, the determined effort to get close to him, the sweet, fever-building kisses—it had all been deliberate, had all been laced with malice and derision. And it had all been leading to one thing: public humiliation. Shame. Hatred.

He closed his eyes, retreating for a moment into cool darkness. What was he doing here with this woman he couldn't trust? He couldn't forget what she had done to him, couldn't forgive what she had cost him…but God help him, he couldn't walk away from her, either. He couldn't give up his one chance to possess her.

Twenty-one years ago he had wanted a lot: respect, acceptance, trust and Shanna. He couldn't have the other three; no one who'd known the boy he had been would ever respect, accept or trust him. But he could have Shanna. He could show everyone in town that he had achieved the most important goal of all, and in so doing, he could repay her for the humiliation and the shame and the hatred. She would have to endure the snickers, the leers, the whispered gossip, as he had, and she would know what it meant to feel humiliation, to be shamed.

And she would hate him for it.

"Rory? Are you hungry?"

He flinched at the sound of his name in her soft, weary voice. "No."

"If you change your mind, you can help yourself." She paused in the doorway, shifting uncomfortably from one foot to the other. "I'll be in the office if you need anything." She moved toward the stairs, then stopped once more. "Rory?"

He turned his head just enough to see her.

"Do you think they'll try to kill me?"

He heard the fear behind the hesitance and felt the muscles in his belly clench in response, but he didn't try to soften his answer, didn't try to cloak it in maybes. "Yes." Then he turned to face her head-on. "If you let this go, if you forget it, if you don't do anything, you won't be a threat to them and they'll leave you alone. But if you push it, they're going to do their damnedest to kill you."

"That's what I think, too," she said with a slow nod. Then she smiled just a little. "Good night."

The nightmare came as usual, jarring her awake in time to stop the terrified scream building in her throat. Her heart was thudding painfully, and her breathing, harsh and raspy, was echoing in her ears. She was both hot and cold, sweaty and shivery. For a long time she huddled underneath the covers, staring with gritty eyes at the ceiling.

She'd been telling herself that the dream would fade with time until eventually it was no more than a memory, but tonight it had been as vivid as ever—the sounds, the smells, the horror. *When* would it fade, *when* would it end? she wondered, then despairingly rephrased the question: Would it *ever* end? Would she ever forget what she had witnessed? Would she ever sleep again without reliving the horror? Would she ever get over her grief and her loss and go on with her life?

Her heart rate slowing to normal, she sat up, swung her feet to the floor and went to the closet for her robe. She didn't look out the window as she normally did—the scene, so peaceful now and so gruesome a week ago, was forever etched in her mind—but belted the robe around her waist, opened the door and silently made her way through the dark along the hall, down the stairs and into the kitchen. There she turned on the single fluorescent bulb over the sink, filled a juice glass half full with Scotch and sat down at the narrow wooden table.

It felt familiar—this sense of having to be quiet because someone else was in the house. But it felt downright odd knowing that that someone else was Rory Hawkes and that he was asleep right now in Alex's bed. In all the years she'd known him, this was the first time he'd come to her house. As an adult, he'd had no desire for contact with the Cassidys, and as a boy, he'd known he wouldn't be welcome. If he had shown up here then, her father would have . . .

She smiled faintly. She didn't know exactly what he would have done, but he probably wouldn't have let him in the door. No doubt he would have handled things differently, she thought as she sipped the whiskey. His opinion of Rory Hawkes had been a hundred and eighty degrees different from hers. To him Rory had been a juvenile delinquent, an incorrigible youth with no future ahead of him.

But Shanna had seen a gentle boy who had taken care of his father and helped his mother, who had treated *her* with more tenderness and consideration than she had deserved. She had looked forward to her afterschool visits to Grandmother Cassidy's, knowing that she would at least catch a glimpse of him when he came to meet his mother after work, that usually he would come a few minutes early, that he would talk to her, tease her and, later, kiss her so hungrily.

Then it had ended.

No, she amended. Then *she* had ended it.

She took a long swallow of the liquor, grimacing as it burned its way down her throat, letting it burn away the memories with it.

He hadn't changed much, she thought, blinking away the moisture that stung her eyes from the drink. The charm had been replaced by bitterness, the niceness by anger, but he was still handsome, with those cool blue eyes, that perfectly straight nose and that unruly hair, a half-dozen shades of brown and cut military-short. Every one of his thirty-nine years showed on his face, but yes, she admitted, he was still handsome.

She drained the glass and set it down carefully, then laid her hands flat on each side of it while she contemplated refilling it. Maybe later, she decided as a warm fuzziness reached her brain, after she'd thought more about Rory. More about the break-in.

Protection—that was what she'd told Rory she wanted from him. But did she really need it, or had her father's senseless murder affected her judgment? Whoever had broken in here had been hateful and malicious, but he—or they—had been careful to do it when she wasn't home, so they weren't interested in her. Chances were very good that they had found whatever they'd been looking for, since nothing of Joseph's was left in his office and his truck had been destroyed in the explosion. His home was the only other option, and now it had been searched. If they hadn't found it here, then most likely it had been blown up in the truck.

So if she let it end here, if she forgot about punishing Channing, she would be safe, and she wouldn't need Rory Hawkes's protection.

But she couldn't let it end here. She couldn't forget about punishing Channing. He had already killed once to stop the investigation into his activities, so she had to assume he would kill again if the investigation was resumed. To believe otherwise would be foolish—and deadly. So the answer to her question was yes, she needed Rory's protection—needed it enough to sleep with him to get it. Needed it enough to sell herself, body and soul, for it.

Then she smiled grimly. All he'd asked for was her body. He had no interest in her soul. Still, she thought, she'd gotten the better end of the deal. All she had to risk was her pride and maybe, for that part that still remembered the boy he'd been, a little of her heart. Rory had to risk his life.

Slowly she stood up, swaying unsteadily, gripping the table edge to stay on her feet. Maybe she'd had too much this time, she thought as she made her way down the hall to the stairs. Too much whiskey and too many memories.

She didn't notice Rory, dark and quiet, inside the door of the den. He waited until he heard her steps on the stairs; then he went into the kitchen.

He never would have pegged the perfect princess for a drinker, he thought, sniffing the glass she'd left on the table. Oh, maybe a glass of wine with lunch or an occasional cocktail before dinner, but not serious drinking. Not three-ounces-of-straight-Scotch-in-the-middle-of-the-night drinking.

Apparently she wasn't dealing well with her father's death. He wasn't surprised. He could remember getting word at Fort Bragg nearly ten years ago that his mother had died. Even though he'd seen her only at odd intervals since he'd joined the Army, he had felt an intense sense of loss, an anguish that one of the two people he loved in the world was gone. Dealing with the immediate matters of her death—arranging her funeral, settling her affairs, finding a facility that could care for his father—had been difficult, completed in a daze brought on by grief, sorrow and regret. How much worse would it have been to know that she'd been murdered for no reason other than an immoral man's greed?

Setting the glass down again, he opened cabinet doors until he found the Scotch. About four inches of the amber liquor remained. He would check it again tomorrow, he decided. If he was going to risk his life to keep her safe, he wanted to know exactly how much she was drinking and when.

He returned the bottle to its place in the cabinet, then shut off the light over the sink. He moved with assurance through the cool, dark house, circling the grandfather clock and the Queen Anne table in the hallway, avoiding the third stair that creaked in the middle.

In the upstairs hallway he hesitated. Shanna's room was on the left, his own on the right. After a moment, he turned the knob on the left and soundlessly swung the door open. She was lying on her back, her black hair a tangle around her. A combination of pale yellow moonlight and harsh white lamplight shone through the sheer curtains at the windows, touching her face, creating a mysterious picture of light and shadow, soft and strong, cool and warm.

He didn't know how long he stood in the doorway, motionless, not daring to move a muscle. Years of harsh training had taught him to ignore his body's responses—pain, hunger, thirst, exhaustion. But one response he couldn't ignore, one he'd never even imagined in Special Forces, was the arousal that was swiftly spreading through him, making his muscles knot, pulling his jeans taut. How could he ignore the changes—the softening inside, the hardening outside—taking place in his body? How could he ignore the fact that more than anything else in the world, he wanted to crawl into bed beside her? He wanted to touch her, to glide his hands all over her, across her breasts and down her spine and between her legs. He wanted to make her skin hot, to spread a fever through her that made her forget who she was, who he was, that made her forget everything except the pleasure his body could give hers.

The need to bury himself inside her was so great that he almost groaned aloud with it, but he gritted his teeth on the sound. He could seduce her now—could sit there beside her and gently stroke her until she awoke again, sleepy and warm, her body ready to accept his. But it wouldn't be fair. She would be vulnerable, more asleep than awake, less capable of understanding the consequences of what he was doing, of what she was letting him do. She would give in to the desire without considering who or what he was, and when it was over, when she was awake and clearheaded, she would hate him for taking advantage of her.

It would almost be worth it.

Swearing silently he swung around and left the room, closing the door quietly behind him, and went into his own room. There he took a cigarette from the pack on the nightstand, shucked his jeans, sat down on the bed and lit the cigarette with trembling hands.

He'd gotten himself into a real mess this time, he thought grimly, watching the smoke filter through the air toward the window. While he was well equipped to deal with the physical danger that was sure to come from Lawrence Channing, he didn't have the experience to deal with the emotional risk Shanna represented. She had hurt him once before, and he had paid dearly for it with his pride, his home, his family. A few times it had almost cost him his life. What price would he pay this time?

Nothing, he admitted bleakly, compared to what he would pay if he didn't help her, if he walked away and let Channing kill her. He could survive anything, could endure anything, but, God help him, not that.

Shanna sat at the desk in her office Thursday afternoon and thumbed through her father's appointment book until she reached the telephone directory at the back. She was familiar with most of the names listed there. Except for a few friends here in Sandy Spring, they were scattered all across Texas: judges and lawyers in Dallas, El Paso, San Antonio and Houston; an accountant in Midland; a private investigator in Odessa; and an FBI agent in El Paso.

Had Joseph turned to one of them for help? Had he hired the accountant to comb through financial records or the private investigator to check Lawrence Channing's background? Had he confided the town's problems to the FBI agent?

Since he hadn't been out of town in recent months, she knew any contact would have been by mail or telephone. She also knew he wouldn't have made such calls from the courthouse, where he was surrounded by people on Channing's payroll. That meant checking the long-distance calls billed to their house in the past few months against the numbers listed here...once she found them among the thousands of papers on the office floor at home, she thought bitterly.

Closing the date book, she swiveled her chair around to look out the window. Main Street was quiet at three o'clock on a March afternoon, just as her office was quiet. After several years of the constant rush and bustle of a Dallas law firm, the pace of a small-town practice had appealed to her. Although the clients were few and she would never get rich from her fees, she had the satisfaction of knowing that she'd given every case, no matter how trivial, her fullest attention, and time off for personal needs was easy to come by.

But she'd found that there were times when the hustle of a big office would be a blessing instead of a burden, times when she would welcome being too busy to think about anything except her job. Times like today when everything she could think about was disturbing: her father's murder, his investigation, Lawrence Channing, Rory Hawkes.

Rory Hawkes. She didn't quite know what to make of him. He'd been no more talkative, no friendlier, no more forthcoming today than he'd been last night. When she'd eaten breakfast this morning, he had sat across from her at the kitchen table, drinking strong black coffee, smoking and answering her questions in single syllables whenever possible. His hostility had been an actual thing, shimmering between them, making her question not for the first time the wisdom of placing her trust in him. He hated her, yet she was counting on him to keep her alive.

Why was he doing it? Why was he risking his life to protect hers? Last night she had decided that vengeance was the logical answer. After all the snubs, the insults and the cruelty he had endured as a boy, how could he pass up the opportunity to possess one of the things denied him then and to flaunt that possession to everyone who had looked down on him?

But was that the only answer? She wanted to believe there was more to it than that—more to *him* than that. She wanted to believe that he was helping her because it was the right thing to do. Because, in spite of the lack of emotion he'd shown upon hearing of her father's murder, he didn't want to bear the burden of knowing that someone else had died when he might have prevented it.

Was she crediting him with a goodness and decency he didn't possess? For the sake of their past—for the sake of their future—was she inventing qualities for him that simply weren't there?

He was a puzzle, she acknowledged with a weary smile. Even as a teenager, he'd had a reputation for being wild and tough, yet no one could have been gentler with his poor confused father. He had mocked authority, had laughed at the rules and broken the laws, yet he had obviously loved his parents and respected *their* authority. He had been called worthless and no good, yet he had worked—whenever he could find a job—from the time he was fifteen, turning his wages over to his mother, and when there was no work, he'd taken on the burden of caring for his father. By the time he was eighteen, he'd been supporting both parents, facing an ordeal most adults couldn't have handled.

If he'd been anyone else, if he'd had any name other than Hawkes, the people in town would have admired him. They would have respected his willingness to work hard and to take care of his parents, and they would have overlooked the wildness that occasionally surfaced as simply a boy's need to have fun once in a while.

But he hadn't been anyone else, and he hadn't had any other name. He'd been a Hawkes and damn proud of it, even though the name had cost him a lot.

She had cost him a lot, too, Shanna sadly admitted. To please her father, to maintain the family reputation, to salvage her own pride in front of her friends, she had stripped him of *his* in front of half the school. Even now, twenty-one years later, the taunting words echoed in her mind: *It was a game. I was having some fun, that's all. You didn't believe I was actually interested in you?*

She surged to her feet, rubbing the ache in her temples with both hands. "No," she whispered, then repeated the word in a stronger voice. "No, I didn't mean—"

"Didn't mean what?"

She whirled around to find Rory sitting in one of the two chairs in front of her desk. There was an instant's fright on her face, but it quickly disappeared, replaced by a hot flush. "That makes twice you've walked into a room without me hearing you."

He shrugged. "You weren't listening."

She came around the desk and leaned on the edge, her arms folded across her chest, her long legs crossed at the ankle. "Did you get everything taken care of?"

Reaching into his pocket, he withdrew two identical keys and tossed first one, then the other, onto the desk beside her. "Front door, back door. The Barely Pink goes to the front door."

She picked them up and held them flat in her palm. One key was painted with a circle of the pale pink nail polish she was wearing today. The other was bare. "Thanks." She slid them into her jacket pocket, then folded her arms again and studied him. This morning he'd had on faded jeans and a worn red T-shirt, his hair had looked as if he'd combed it with his fingers, and he'd needed a shave. His jeans now were newer, and so was the T-shirt, this one black, and he'd shaved, but his hair still looked as if he'd combed it with his fingers—the way it had always looked, she remembered, a little wild and disheveled, the way *he* had always looked.

He returned her even gaze, treating her to the same inspection he was receiving, starting with her long, straight black hair and moving down to her clothes: a slim, thigh-hugging skirt of palest pink and a matching jacket worn over a white blouse of some soft, silky-looking material. This outfit was more feminine than yesterday's severely tailored suit that had all but growled "businesswoman." Today she looked like a woman, pure and simple—soft, approachable, touchable.

But he didn't touch her. Even though he wanted to, even though his fingertips itched to make contact with her soft, warm skin—for those very reasons, he didn't touch her.

Scowling, he settled into a comfortable slump in the chair. "Where is your secretary?"

Shanna glanced at her watch. "She went to pick up her daughter from school."

"Does she do that every day?"

"She leaves about 3:10, takes Candy to her dance class on Mondays, Wednesdays and Fridays and to her grandmother's on Tuesdays and Thursdays, and she's usually back here by 3:45."

"And you're alone in the office during that time."

"Unless I have an appointment."

"So anyone could just walk in."

She smiled before she thought to stop it. "Anyone just did." Moving gracefully, she stood up and started around the desk, then chose instead to sit in the other chair. "I'm a lawyer. My business requires being accessible to my clients. I can't lock the doors and cower in the corner every time Susan has to go out."

Ignoring her response, he looked around the office. "Either keep the blinds partially closed or move your desk away from the window—preferably both."

She followed his gaze to the big picture window. The layers of dust on the slats attested to the fact that the blinds were never closed. She needed the sun that streamed through in the morning and the contact, however distant, with the rest of the world when she was in here working. Her office with the Dallas firm had been a tiny windowless cubicle, and the closed-in feeling it had given her had been nearly unbearable.

Shifting back to Rory, she asked flatly, "Why?"

"There's a saying to the effect that if you can be seen, you can be killed. You're pretty damn visible."

She stiffened at the derision that softly shaded his comment, but refused to defend herself. Instead, she responded in a similarly derisive tone. "What do you think Channing's going to do? Throw a bomb through the window?"

"Possibly. But if I were him, I'd use a sniper."

A quick glance showed that he was deadly serious. With an open hand she gestured to the view outside. "There's nothing across the street but the park and the church on the other side. Where is a sniper going to hide and still be close enough to hit me?"

He didn't look away from her. He knew the scene outside well enough to recall every detail without looking: a scruffy, empty lot, whose few wooden benches and playground equipment qualified it as a park, even if its grassless, sand-and-dirt surface didn't, and across a side street, St. Paul's, a stuccoed two-story church with a cupola rising another ten feet above the roof. "How far away would you say that church is?"

"One block."

"In feet."

She sighed impatiently. "I don't know. Fifteen hundred, maybe two thousand feet."

"Using an M14 rifle, I can hit my targets ninety-eight percent of the time from a thousand yards. That's *three thousand* feet away. From the roof of that church, I could put a bullet—" he raised his left hand in a simulation of a gun and touched just the tip of his outstretched finger to her forehead "—dead center in your brain without even trying."

She swallowed hard as he drew his hand back. "Well...aren't we lucky that you're not the one who will be trying to kill me?" she asked, the huskiness in her voice ruining her attempt at sarcasm.

"Channing won't find anyone as good as me. But he can get someone who's close."

"So you'll have to be better."

"I will be...but that doesn't mean it will keep you alive."

Shanna stood up and walked to the window to stare out. Her spine was straight, her arms folded across her chest. "I was under the impression that that was our deal—that you would protect me. That you would keep me alive."

"I installed dead bolts on the doors and extra locks on the windows at your house, but that doesn't mean someone can't kick a door in or break a window and gain entry that way. I put the alarm on your car, and that will probably protect you from someone wiring a bomb to the electrical system or tampering with the steering or the brake lines, but it won't stop someone from attaching a bomb with a timer to the undercarriage. I can move your desk, cover that window, put extra locks on these doors, follow you everywhere you go. I can make you *safer*, but I can't guarantee anything. The only way I can give you guarantees is to put you in hiding someplace. But you can't investigate Channing that way, and if you're not investigating him, you don't need protection."

She looked at him over her shoulder for a long moment, then gave him a sickly smile. "I understand. No guarantees." Then, in an attempt to lighten the conversation, she added, "But if you let them kill me, I'm going to be really disappointed in you."

Impatience passed through his eyes quickly; then they were blank again. "I'm not going to 'let' them do anything. But look at it this way: if they kill you, at least you'll have the satisfaction of knowing that I'm already dead."

His cool, emotionless words made her shudder. How could he think for a moment that she would take satisfaction from his death? Then she answered her own question with brutal honesty. How could he think otherwise? She had gone to him for help, had asked him to protect her while she gathered information against Channing. She'd given little thought to the fact that his acceptance would put him in even more danger than she faced. She hadn't considered that once Channing realized Rory was protecting her, his obvious first move would be to eliminate *him* before coming after her.

"Why are you doing this?"

He grinned slowly. "Fun and games."

It was a game. I was having some fun, that's all. She turned her back on him once more, too ashamed to meet his gaze any longer.

His grin turned bitter before it faded. She remembered—he'd seen it in her eyes before she'd turned away. She remembered what she'd said, what she'd done to him, and she had turned away as if it meant nothing. The way *he* had meant nothing twenty-one years ago.

He wished he hated her. He wished he didn't want her. He wished he didn't care if Lawrence Channing splattered her brains all over these walls. But he'd learned a long time ago that wishes didn't come true, at least not for people like him. He couldn't count how many wishes he had made, how many prayers he had prayed—for his father to wake up one morning and be normal, to take care of his mother, for heat in the cold desert winters, to never go hungry again, for one friend, just one, who saw past his tough act to the loneliness inside, for Shanna to be that friend. His last wish twenty-one years ago had been to disappear off the face of the earth, and when that hadn't happened, he'd given up on wishes and prayers, on hopes and dreams.

He turned his attention from the woman determinedly ignoring him at the window and looked around her office. It was small and plain, not at all what he'd expected for the princess Cassidy. Her degrees from Texas Tech and the University of Texas hung on one wall, along with photographs of her family. Two large bookcases stood side by side on the back wall with two tall filing cabinets, their gray paint scratched and peeling. The carpet was brown and worn, as were the chairs and the love seat against one beige wall, and the desk was inexpensive, old and well used.

"Kind of a step down, isn't it?"

His lazy drawl jolted Shanna out of her thoughts. She turned, blinked, then focused on him. "What?"

With an easy grace, he opened his arms wide to indicate the room. "This place. I bet you didn't know until you moved in here that people actually live like this, with cheap furniture and shabby carpet. It's a far cry from all the oak and mahogany and plush carpet and polished wood floors and fancy upholstery that you're used to."

"You think I'm a snob," she said quietly.

He smiled with malice. "Now what would give me an idea like that?"

"Do you want to talk about it?"

"About what?"

"That day at school."

That day at school. It sounded almost harmless the way she said it. But there'd been nothing harmless about it. It had affected the next twenty years of his life. It was still affecting him.

He'd been used to the teasing. For as long as he could remember, the other children had mocked his crazy father; they had made fun of his shabby clothes and his shabbier house, had insulted and belittled and taunted him. And they had succeeded in hurting, angering and even embarrassing him. But Shanna had taught him the meaning of shame. She had taught him how it felt to be stripped of everything—pride, ego, defenses, even anger. She had left him with nothing but shame: of being a Hawkes, of being poor, of being foolish enough to believe she cared, of wanting her even when he knew she didn't.

Did he want to talk about it? Did he want to give her a chance to repeat the words that still haunted him? Did he want to give her an opportunity to make an apology that wasn't sincere, to watch her lie about how she regretted it and know that she was lying? Did he want further proof that he couldn't trust her?

Before he could decide, there was a tap at the door, then Susan walked in. She stopped short when she saw Rory sitting in the chair. She blanched when she recognized him.

Embarrassed by her secretary's reaction, Shanna rushed into introductions. "Susan, you remember Rory Hawkes. Rory, this is my secretary, Susan Miller. She used to be Susan Sanders. She was a couple of years behind you in school, but her husband, David, was in your class...."

She let her words trail away when she realized that neither one was listening to her. Instead they were watching each other, Susan's expression wary, Rory's smugly challenging. After a moment, the secretary looked to her boss. "I didn't know you'd taken on a new client. I'll prepare a file—"

Rory waited for Shanna to set the woman straight, and she did so haltingly. "He's not a client, Susan. He...he came by to visit and to—to..." Her gaze fell helplessly on the clock, and she blurted out the first thing that came to mind. "And to give me a ride home. I—I plan to leave early today."

"I can give you a ride, Shanna. It's right on my way."

"No, thanks," she said abruptly. "You see..."

A heated flush made her cheeks pink, and the look in her eyes bordered on panic, Rory thought unsympathetically. He pulled a cigarette from the pack in his breast pocket, lit it and blew a stream of smoke into the air. "It's right on my way, too."

"But you live out north of town," Susan disagreed. "Shanna's house is on the east side."

Shanna moved to stand beside Rory's chair and rested her hand lightly on his shoulder, drawing the secretary's gaze there. "Susan," she began awkwardly, "you're probably going to hear some gossip in the next few days, so let me tell you now—Rory and I have been..." She cleared her throat and forced the rest of her explanation through tight vocal cords. "We've been involved since he came back. Of course, my father never would have approved, but...he's gone now, and I—I asked Rory to move in with me."

"You're kidding!" As soon as the thoughtless words burst out, Susan blushed. "I didn't mean... That is..."

"So we'll be going home soon," Shanna continued, relieved to have the worst part over. "If you want to close up early and take off, too, feel free."

The secretary looked wide-eyed from one to the other, then left the office with a murmur.

The hand on his shoulder had been a nice touch, Rory thought cynically. While he could feel the tension radiating through those long, slender fingers, all the secretary had seen was the simple, proprietary gesture her boss had intended.

He reached up, lifted her wrist with two fingers and pushed her hand away. "That wasn't a very convincing act, princess," he warned as he got to his feet. "Your secretary was too surprised to be suspicious. Most people will be at first. But after they get used to seeing us together, if you don't start acting like you're willingly and happily sharing my bed, they're going to wonder exactly what's going on."

"You could help, you know," she said in a low, heated voice. "You didn't have to sit there with your mouth shut and looking so damn smug."

"That's exactly how they'll expect me to look. Smug and—" he let his gaze move over her, from her princess-pretty face all the way down her long, long legs "—satisfied."

"And how am I supposed to look?"

He shrugged carelessly. "*Not* frightened half out of your mind."

She studied him for a moment, then quietly disagreed. "I'm not afraid of you." And it was true. She was afraid of what he would do to her, but not of him. Maybe it was a silly distinction, but valid for her nonetheless.

"No, you're afraid of what people think. You're afraid of what they'll say. You're afraid they'll gossip about you, that they'll whisper nasty things behind your back and point fingers at you when you walk by. You're afraid of harming your reputation, of tarnishing the great Cassidy name." His smile was cold and cruel. "But you know what? You *should* be afraid of me. What these people think, what they say— that can't hurt you, not really. But *I* can. I can be more dangerous to you than anyone in this town except Lawrence Channing. I can take everything you value—your reputation, your self-respect, your body—and I can leave you with nothing."

Nothing except the satisfaction of knowing that her father's murderer had been punished. And *that*, Shanna thought bleakly, would be worth risking everything else. It had to be.

Chapter 3

When they got home, they went to the back door where Shanna fumbled for a moment with the unfamiliar lock before it clicked open. She started to go inside when Rory stopped her. "This is where your visitor came in yesterday."

"How do you know?"

"See for yourself."

She set her purse and briefcase on the washing machine, then crouched in the open doorway. After studying the area around the lock plate for a moment, she found a scratch across the metal and a place on the door frame where a chunk of wood had been gouged out. She rubbed her finger over the scratch. "You forced this lock last night yourself," she reminded him, "and put the new lock on today. How do you know *you* didn't do it?"

The long, vaguely amused look he gave her was the only answer he offered.

Shanna slowly got to her feet, found herself only inches from him. One step forward, and they would be touching, his hard, warm body snug against hers. The thought made her mouth dry and caused her throat to tighten. Instead of taking that one step forward, she took two back, then another for good measure, and forced her mind from Rory the man—soon to be her lover—to Rory her protector.

He was a sharpshooter. He could pick a lock without leaving a mark. He knew a few things about security and alarms, and he moved in deadly silence. Those sounded more like the qualifications for a crook than a soldier. "Just exactly what was it you did in the Army?" she asked, trying unsuccessfully to hide the suspicion in her voice.

"You've heard of a jack of all trades?"

"Of course. But the saying *I've* heard is, 'jack of all trades, master of none.'"

He smiled faintly. "*I* mastered all of them."

"Seriously, what did you do?"

He held his hands out, palms up, in a shrug. "Seriously, a little bit of everything."

Shanna scowled at his evasion. "That's not how the Army works. You're given a specialty, and you do it. *One* job. *Real* jobs, not shady skills like yours."

His smile turned sarcastic. "Thank you for telling me that. You'd think after more than twenty years in the Army, I would have learned that bit of information, but what can I say? We Hawkeses were never quite as quick to learn as you Cassidys."

His words stung, but she hid it behind her even stare. "What are you?" she whispered.

Rory leaned forward until he was right in her face. "As long as you persist in this notion of sending Channing to jail for your father's death, I'm your only chance of staying alive."

Shanna stared at him for a moment, then with a shudder, spun around and went inside. He remained there a bit longer, staring up into the darkening sky, wishing he was somewhere, nowhere, anywhere but here.

When he finally went into the house, she had changed into jeans and a T-shirt and was standing in front of the stove, placing chicken breasts in a skillet. She heard him come in, heard the door to the laundry room close with a click, but she didn't glance at him. He stopped somewhere behind her and leaned against the opposite counter.

"I was in Special Forces," he said, his voice flat and empty of emotion. "I'm an expert shot with virtually every kind of handgun, rifle and automatic weapon the Army uses. I can pick practically any lock. I'm jump- and dive-qualified—skydiving and scuba. I can hot-wire an engine, and I can drive a tank, a bulldozer or an eighteen-wheeler. I can provide emergency medical care, stabilize an injured person and evacuate him to safety. I can look at a set of blueprints and instantly memorize the number and location of every exit. I can memorize the layout of a room, a building or a city. I can navigate from point A to point B on foot in the least amount of time possible without detection. I can rappel from a cliff, a fifty-story building or an airplane, and I speak fluent Turkish and Farsi."

But he deliberately left out part of his background: that before Special Forces, his original MOS, or Military Occupational Specialty, had been demolitions; that he could put together a bomb like the one that had killed her father in a matter of minutes; that he could tell by looking at a building or a car exactly what kind of explosives and how much he needed to destroy it.

As he'd spoken, she had slowly turned around to face him. He identified the speculation in her eyes. She had probably heard occasional news stories about military teams who had operated in Grenada, the Middle East, Central America and Panama, teams with special training and special skills, teams created for crisis intervention, for hostage rescue, for counterterrorism. She knew they existed, but what she was having trouble with, he suspected, was accepting that *he*, a Hawkes, could have been a member of such an elite unit.

But he had been. Special Forces Operational Detachment—Delta, better known as Delta Force, was *the* elite, the best of the best. It was the Army's—in fact, the U.S. government's—primary weapon against terrorism. Being recruited by Delta had been quite an honor for him, and passing their long and grueling selection process had been the most significant accomplishment of his twenty-year career. No matter what he did with the rest of his life, he would always know that he'd been one of the best.

"Why are you telling me this?" she asked softly.

"Because if you're going to depend on me to protect you, you have a right to know what my qualifications are."

She studied him for a moment, her gaze moving over the taut lines of his face, the hard set of his mouth, the smooth blue glass of his eyes. "Is that my cue to say, 'If you're going to risk your life to protect me, you have a right to know what you're getting in return'?"

It was his turn to study her—the straight black hair that fell down her back, the lemon-yellow T-shirt that clung to her breasts, the faded jeans that fit snugly over her hips and her long legs, all the way down to her bare feet that shifted uneasily on the small yellow throw rug.

When he spoke, his voice was husky with desire. "I know what I'm getting." A teenage boy's dream. A grown man's fantasy.

Before she had time to analyze the change in his voice, it was normal again, low and deep and sharp-edged. "Do you need help with dinner?"

Wordlessly she shook her head.

"Then I'll be in the living room."

She watched him leave, then slowly turned back to the chicken browning in the skillet. Had she imagined that hoarseness in his voice that had hinted of desire, of needing and wanting and not having?

Probably. Whatever desire Rory Hawkes might feel for her, it had nothing to do with her as a woman. Once, over twenty years ago, he had looked at her and wanted her. But when he looked at her now, he didn't see the girl he used to kiss so sweetly, so hungrily, and he didn't see the woman she had become. Instead he saw a symbol for everything bad in his life, for many of his parents' troubles and for all of his own.

He saw a Cassidy.

She shuddered uncontrollably. For the first time in her life she understood a little of what living in Sandy Spring had been like for him. All his life he'd been condemned for being a Hawkes without any consideration for the person who bore the name. Now he was treating her to the same judgment, the same damnation. Just as the townspeople couldn't look at him and see a decent, intelligent, trustworthy man, he couldn't look at her and see a woman—sometimes foolish, sometimes weak, but basically decent and very sorry for hurting him.

With a sigh she put the chicken into a baking dish and placed it in the oven, then went to the pantry to choose a side dish. Cooking wasn't one of her favorite jobs, but she'd taken it over when she'd moved back to Sandy Spring from Dallas, relieving Joseph's housekeeper of the task. Since she had to eat, it was nice to have someone to cook for again, even if it was only temporary.

Once everything else was ready to heat at the last moment, she went down the hall to the living room, stopping inside the wide door. Rory had cleaned the room today, stacking the broken items in a wicker basket, vacuuming the broken glass and crushed flower petals, replacing knickknacks on shelves and tables. Now he stood at the picture window, staring outside, drawing one finger back and forth over the fresh caulking.

When would he want payment from her? she wondered. When would he come to her and tell her it was time—time to touch, to be intimate, to become lovers? She wouldn't have been surprised if he'd insisted on it last night. He had been treated badly by enough Cassidys to be justified in distrusting all of them, most especially her. He could have demanded payment up front, before he lifted one finger to help her, before he endured one insulting look, before he risked his life.

And what would she do when he came to collect? Why, she would pay, of course, she thought with a bitter smile. Just how dearly would depend on him. Would he seduce her or just take her? Make love or have sex? Be gentle, as she knew he could be, or cold, as she knew he was?

She wished she could deny that the prospect of finally making love with him held any appeal to her, but it would be a lie. At fifteen she would have given her virginity, her heart and her soul to Rory. He had been the only boy in Sandy Spring to kiss her, the only one to make her tremble with yearnings she didn't understand, with desires she couldn't control. Only his restraint had kept her virginity intact, to be given instead to a clumsy college sophomore who'd meant little to her at the time and nothing now.

Twenty-one years later she still found him handsome, still found herself drawn to him. In spite of his bitterness, in spite of his highly-justified derision of all Cassidys, she suspected he could still make her tremble. He could still send her desire spinning out of control.

Rory Hawkes was a dangerous man, her father had warned her. In more ways than one, she grimly agreed.

Rory knew she was behind him—had heard the soft slap of her bare feet on the wooden floor, could now hear the softer in-and-out of her breathing in the quiet room. He knew, too, that she was watching him, probably hating him. Cassidys had always hated Hawkeses—it had been that way for a hundred years. Cassidys had been morally, financially and socially superior to Hawkeses. Cassidys had never befriended Hawkeses—without ulterior motives—and they had certainly never needed them.

But *this* Cassidy needed *this* Hawkes—at least for a few days, probably for a few weeks, maybe even a few months. And what did *he* need?

He refused to give the question any consideration.

Stiffening as a deputy drove slowly down the street, he said, "Bombings have to be reported to the Bureau of Alcohol, Tobacco and Firearms. Did the sheriff do that?"

Shanna came into the room, choosing to sit in the easy chair where she could see at least a portion of his face. "I don't know."

He glanced briefly at her. The way she was looking at him reminded him of the thoughtful expression she'd worn last night when he'd taken one look at the street outside and known immediately that a bomb had exploded there. She had wondered then how he'd known it so quickly, with such certainty, just as she was wondering now how he knew about the reporting requirement.

"I suppose in between learning to pick locks and rappel from fifty-story buildings and speak Turkish and Farsi, you studied up on federal laws, too."

He shrugged. Army EOD—Explosive Ordnance Disposal—specialists often worked closely with the ATF. They were familiar with every law pertaining to explosives.

"What exactly is Farsi?" she asked, settling more comfortably into the chair.

"A language."

"No kidding. To speak three of them fluently, you certainly don't say much."

"Farsi is a language widely spoken in the Middle East, primarily in Iran and Afghanistan."

"I remember when you were failing Spanish, in a town with a large number of Hispanic residents and located only minutes from the Mexican border." She gave a wry shake of her head. "I'd love to know what secrets you have hidden in that brain of yours."

"No," he said flatly. "You wouldn't." He directed his attention back to the deputy, who had pulled into a driveway down the street, turned around and was coming by again. "You've got someone's attention."

She joined him at the window as the car came to a stop in front of her house. "He's probably wondering who's visiting."

"He already knows. If your secretary did her job, the entire town already knows."

She glanced up at him. "Susan would never gossip about my personal affairs."

He gave her a look that called her naive. "Susan told her husband, who will tell his buddies, who will tell their wives, and so on. Gossip spreads fast in any small town. Gossip about a Hawkes spreads especially fast in this small town, and gossip about a Hawkes *and* a Cassidy spreads like wildfire. Take my word for it."

He knew, because he'd been through it before, she realized. Her family, her friends, her *name*, had protected her, but he had taken the full brunt of the malicious laughter and taunts and jeers.

"Rory—" She reached for him, had almost touched her fingers to his arm, when he subtly shifted away.

"Do they normally keep a close watch on you and your house?" he asked, gesturing toward the deputy with a nod of his head.

Her frustration was manifested in a sigh as she let her hand fall back to her side. "Years ago they did, but not since Channing came."

"How long ago was that?"

"Six years." Like him, she watched the deputy. "Maybe we should be friendly and wave," she suggested, attempting to tease and failing.

"He doesn't want to be friendly with you. He might get orders to kill you."

She returned to the chair, tucking her feet beneath her. She didn't know whether he made blunt statements like that to frighten her, to annoy her or to make certain she didn't forget that her decision to finish her father's work put her in danger. Whatever his reason, she wished he would stop.

"The nearest ATF office is probably in El Paso," Rory said, drawing the drapes over the big window as the car drove away. "They'll send a couple of agents—"

"No." She waited until he sat down on the sofa to continue. "If federal agents come around here asking questions, it will make everyone nervous. I think one of Dad's— one of my father's—" She broke off and stared sightlessly for a moment, then forced herself to continue. "I think one of my father's mistakes was being too open. He made no attempt to be discreet. I want to keep this quiet. I don't want to put either of us in any more danger than necessary."

He'd heard her falter. Now he referred to it, his voice sharpened by mocking. "Hurts to find out he wasn't perfect, doesn't it?"

Although she wanted to hide her face in shame, she raised her chin and met his taunting gaze with quiet dignity. "I've known that my father could make mistakes since I was fifteen. I know that he was wrong about you. I know he shouldn't have been so hard on you. He wasn't perfect, but that didn't stop me from loving him, any more than your father's imperfections stopped you from loving him."

"Imperfections?" he echoed derisively. "I take it by that you mean the fact that he was crazy? Unbalanced? Daft? Unhinged? Insane?"

Shanna blinked away the sudden stinging in her eyes. There was pain behind every word, every mockingly offered label that had been applied to Joe Hawkes, pain that Rory had kept buried inside for years. She scooted forward in her chair, lowering her feet to the floor, then paused before standing up. "You're a very angry man, aren't you?" she asked, her whisper unsteady and teary. "Maybe that's what keeps you going—anger and bitterness and hate. But if you don't let it go . . ." She got to her feet and walked to the doorway. There she paused long enough to finish. "It's going to destroy you."

* * *

Rory stood at the window in his room—in Alex Cassidy's room—with both hands braced high on the frame. It was well after midnight, and the house was quiet. Shanna had gone to Joseph's office shortly after dinner, shutting herself inside, and had remained there until a couple of hours ago when she had showered and gone to bed. She hadn't spoken more than a few words to him all evening. Whether she was annoyed or angered or put off by their earlier conversation, he didn't know, and he didn't care. The less contact he had with her, the better.

Keeping his hands flat on the painted wood, he stretched, curving his spine first inward, then out. He dropped his arms, rotated his head to ease the taut muscles in his neck, then reached for the package of cigarettes and the matches on the windowsill. He rarely smoked more than three or four cigarettes a day, he thought as he lit one, then exhaled, but in the past twenty-four hours or so, he'd gone through almost a full pack.

It was restless energy that was causing him to smoke. He knew a dozen different ways to channel it, to use it effectively, but not one of them had worked for him tonight. Because of *her*. Shanna.

He'd told himself he didn't care why she was avoiding him, but he had lied. That was something new for him. As a kid, he had frequently lied to his teachers and to the sheriff's deputies, to his bosses and to Joseph Cassidy. He had lied to his father, and occasionally to his mother, but he'd never lied to himself until tonight.

He cared why she was hiding away from him. He had wanted to follow her into the office, to force her to acknowledge his presence, but he hadn't done it—because she would be offended by his presence in the sanctity of her precious father's office. Because forcing his company on her was wrong. Because he'd wanted it too much.

She'd been right in the living room. He *was* filled with anger and bitterness and hatred. It seemed that life held nothing but injustice for people like him, while others like

Shanna were blessed. Until her father's death, the most traumatic event in her life had probably been losing the election for sophomore class president and having to settle for vice president. She had been sheltered and protected, cossetted and coddled, all her life. She had been born with everything she needed, had been given everything she wanted, and what she wanted now was his services. She had felt it was her right to ask, to expect him to risk death so that Joseph Cassidy's murder could be avenged.

She had used him before, and he had suffered for it. She was using him again, and he would probably suffer for it again. But this time he would have something to show for it. This time he would have *her*, however briefly, however much she hated him, however little she wanted him.

He closed his eyes on the longing stirred inside him by that knowledge. How long had he wanted her? Always, from the time he'd been old enough to know what wanting was. He'd always been fascinated with her, with her delicate air and her big brown eyes, with her soft black hair and her easy, gentle smile. Once he'd thought he could have her, free and willing; then he'd known that she would never come to him willingly. She would fulfill her end of the bargain because her father was that important to her, but that couldn't be considered willingly.

The sound of a car on the street opened his eyes in time to watch a deputy cruise by slowly. Was this a routine patrol, he wondered, or were they keeping an eye on Shanna? Or had they come back to see if his truck was still parked outside, if the rumors that he'd spent last night here were true?

When the deputy disappeared around the corner, Rory breathed out slowly. His muscles had gone taut when he'd seen the deputy earlier this evening, and now he'd been holding his breath. They were familiar responses—to become motionless, unmoving and unbreathing, at the sight of a sheriff's car, as if his very stillness would keep him from being noticed. He thought he had outgrown that—and the sweaty palms and the sick feeling that built inside him—but he'd been wrong.

It had started when he was thirteen. He'd been outside his house playing one day when the sheriff had pulled up in his big police car, and he had known immediately, from the dread that had rushed over him, that something was wrong. The owner of Wilson's Variety had accused him of stealing, the sheriff had announced and demanded to know if Rory had been in the store that day.

Yes, Rory had replied, stammering in his fear. He and the few kids he could claim as friends—other poor kids, other outcasts—often stopped in the store on their way home from school, even though they rarely had money to spend. But he hadn't stolen anything. He'd never stolen anything in his life.

That was God's honest truth, but he'd learned that, when your name was Hawkes, the justice system cared little about truth. He had gone to court and faced Joseph Cassidy for the first time—but not by any means the last. Even though there was no evidence against him, even though the merchandise Wilson claimed he had stolen wasn't in his possession, even though he swore on his life he hadn't taken it, he was found guilty by the court and by the entire town. Only his parents—his mother who loved him and his sweet, simple father who knew nothing of evil—had believed in his innocence. Shopkeepers had watched him suspiciously any time he dared venture inside. They'd called him a thieving brat and followed him, ignoring their other customers, their *paying* customers, until he left again.

He'd learned another lesson then, one he couldn't have put into words at thirteen but understood all too well now: people rise—or sink—to the level of expectations. Innocent or not, he'd been branded as a thief, and so then he'd stolen. He'd already been convicted of the crime, and so then he had committed it. Another dozen arrests followed— mostly shoplifting, the rest trespassing, malicious mischief, an occasional public drunk.

Then had come the final arrest: grand larceny. A felony, and right at the age where he would have been tried as an adult.

He became aware of the heat from the cigarette between his fingers and glanced at it. It had burned down to the filter without him taking a single puff. Memories had a way of doing that to him, he thought with a wry grin as he stubbed it out. He got lost in the past—in the deprivation, the injustice, the anger, the shame. He wished he could live his life over again, but he knew there was no other life a poor young kid named Hawkes could have lived at that time in this place.

At least he had straightened up in the Army. He, who had long despised authority, had learned to respect it. He'd found he could not only survive the harsh conditions and strict discipline of Army life, but he thrived under them. His drill instructors, his first sergeants and his company commanders knew nothing of his background. They didn't know he was a kid entitled only to disrespect and mockery and scorn, and so they didn't offer those things. Instead they judged him solely on performance. If he was a good soldier, they gave him the respect and common courtesy a good soldier deserved. For the first time in his life he'd belonged someplace. He had fit in.

He had achieved much to be proud of in the Army. He had survived two hellish years in Vietnam. He had retired at the coveted rank of master sergeant with a chestful of badges, ribbons and medals. His selection for Special Forces had been an accomplishment exceeded only by his selection for Delta. He had earned respect from his fellow soldiers.

He had made something of himself.

Then he had retired and come back here—only temporarily, he reminded himself. Only to rest and put the house on the market and make a decision about his future. But then he'd gotten involved with the Cassidys again, and he'd let all the hurts and disappointments and sorrows of the past swallow him up. He had once more become that boy accepted by no one, wanted by no one, trusted by no one.

Except Shanna. She didn't want him, and she had accepted his presence in her house and her life only because she'd had no other choice, and she trusted him for the same reason. But at least it was a start. It was more than anyone had offered him twenty-one years ago. It was more than he could offer her. He hadn't accepted her, hadn't been able to see past the fact that she was the princess Cassidy, and he didn't trust her.

But he wanted her. God, how he wanted her!

As if called forth by his thoughts of her, he heard the soft click of her bedroom door opening across the hall. He waited a moment, knowing that she was headed for the kitchen, making her way as quietly as possible through the darkened house.

He thought of the bottle of Scotch in the cabinet and wished he'd emptied it last night instead of leaving it there. Most people would say he was overreacting, that he had no reason to believe she was drinking enough to be at risk, but in his mind, anyone who drank for a reason was already at risk, and Shanna's reason, he suspected, was to forget. To forget that her father was dead. To forget that the person she'd lived her entire life for was gone. To forget that for the first time in thirty-six years, she was truly on her own, with no one to look out for her, no one to make life easier for her.

He slipped out of his room and down the stairs in silence. He knew which stair creaked and where to step to avoid it and how to muffle the sounds of his bare feet on the wooden floor.

When he entered the kitchen, Shanna was surprised but not startled by his appearance. She was growing used to his stealth, used to his presence in her house. She offered him a taut smile and slid the bottle to the center of the table. "Help yourself."

Her words were softly slurred, but from weariness, Rory judged, rather than inebriation. There were shadows under her eyes, dark and fragile-looking, that she skillfully covered with makeup during the day. He wondered how long it had been since she'd had a full night's sleep, then answered his own question: nine nights. Since Joseph's death.

He laced his fingers around the bottle but made no move to unscrew the cap. "I don't drink."

She smiled again. "That's okay. Neither do I." She lifted her glass, swirling the contents, then sipped from it. She'd started these nightly sessions with more water than Scotch in the glass, but in little more than a week, she'd graduated to straight Scotch, fiery and potent. Later, in the bright light of day, she might be concerned about that, but not tonight. Not when the images of the dream were still fresh in her mind.

He watched her drink again, pinning her with his solemn blue gaze, making her nervous, making her feel vulnerable. She avoided looking at him, concentrating instead on her glass, turning it in slow circles, making the liquor inside slosh and swirl.

Finally she raised her head. Her eyes were as soft as his were hard, as hazy as his were clear. "You don't have to wait here. I'll get to bed under my own power."

"You drink all that," he said, gesturing to her glass with the tapered neck of the bottle, "and I'll find you on the floor in here in the morning."

"I'm not going to get drunk."

"Of course not. Cassidys don't get drunk, do they? They just get tipsy. Instead of passing out, they drift off to sleep. And instead of hangovers, they have headaches." He paused. "You have a lot of headaches, princess?"

Shanna looked away but couldn't hide the hot flush of guilt that colored her face. "I don't have a problem," she said imperiously, pronouncing each word slowly and precisely.

"Well, congratulations, because all the rest of us have them. I guess Cassidys are superior in that aspect, too, aren't they?"

Finally releasing the glass, she leaned back in her chair and folded her arms over her chest. With a scowl, she asked, "Did you come down here for the sole purpose of being spiteful? Because frankly, I can't handle it on less than three hours sleep at three in the morning."

"I came down here to talk."

"About what?"

"This." Once again he gestured with the bottle. He dropped his gaze to the label. "This is a good brand. Expensive."

"Cassidys have expensive tastes, right?" she asked flippantly. "If you can afford it, always buy the best—that's our family motto." She paused and let her lips curve in a malicious smile. "That's what I did with you."

He responded with his own cool smile. "You didn't buy me, princess. You traded your services for mine."

Somehow that sounded even worse in her ears than her claim to have bought him. But she focused instead on the name he'd called her twice tonight and only God knew how often when she wasn't around. "Don't call me that. I hate it."

"Why? It's accurate. If Sandy Spring had ever had royalty, it would have been the Cassidys. Then you would have been a princess by birth and not simply by nature."

Her scowl returned, darker and more hostile than before. "If accuracy is all that counts, why don't I just forget your name and call you thief?"

His smile slowly faded, and his fingers tightened around the bottle. "And a Cassidy never forgets someone else's shortcomings. How long have you been drinking like this?"

"That's none of your business."

"When you accepted the terms of our agreement, everything you do became my business."

"I told you, I don't have a drinking problem."

"When you can't sleep through a single night without getting up for a couple of belts of this stuff, you have a problem."

She stared at him for a moment, then pushed away from the table, took her glass to the sink and poured the remaining Scotch down the drain. She set the glass on the counter with a thump, then defiantly asked, "Are you satisfied?"

"It takes a hell of a lot more than that to satisfy me—" He bit off the "princess" before it made it out and left the comment dangling, sounding unfinished.

"You seem to have misunderstood the terms of our agreement." She returned to stand at the end of the table, pushing her hands inside the pockets of her robe. "You're supposed to protect me from Lawrence Channing. You're not supposed to pass judgment on me, criticize my behavior or snoop into things that don't concern you."

"Wrong. You asked for my help—to do whatever Joseph would have asked me to do. To make sure that another break-in doesn't happen. To keep you alive long enough to make Channing pay. That's a pretty broad agreement."

She recognized her own words and swore silently. He had told her last evening that he had an exceptional memory, and now he'd demonstrated it. "Then maybe I'll modify it."

He stood up, too, slowly taking the two steps needed to put him close to her. "You're a lawyer, princess. You should know that an oral contract is binding."

As he said the word "oral," his gaze dropped to her mouth—she could feel it as surely as a touch. She nervously touched the tip of her tongue to her lips, then, when he smiled, quickly withdrew it. She found herself studying his own mouth and looked away—to the no-less-enticing view of his bare chest.

How had it not registered through this entire conversation that he wasn't wearing anything but jeans? she wondered dumbly. His chest was bare and brown and smooth, not too broad but hard muscled, and his arms were strong, also brown, as dark as her own skin. She thought briefly of touching him, and her hand trembled. The time would come when she would get to do that—*get* to, she silently stressed, not *have* to. When she would find out for herself if his skin was as warm as it looked, his muscles as powerful as they appeared.

Slowly, cautiously, she let her gaze wander lower, over his unbelted jeans. Jeans that had faded to a soft blue, that fit him as superbly as his skin did, that gloved his slim hips and long, lean thighs. Jeans that couldn't hide the slight swelling that grew beneath her curious gaze.

"And how would you modify our agreement—*if* I were inclined to let you?" he asked in a husky drawl. "Would you spell out your rules—no judging, no criticizing, no snooping? Would you tell me when I could touch you and how and where? Would you regulate how I look at you, what I say to you, what I think about you?"

She couldn't answer, couldn't find sufficient air to fill her lungs to form the words—words that refused to come to mind. She raised her eyes to his face, searching for something there to help her—some derision, some of that icy coldness he wore so well—but his lashes screened his eyes, and his features gave away nothing.

"It doesn't matter," he said when she failed to answer, "because I'm not inclined to let you change it. And as for rules, I'm as good at breaking them as I am at following them. We made a deal—my services for yours—and you'll keep your end because Cassidys don't break their promises." Then he smiled and some of the chill was back. "At least, this time you won't."

He was remembering her promise twenty-one years ago to attend the spring dance with him, Shanna knew. Not only had she broken it, but she had done it in front of kids who had taunted and tormented him all his life. "Can we talk about the last time?" she asked hesitantly.

"No."

"Just let me explain—"

"You explained it quite well then."

"But what I said—"

He interrupted her once more as he returned to his seat. "What you said was no more than I expected from a Cassidy. My only regret was that it happened before I'd had a chance to get you into bed.''

Shanna sank into the chair at the end of the table. "That's not true. You'd had plenty of chances, but you refused to take advantage of them...just as you've refused to take advantage of it now. I agreed to—to sleep with you whenever you wanted for as long as we're working together, yet you haven't touched me. Why?''

He grinned sardonically. "Been a while for you, too, has it? Of course, there aren't too many princes running around Sandy Spring, are there?'' He didn't give her a chance to answer. "Tell me something. Do you think a Hawkes can screw a Cassidy? It's been the other way around—you people screwing us—for so long that I'd begun to think anything else would be unnatural.''

She sighed, tired of his insults, tired of arguing with him, so damn tired of everything. "I'm going to bed.''

Suddenly, grimly serious, he extended his arm, not touching her but stopping her from standing up. "We haven't finished our conversation. Why are you getting up in the middle of the night to drink?''

"It helps me relax.''

He shook his head. "It doesn't help you relax. It doesn't make you sleep. It doesn't let you rest. One look in the mirror would tell you that.''

She stared at him for a moment, resentment shadowing her eyes, then said flatly, "I have dreams.''

"About the explosion?''

She nodded.

"Tell me about them.''

She tried to focus her thoughts on the memories, then cringed. She couldn't do this, not now. "I don't want to talk about this.''

"Where were you when it happened?''

She stared at him mutely.

"What did you see?''

He wasn't going to leave her alone—she could hear it in his relentless questions, could see it in the implacable lines of his face. But she couldn't tell him everything he wanted to know. She couldn't willingly relive the horror for him.

She pulled her hands from her pockets and folded them together on the tabletop, squeezing them so tightly that her fingertips whitened. "It happened a week ago Wednesday at a quarter to eight. We normally left for work at the same time, but I had overslept and was barely dressed when Dad left. He got into the truck, and it—it blew up."

Rory sat silent for a moment, considering all the questions he wanted to ask, all the answers she hadn't given; then he looked at her and knew he couldn't force the answers from her now. She was on the verge of physical exhaustion, and if these dreams—these nightmares—had been bothering her every night since Joseph's death, she was probably close to emotional exhaustion, too.

"So you wake up from the dream, you think a little whiskey will make falling asleep again easier and you have a drink. Only each night it takes a little more to achieve the same effect, and soon you've got a problem, princess, because that bottle of Scotch doesn't give a damn whether you're a Cassidy or not. It will affect you as easily as it affects us common folks, and the need for it will destroy you as surely as it destroys us." He picked up the bottle, gave it a long look, then offered it to her. "Once you start actively investigating Lawrence Channing, he's going to try to kill you. If you keep drinking this stuff, the best you can hope for is that when he *does* kill you, you're too drunk to feel anything. It's your choice."

She wrapped her fingers around the neck of the bottle but didn't pull it from his hand. "And what am I supposed to do without it? How am I supposed to sleep?"

"Maybe you won't for a while. Maybe the dreams will go away soon. Maybe you'll get counseling if they don't." He shrugged and offered a half smile. "For the time being, you can get out of bed and argue with me." Though he wasn't

Now the weekend was here. For two days there would be no office to spend the better portion of each day in, no excuse to be away from him for nine hours each day. She was curious how they would handle two entire days together—and a little bit fearful, too, she admitted.

He was waiting in the kitchen, as he was every morning. In such a short time she'd grown used to the sight of him sitting at the small table, to the aroma of the strong black coffee he made so well. But this morning there was no coffee, and he wasn't sitting, barefoot and relaxed, at the table, but was standing near the sink, leaning against the counter, boots on his feet and jacket dangling from one hand.

She stopped near the table and studied him. "Going out?"

"Yes. For breakfast."

"You don't eat breakfast."

"No, but you do."

After a moment she nodded. She knew without asking that he intended to take her to the Main Street Café. It was a small restaurant located only two blocks from her office. Everyone who worked in Sandy Spring's small business district had breakfast, breaks or lunch there during the week, and it seemed like the entire town stopped in on weekends. It was the perfect place to see your neighbors and friends and to pick up the latest gossip. It was the perfect place to confirm the rumors that were surely circulating about them.

She went back down the hall and found the tennis shoes she'd left in the living room. After putting them on, she got her purse and a dark brown jacket, similar in style to the black jacket Rory was holding, then returned to the kitchen. "How am I supposed to act?" she asked in a conversational voice as she put the jacket on, then lifted her hair free.

He smiled sardonically. "Like you're horny as hell."

She smiled, too. Sometimes, when she looked at him, when she thought of the agreement she'd made with him, that wasn't a difficult state to achieve. After all, he was a sexy, handsome man, one who'd played an important role in her life, one who'd taught her more about passion as kids than any of the grown men she'd known. Wanting him was definitely easy. "Wouldn't you prefer satisfied?"

"That's *my* role, princess."

She frowned at him but didn't waste her breath asking him once again not to call her that. As nicknames went, it wasn't pleasant, and it certainly wasn't complimentary, but it wasn't as bad as the other names he surely must have called her in the past.

When they left the house, Shanna waited patiently while Rory inspected the truck. Such caution was second nature to him, but she was still learning. She'd set off the alarm on the truck yesterday morning, giving her neighbors an unpleasant jolt, and she had forgotten to lock the dead bolt when he'd brought her home from work yesterday. That would be his responsibility now, he had informed her, one she was more than willing to give him.

When he leaned across the seat and unlocked the door, she opened it and climbed inside. "What else do you have planned for today?"

He fastened his seat belt, started the engine, then answered her with his own question. "What do you normally do on Saturdays?"

"Housework, laundry, errands."

"What kind of errands?"

"I take clothes to the dry cleaners or pick them up, buy groceries, go to the post office—whatever I haven't had time to do during the week."

"I can do the housework and the laundry during the week."

"Great," she said dryly, then thoughtlessly added, "You can hand wash my lingerie."

He glanced at her with the first genuine smile she'd seen playing over his lips. "You really wear all those little bits of ribbons and lace I saw on your floor Wednesday night?"

Shanna felt a heated flush spreading up her throat and into her face. She'd forgotten that he'd been in her room after it had been searched, when every teddy, every camisole and slip, every chemise and gown and every pair of lacy silk panties had been dumped onto the floor. She loved sexy lingerie and, since no one ever saw it, indulged herself with the prettiest, the laciest, the raciest. At least, until now no one had ever seen it.

Rory didn't wait for an answer—her blush had been answer enough—and he didn't pursue the subject. Just the thought of her wearing nothing but those tiny, silky, lacy scraps was enough to start an ache that he couldn't deal with, not this morning. "So we'll get groceries after breakfast. What else?"

"I've got to stop by Elaine Martin's gift shop next to the courthouse and get some cards. I also thought—" She dared to glance at him and saw that he seemed to have forgotten the subject of her lingerie. "I thought maybe we could go by the office and rearrange the furniture."

Her suggestion brought him a warm sense of satisfaction. After her reluctance, he had dropped the subject of closing the blinds and moving her desk away from the window. She hadn't thought much of the idea, and he hadn't argued the point. What was the use of giving advice that was ignored? He had decided to look out for her the best that he could without her full cooperation and had hoped that nothing would happen to make him regret that decision. Now they could tip the scales a little bit more in their favor.

Main Street, when he turned onto it, was busy. Virtually every business in Sandy Spring was located on the two-mile street formed by the highway as it passed through town on its way to Mexico. He found a parking space halfway between Shanna's office and the restaurant, switched off the engine, then turned to look at her. "Are you ready for this?"

She sighed softly. She had always liked living in a small town—had liked knowing practically everyone she met, what they did for a living, who their families were, how many kids they had. But benefits could always become drawbacks, advantages turn into disadvantages. Everywhere they went today, they were going to see people she knew, people who had known her family, people who remembered Rory's family. And everyone was going to judge them.

"I'm ready." Then she added thoughtfully, "You know, Rory, depending on who we see, I'm probably going to have to touch you."

His face was expressionless.

"The few times I've tried that, you've backed off real quick."

He remembered each time, remembered the soft, gentle strength of her fingers. It seemed foolish that a simple touch could give birth to intense need, intense hunger, but every tiny bit of contact with her made him want more. It was only because no one had touched him in so long, he tried to tell himself—not a caress, not a handshake, not even an accidental bump in the grocery aisle. But that was just one more lie. No one's touch, not even a woman's most private caresses in the most intimate places, had ever made him ache the way the slightest brush with Shanna did.

"Don't worry," he said, then climbed out of the truck.

"Don't worry," she mimicked under her breath as she slid to the ground. She locked the door and shut it hard, then circled the front of the truck while he activated the alarm. "We're supposed to convince these people who have known us all our lives that we're lovers when we hardly speak to each other and never touch each other, and you say, 'Don't worry.'"

"You're the one who has to act. No one in this town knows me. They don't have the vaguest idea in hell what to expect from me. Half of them think I'm as crazy as my father was, and the other half think I'm too dangerous to walk the streets." He gestured toward the café on the next block, and they began walking in that direction.

"Are you?" Shanna asked quietly.

"Crazy? Or dangerous?"

"You're obviously not crazy," she said scornfully.

He looked at her, her long legs matching his stride, the ends of her heavy black hair swinging with each step, and thought of their bargain—her body for his protection—and the restless nights he'd spent alone in brother Alex's bed. He gave a rueful laugh. "I'm not so sure about that."

"I am."

"Why?"

"Because the Army wouldn't let you be in Special Forces if you were the slightest bit unstable. They wouldn't have taught you to do what you learned to do."

Again he glanced at her. She was serious. It was nice to have someone showing a little faith in him—even if it was Shanna Cassidy, who had once betrayed his trust, who had treated him worse and hurt him more than all the residents of Sandy Spring combined. "Well, if it's any reassurance, you're right. My job required regular, routine psychological evaluations. I'm probably more sane than anyone in this town—and I've had the tests to prove it."

Their steps automatically slowed as they approached the café in the middle of the block. Shanna looked up at him, narrowing her eyes against the sun rising overhead. "You didn't answer my question," she reminded him, her voice once more quiet and serious. "Are you dangerous?"

Rory stopped, his hand on the heavy glass door, his fingers curled around the handle. He started to pull, then instead tightened his grip and met her questioning brown gaze head-on. "You'd better believe it, princess," he replied, the grimness of his expression echoed in his voice. "After all, you're betting your life on it."

She considered his answer for a moment and smiled just a little. "Good. I'm glad." Then, in a gesture so natural that it would have fooled even Rory if he'd been watching instead of participating, she reached for his hand, twined her fingers through his, and gave him a bright, warm smile. "Shall we go inside?"

She was good, very good. Rory sat across from her in the booth for nearly an hour, watching her respond to each person who stopped by to say hello or to offer condolences on her father's death—and to get a closer look at the two of them together. He learned quickly which ones were her friends, which ones were merely acquaintances and which ones she didn't like, even though the differences in her behavior were subtle. She introduced each of them to Rory, evoking long-forgotten memories, memories that could have stayed forgotten for all he cared. None of these people had ever been friendly to him, and few of them offered even the faintest courtesy now.

She had eaten little of the breakfast she'd ordered, and Rory had long since finished his last cup of coffee. Reaching across the table, he pulled the fork she was using to mutilate her pancakes from her hand and laid it across the plate. "Are you through?"

She nodded.

"Ready to go?"

She looked up, hoping her relief was hidden to everyone but him. "Yes, please."

He left a tip on the table and took the greasy ticket to the cash register near the door. Shanna followed, staying close but not touching.

"That'll be $4.17," the waitress said.

From the corner of his eye, he saw Shanna start to open her purse, and he stopped her with the slight shifting of his body. She looked up at him, saw the barely perceptible message in his eyes and drew her hand away from her purse.

The woman took the five-dollar bill Rory offered and counted out the change, dropping it into his palm.

On the sidewalk out front, Shanna stopped. "Keep track of everything I owe you—for breakfast, the locks, the alarm—so I can pay you back, okay?"

He nodded. If the breakfast between them had been what they'd pretended it was, he would want to pick up the tab. But this was business. The smiling, the touching, the affection were all pretense, all part of the job—something he couldn't let himself forget—so he would let her pay the expenses of that job later.

"The gift shop is that way," she said, gesturing with her right hand, "and my office is back that way. Which one first?"

"It doesn't matter."

She still hesitated. "Do you want to take my keys and wait at the office? It won't take long—I just need to pick up some cards."

"No, I don't want to wait at the office." His steady gaze turned dark and suspicious. "This Elaine who owns the gift shop wouldn't happen to be the same Elaine you were such good friends with in high school, would she?"

"Yes," she admitted, "it's her. But that's not why I suggested you meet me at the office."

He didn't believe her. She hadn't objected to putting on an act in the café for her friends and acquaintances, but maybe she drew the line at lying to the woman who'd been her best friend through twelve years of school. Maybe she was afraid that someone who knew her as well as Elaine did—someone who had probably known all about her sick little game twenty-one years ago—wouldn't buy the pretense.

Or maybe she was ashamed.

"I thought you might not want to go to Elaine's shop because..." Shanna looked up at his hard, doubting expression and sighed. "Because in case you've forgotten, Elaine Martin is Donald Tyler's daughter."

Donald Tyler. For a moment Rory was eighteen years old again, facing his boss, the money he'd stolen still in his hand. He'd been sick over what he'd done—what he'd *had* to do—and so terrified at getting caught that he had hardly felt the pain when Tyler, a good seventy pounds heavier, had punched him and sent him crashing to the floor, ten- and twenty-dollar bills scattering around him. He would go to prison for sure this time, he'd thought when the deputies hauled him off to jail, but Joseph Cassidy had offered an alternative, and Donald Tyler had enthusiastically endorsed it. *Maybe he'll get killed over there in Vietnam,* he'd said with a malicious smile, *and save the state the trouble of executing him when he gets back.*

He shuddered with the memory, then forced it into a dark corner of his mind where it had no power over him, where it couldn't hurt him. "Are you suggesting she won't want me inside her store?"

"No. But sometimes one of her parents fills in when she needs time off, so. . . be prepared for a little hostility."

His smile was meant to be mocking, but she saw the bleakness underneath. "Hostility, distrust, suspicion, hatred—that's all I ever got around here. It's nothing new."

She wanted to reach out to him as they began walking, but without an audience, she wasn't sure he would accept her touch, and she didn't want to risk his rejection, so she pushed her hands deep into her jacket pockets and simply walked at his side.

She had watched him from time to time through breakfast. She had seen the muscles in his jaw clench when someone approached, had watched his eyes grow dark and shadowy at each subtle snub, then turn to a cool blue that reflected nothing—no feelings, no thoughts, no life. He had said little, had simply sat there, his expression and even his body language smug and arrogant, but she sensed that inside, the meal had been more of a trial for him than for her. At least everyone had spoken to her; none of them had ignored her the way some had ignored him—not as if he didn't exist, but as if he simply wasn't worth noticing.

She felt pity for him and all that he had endured and all that he endured now, even though he would hate her if he knew it. The hostility, distrust and suspicion must have been a terrible burden when he was a child, but how much worse it must be now. He had accomplished so much in his Army career, had achieved a measure of success that far exceeded that of the people in town, but to them, it meant nothing. No matter what he did, no matter what he accomplished, he was still a worthless Hawkes.

"You did okay back there," Rory said, more to break the silence than to compliment her. "Maybe you should take up acting."

She smiled faintly. "All lawyers have a theatrical flair, I think. It helps them in front of a jury."

"Do you like being a lawyer?"

Surprise quickly passed over her face before she controlled it. Other than her lingerie, this was the first time he'd shown any interest in her personally. "Yeah, I do. I don't even mind that I'm not very good at it."

The look he gave her was doubting, but she didn't see it because she was turning into the small store that was their destination.

The shop was empty when they entered, but she knew the tinkle of the small bell above the door would bring someone from the back room. Let it be Elaine, she silently prayed, but her plea went unanswered as Audrey Tyler came out of the storeroom.

"Well, hello, Shanna, how are—" The welcoming greeting faded as the older woman's gaze settled on Rory. "What is he doing here?"

"I need some cards, Mrs. Tyler—a plain white, I think. I need to send notes to the people who sent flowers for my father's—"

Mrs. Tyler interrupted her. "He isn't welcome here, Shanna."

"Mrs. Tyler—"

"And if you're with him, you're not welcome, either."

She felt a flush burning into her cheeks—not of embarrassment or shame, but of anger, pure and hot and bitter. "Why not?" she demanded.

"Why not?" The older woman's face turned even pinker than Shanna's. "You know who he is—you know *what* he is! He's a thief, plain and simple—a no-good, lying thief! My husband felt sorry for him and gave him a job when no one else would let him in the door, and how did he repay him? By stealing every penny he could!"

"Knowing how cheap your husband is, what he took was probably a lot less than he'd earned," Shanna said icily. "You surprise me, Mrs. Tyler. I thought you had some decency, but apparently, I was wrong. You are a narrow-minded, bigoted, hateful—"

This time it was Rory who cut in, his voice flat and empty. "Let's go."

Audrey Tyler folded her arms across her chest. "I'd heard the talk around town about you and him, but I'd hoped, for your poor father's sake, that it was just talk. Why, if Joseph had known that you'd taken up with this—this trash, he would have—"

"Don't tell me what my father would have done," Shanna warned in a deadly low voice. "He was capable of admitting when he was wrong, when he'd misjudged someone, but you—you're so shortsighted that you can't see anything but your own prejudices."

"Are you going to leave, or do I have to call the sheriff?"

"Don't bother," Rory said, catching Shanna's arm in a firm grip. "We're going."

Shanna let him pull her to the door and outside onto the sidewalk. They crossed the street in midblock, then turned in silence toward her office. They'd gone only a few feet when she pulled her arm free and looked up at him. "I'm sorry."

"If you go back and apologize, she'll probably overlook your outburst. She'll figure it was just evidence of my bad influence."

She stopped short, forcing him to pull up and turn around to face her. "Apologize for what?" she demanded. "She's a hateful, narrow-minded, bigoted old woman!"

"You used all those adjectives before," he said mildly. "I thought, in addition to a theatrical flair, lawyers also had an exceptional command of the English language."

Her smile came slowly and was rueful. "Not when I'm angry."

"Angry? Or ashamed?"

She studied his face for a long time, but found nothing there—just an emptiness that was more painful to see than all the anger and bitterness and hatred she knew he harbored inside. "I'm not ashamed of you, Rory," she said quietly. "I'm not ashamed to let people believe I'm having an affair with you. And I'm not ashamed of what happened just now. I'm sorry it happened. I'm sorry people treat you badly, and for that reason, I'm sorry you came back to Sandy Spring. But for my own selfish reasons, I'm glad you did."

"It's going to cost you."

She smiled faintly. "Probably." But not in the way he meant. Sleeping with him—trading her services, as he'd so bluntly put it—wasn't going to strip her of her pride. It wasn't going to be a thing to endure.

No, she expected the price she would eventually pay to come from a completely different quarter—not from her pride, her self-respect or her dignity, but most likely from her heart. Because by the time he got around to demanding his payment, more than her body would be involved. Already when she looked at him, she was drawn to him, and when she touched him . . .

She wondered how his hands, strong and callused and long-fingered, would feel removing her clothes, cupping her breasts, stroking her body. She wondered if his lovemaking was as fluidly, masculinely graceful as his movements out of bed. She wondered if his eyes ever warmed with passion, if he ever felt or wanted or needed so badly that he lost his rigid control.

She wondered if he was going to break her heart.

That would be the ultimate victory for him. Using her, pushing her into an affair, then walking away—that could assuage a lot of bad feelings, she suspected, but walking away if he knew she loved him... What better vengeance could a man ask for?

Rory watched the expressions cross her face—sadness, acceptance, something that looked like despair. If he told her to forget their agreement, that he would help her and she wouldn't have to give him anything but cooperation in return, would that chase away the sadness and despair and make her smile again? It was almost worth a try.

But damn it, he couldn't do it. Just once he had to beat the Cassidys. Just once he wanted to play Shanna's game and win, and there was only one way to do that: to possess her. Not make love to her, not have sex with her, although the act was the same, but to *possess* her, to take her, to know that for that very brief time, she was *his*.

That was all he needed.

That was everything.

"Come on," he said gruffly, and they started walking again, side by side but each basically alone. It wasn't anything new, he thought stoically. He'd spent much of his life alone. It had stood him in good stead in the Army. We're looking for loners, the Delta selection team had said, men who can operate independently and without orders. That description had perfectly fitted him. He'd been alone and independent longer than he'd wanted to remember. But he found it a bleak thought now that he would probably spend the rest of his life that way.

When they reached the office, he waited patiently while Shanna unlocked the door. "Why do you have better locks at your office than at your house?" he asked idly, watching the traffic pass as she turned the key in the second lock.

"Because the records I keep here are confidential. There's nothing really important at the house."

"Except you."

She became still for a moment, considering his response, then pushed the door open and went inside.

The office was cool and quiet. Shanna turned on the lights in her private office, shrugged out of her jacket and hung it on the brass rack behind the door. She extended her hand for Rory's jacket, and after a moment's hesitation, he removed it and handed it to her. When he turned away, she saw the gun and holster clipped onto the waistband of his jeans in back. She'd never known anyone who carried a gun before. There was something intimidating about it—and something sexy, too. Unexpectedly she chuckled softly.

Rory glanced over his shoulder at her. "What's so funny?"

"Considering the paranoia this town exhibits when it comes to you, imagine how they would have reacted this morning if they'd known you were wearing a gun underneath that jacket."

"I'd prefer that they not find out."

"I won't tell anyone," she promised, going to stand beside him. "How do you want to rearrange the furniture?"

He gave the room a quick study. The wide window was off center, and Shanna had placed her desk to take advantage of its light. All he had to do was reverse the arrangement by moving the love seat to the window side of the room and placing the desk where the love seat now stood. With an adjustment to the blinds, she would be about as safe as possible. "Grab that end of the love seat," he directed. "We'll move it over there for now."

She did as he commanded, struggling with her share of the burden. When they set it down, he began clearing her desktop and taking out the drawers while she moved the three chairs to join the love seat. As soon as he finished, she went to help him with the desk. By the time they turned it around and carried it across the room, she was breathing unevenly.

"You need to get some exercise," Rory commented as he started replacing the drawers.

"I know, but I'm a klutz at aerobics, I can't hit a tennis ball, I hate jogging, there's no place to swim, and I'm too lazy to ride a bike." She plopped down on the love seat and watched him. His heart rate hadn't increased by a single beat, she thought enviously. "What do you do?"

"Run, lift weights, taekwondo."

She studied him with a critical eye. "By 'run,' I take it you don't mean jogging?"

"No, I don't." He gestured for her to stand up, and together they moved the love seat to the wall opposite the desk.

"Well, that explains it," she said mostly to herself.

He picked up one shabby chair in each hand and positioned them in front of the desk. "Explains what?"

She shrugged awkwardly. "You."

"What do you mean?"

A faint tinge of color accompanied her next shrug. "The body. The muscles. The grace. You're obviously in very good shape, and you move very gracefully but with a great deal of control."

That control relaxed almost enough to allow him to smile—almost. "I wasn't aware you'd noticed."

"You're not the only observant one." She went around to sit behind her desk and moved several items he'd placed there an inch or so to one side.

He adjusted the blinds, stepping back to avoid a shower of dust from the slats as they tilted, then warned, "Leave these just like this."

"Yes, sir." She offered him a mock salute. "You give orders very well. Did you get to do much of that in the Army?"

"I was a master sergeant. Of course I did."

"I don't know what that is, or I would probably be impressed," she admitted with an apologetic smile.

He sat down in one of the chairs in front of her desk. "There are nine enlisted grades in the military, classified E— for enlisted—one through nine. When you join up, you're an E-1, and you work your way up. I was an E-8 when I retired."

"So you had advanced almost as far as you could. I *am* impressed." She picked up a pen to doodle on her desk pad, found it was out of ink and played with it instead. "I was surprised when I heard you had joined the Army. That was probably the last thing I'd expected of you."

The change that came over him was swift, a brittle chill replacing his earlier, almost-friendly manner. "It wasn't like I had much of a choice, was it?" he asked, his words sharp, his tone bitter.

Shanna regretted the change and wished she could take back the innocent comments that had sparked it. But even more she wanted to understand him, wanted to know why he'd made the choices he had, wanted to know everything. "I'm sorry, Rory, but I don't understand what you mean."

"Prison or the Army. Prison or Vietnam." He drawled out each syllable of the name, placing equal emphasis on them. "There were times over there, when I watched my friends die, when I came within inches of getting killed myself, that I was positive I'd made the wrong choice. A lifetime in prison couldn't possibly have been worse than a year over there."

Twining her fingers around the pen, she sat back and looked at him for a moment before shaking her head. "I've heard occasional stories about people being forced to join the military as a punishment for some crime, but I don't believe them. It's not legal. Besides, you were charged with a felony. Why would the Army want a convicted felon?"

He scowled at her. "I never went to trial, so I was never convicted. Oh, I would have been, since the evidence that would have helped me was destroyed. But instead I was given the option of standing trial on the charge of grand larceny or joining the Army and leaving Sandy Spring with the charge dropped. It was all but guaranteed that if I joined the Army, I would end up in Vietnam before a year was out. But as scared as I was of the war, prison scared me even more." He shook his head in disbelief. "I was a fool."

There was an uneasy feeling in the pit of her stomach—dread that she was going to learn something she didn't want to know, something she was beginning to suspect but couldn't yet confirm. "You were eighteen, out of school, not going to college. You probably would have been drafted anyway."

He shook his head grimly. "I was exempt from the draft. I was the sole support of both parents at the time. My mother was sick and your grandmother had fired her for missing too much work, and my father..."

And poor Joe Hawkes hadn't been able to hold a job since Rory was a baby. Shanna's dread was growing. She was clutching the pen with both hands and staring at him with something close to horror darkening her eyes.

"You really didn't know, did you?" He closed his eyes for a moment, breathing deeply, evenly, then got to his feet, putting on his jacket, tossing hers across the desk. "Let's get out of here."

She stood up too, blocking his way when he would have walked through the door. "What evidence was destroyed?"

"Forget it."

"No. I want to know."

He remained silent.

"Damn it, Rory, you can't start something like this, then get up and walk out. What evidence was destroyed?"

His answer came reluctantly. "A letter to Donald Tyler, explaining why I needed the money—my father was sick. I asked Tyler to withhold it from my future paychecks with whatever interest was fair."

"And who destroyed it?"

He stared down at her, only inches away, but said nothing.

She shook her head in disbelief. "He didn't want to send you to prison," she whispered, only half aware of the hopeful note in her voice. "The letter was an admission of guilt."

"The letter was proof that I intended to repay the money. If it hadn't been an emergency, I never would have taken it. The letter proved the existence of what you lawyers call mitigating circumstances. It could have kept me out of prison, and your father destroyed it. He stood there in front of me and held a match to it and watched it burn. Then he made his generous offer. If I joined the Army, he wouldn't bring charges against me."

The hope faded from her face and her voice. "Why? Why did he do it?"

Rory closed his eyes and remembered the helplessness, the grief, the overwhelming urge to simply cry as he'd sat, handcuffed and under guard, and watched the letter burn. Then he looked at Shanna once more. "Because of you. He sent me to Vietnam to keep me away from you." He stepped around her, walked through the reception area and stopped to wait for her at the front door.

Shanna took a step back, then another until her back was against the wall. Slowly she slid down to sit on the cheap brown carpet, her knees drawn to her chest. She didn't believe him. She didn't believe her father would destroy evidence in a case, didn't believe he would offer such a deal to a frightened boy—and, his age notwithstanding, that was what Rory had been: a frightened boy trying to shoulder a man's burdens. She didn't believe Joseph would offer him a choice that was no choice at all, knowing that joining the Army would mean fighting the war, knowing that he very well might be condemning Rory to death. It was illegal. It was immoral.

But what did legality and morality mean to a Cassidy when dealing with a Hawkes? What did decency and goodness and justice matter to Joseph Cassidy when his daughter was at stake? He had pulled strings for her all her life, had made things easier, greased the wheels, smoothed the wrinkles, protected her. And the one thing in this world that he'd thought she needed protection from the most was Rory Hawkes. He had known that she cared for Rory, had known that Rory attracted her in a way no boy ever had before—and no man had since. He had known that she was willing to risk anything for her friendship—her relationship—with Rory...anything except her father's displeasure. And he had known that as she got older, she would risk even that.

Rory hadn't lied. Joseph had used—had *misused*—his position as district attorney to force him to leave town. He had used the threat of a felony conviction, of years in prison, to coerce him into joining the Army and risking his life. *He sent me to Vietnam to keep me away from you.*

She closed her eyes tightly and covered her face with both hands, but she couldn't shut out the truth. Because of her Rory had been forced to leave his hometown. Because of her he'd had to leave his sick mother and his helpless father. Because of her he'd had to fight the war he could have legally avoided. Because of her he'd almost been killed.

"It isn't true—any of it."

She moved her hands and opened her eyes to see Rory crouching in front of her, his expression hard and protected.

"I lied," he continued. "It was *my* decision to join the Army. Your father didn't have anything to do with it. *You* didn't have anything to do with it. I lied about it all."

She shook her head. "You're lying now." With a pathetic attempt at a smile, she asked, "Don't you know lawyers have a talent for knowing when someone is lying to them?"

He looked away from her unbearably sad eyes. Damn it, he had never meant to get into this—had never meant to tarnish her memories of her oh-so-perfect father.

He had never meant to hurt her.

"You know," she said softly, unsteadily, "most men want their first child to be a son—someone to follow in their footsteps, to carry on the family name and the family traditions. But for as long as I can remember, my father was always much closer to me than to Jody or Alex. He always took care of me. He always wanted life to be perfect for me, and he did whatever he thought was necessary to make it that way."

She fell silent for a moment, staring into the distance, then continued in that soft, dazed voice. "But he was wrong—as a prosecutor, as a father, as a human being, he was *wrong* to do that to you. And I'm sorry, because I certainly wasn't worth it."

After another silence, she spoke his name, then waited for him to meet her eyes before going on. "Why are you here? If you had to take sides in this, why didn't you go to Lawrence Channing? Why didn't you offer your help to him instead of me? After everything we've done to you, no one would have blamed you for hating us that much."

He was feeling a lot of things, but hatred wasn't one of them. He was angry with himself for telling her the truth, a truth she'd never needed to know. He was sorry he'd hurt her, and he longed to comfort her. But he didn't hate her. He wasn't sure he had ever really hated her, not even on that day so long ago when she had stolen his pride and shattered his last fragile dream all for the amusement of her snooty, taunting friends.

She was waiting for an answer to her question, and he gave it with his own. "Do you think I would help Channing stop you? Do you think I would kill you or even hurt you for what you've done, for what your family has done?"

"No." She cleared her throat and brushed away a tear that had formed in the corner of her eye. "Because you're a good man—a more decent and more honorable man than my father."

Another tear immediately formed. This time Rory reached out to dry it, touching only the pad of his thumb to her skin. "He did what he did because he loved you."

She shook her head as the tears started in earnest. "He did what he did because he thought it was his right as a Cassidy. So what if it was wrong? So what if it got you killed? You were a Hawkes—nobody special. If a Hawkes had to die to protect Joseph Cassidy's little girl..." She raised her arms to her knees, buried her face and cried— quiet little sobs that shook her shoulders.

Hesitantly he reached out to her again, finding her hand underneath the curtain of her hair and clasping it tightly within his. "I thought you knew," he said, his voice miserably soft. "I never would have said anything..."

It had been years since he'd had any illusions about life or the people in it, and he'd almost forgotten how painful it had been to lose them. But her tears and the desperate grip of her fingers on his reminded him. He had felt almost this bad when he'd found out how she had used him, when he'd learned that she wasn't the sweet, gentle girl he'd come frighteningly close to loving as much as a teenage boy was capable of loving.

He crouched there, holding her hand, ignoring the cramping muscles in his legs, and waited—prayed—for her tears to stop. He wanted to take her in his arms, to hold her close and comfort her, but he wasn't sure she would accept comfort from him, wasn't sure he even knew how to offer it. He'd received little comforting in his life and had never given it. So he simply sat there, holding her hand, and wondered if she knew that was the best he could give her.

The tears slowly passed, but she stayed in the same position, head down, face hidden, while an occasional shudder trembled through her. Finally she wiped her cheeks with her free hand and took a deep, cleansing breath. "I never cried," she said, her voice muffled by her arms and the thick veil of her hair. "Not when he died, not at his funeral, not since then."

"I'm sorry I told you."

"Why?"

"He was your father."

She raised her head then, sniffled and dried her cheeks once more. "But it was the truth, and I needed to know it. It helps explain..."

His hostility? he wondered. His willingness to help her? His demand to sleep with her? She didn't offer further explanation, and he didn't ask for it.

She sniffed again, then met his cool, troubled gaze. "Thank you for telling me...and thank you for lying, too. It was a nice gesture."

He stood up and used his hold on her hand to pull her to her feet. "Go wash your face. We've got errands to run."

She disappeared into the bathroom located in the storeroom, and he picked up her purse and jacket, shut off the lights in her private office and closed the door, then waited for her in the reception area. He'd been there only a moment when the door swung open and three uniformed men walked in.

The sick feeling he'd remembered so well a few nights ago rushed over him as the deputies took up position beside the door, and the sheriff, with a smile about as friendly as a rattler, came toward him.

"What are you doing here, Hawkes?"

"Waiting."

"What are you doing with that handbag? Whose is it?"

Rory stared at him and said nothing, directing his energy and emotions inward, concentrating on maintaining control.

Sheriff Hart stopped directly in front of him, only a few inches separating them, and leaned forward until that small distance was gone. "I asked you a question, boy," he said loudly. "Whose handbag is that?"

The action—the invasion of those few inches of personal space and the loud voice—was meant to be intimidating, but in the Army Rory had been intimidated by people who made

Hart look as harmless as a fat puppy in comparison. In fact, he *was* one of those people. He didn't flinch, didn't tighten a single muscle, didn't even so much as blink.

Shanna came out of the bathroom, patting a paper towel over her face. She stopped short when she saw the sheriff so threateningly close to Rory that *she* flinched. "What are you doing here, Sheriff Hart?" she demanded.

"So you're here, too." He took a step back, then a half dozen more, and smiled heartily at her. "We got a call that someone saw Hawkes here coming into your office. Seeing that this is Saturday and you don't usually work on Saturdays, we thought we'd check it out. We thought he might have broken in, the way someone broke into your house last week." He shifted his attention back to Rory. "You know, if I was to send a couple of boys over to check your house again, Shanna, I'd bet they'd find his fingerprints all over everything—including the lock that was picked to get inside."

"Yes," she agreed, coming to stand beside Rory. "They probably would. And they would find them all over my bathroom—which wasn't ransacked, incidentally—and since it's possible to lift fingerprints from skin, they would find his all over *me*." She leveled an icy stare on him. "Rory doesn't need to pick the lock to get inside my house. He has a key."

"The sheriff knows that," Rory said, his voice steady, his smile thin. "And he knows that I've been staying with you, because he's got his boys driving by every few hours all night long, don't you, Sheriff?"

"Just keeping an eye on the house," Hart replied. "It's a nice neighborhood. Everyone important in town lives in that neighborhood. We don't want the wrong kind of trash getting the idea that they can come in and just take whatever they want. And we don't want whoever broke into your house coming back to do it again, Shanna, do we?"

"No, of course we don't," she said dryly. "If you'll excuse us, Sheriff, we were just on our way out."

He walked to the door, waited until his deputies went out, then glanced back. "If you get yourself into any trouble, Shanna, just give me a call. I'll handle it personally."

Her only response was a smile that faded as soon as the door closed behind him. "I'm sure you will, you pig," she muttered. "Like you personally took care of having my house searched."

"You think he's that closely connected with Channing?"

"He said that whoever broke in picked the lock."

"So?"

"He never looked. He and his deputies came and walked through the downstairs portion of the house with me, asked a few questions and left again. I saw them drive up, and I saw them drive away. They never checked the windows or the doors. They never went around back."

"Maybe it was a lucky guess," Rory said noncommittally, but he didn't believe it. He'd known Hart years ago when he was a deputy, and he'd been corrupt then on a more minor level. Channing had bought him, all right, and bought him cheap. "He arrested me once for vandalism. He picked me up at my house, and I arrived at the sheriff's office a half hour later with a black eye and a few bruised ribs."

Shanna stared at him, her eyes wide. "He hit you?" she asked in dismay.

"Only once. He kicked me in the ribs."

"How old were you?"

"I don't know. Fourteen, fifteen."

"Why didn't you tell someone?"

"Who would have believed me?"

"Your mother."

"And who would have believed her?" When she didn't answer, he shrugged. "Right. Besides, Hart said he would kill me if I told, and *I* believed *him*."

"I'm sorry."

He heard the grimness in her voice, the acceptance that her beloved father, her dear hometown and friends and neighbors weren't perfect, had never been perfect. He could tell her other stories, stories that would shock her, stories that would repel her, but he'd offered enough disillusionment for one day.

Reaching up, he dried a drop of moisture that had remained under her eye, then left his fingers for just a moment on her cheek. Her skin was soft and cool, smooth and unlined. Her eyes were puffy and red from her tears, but she was beautiful.

And in the basest sense, she was his for the taking. His to touch, to hold, to kiss. He could seduce her, could make her entire body throb with need, could give her pleasure so intense that it was painful. Or he could simply take her, with no emotion, no gentleness, no passion, could take from her nothing but the dubious pleasure of a purely physical release and give her nothing, not even that same dubious pleasure, in return.

Or he could make love to her.

Abruptly he pulled his hand back. "You look better," he said gruffly. "Are you ready to brave the grocery store?"

When she nodded, he handed first her jacket, then her purse to her. Outside he waited while she locked the door, then they started across the street. It was just like before, he thought with an old familiar yearning—side by side but not touching. Together but apart.

Then, as they reached the sidewalk, Shanna reached out and hesitantly tucked her hand inside his. It was an effort to keep up their pretense for the few people they passed, he told himself, or maybe just a simple need for human contact—nothing more. It didn't mean she wanted that contact specifically from *him*. It didn't mean she would willingly accept anything more than this, his fingers wrapped protectively around hers, from him. It didn't mean she would *ever* accept anything more.

But maybe someday... He almost smiled at the thought. He, who had long ago given up on wishes and dreams and prayers, who had never lost hope because he'd never had any to lose... he was beginning to believe in maybes and somedays.

Chapter 5

Shanna was putting away the last of the groceries when Rory came into the kitchen. "Do you want some lunch?" she asked, stretching to reach the top shelf of the pantry.

"I want to see what's left of your father's truck."

She froze in the awkward stretch, the box of crackers she held swaying in her unsteady grip. Rory crossed the room and took the box from her, set it on the shelf and waited for her answer. The redness was gone from her eyes, and the puffiness from her tears had subsided, but now she was pale, deathly pale, beneath her bronzed skin. "Why?" she whispered.

"I might find something there that will help."

Slowly she sank from her toes until her feet were flat on the floor, and she hugged her arms to her chest, shivering. "Like what?"

"I don't know. You don't have to go with me. Just tell me where it is."

"At the salvage yard on the way to your house. The sheriff had it taken there."

He knew the place, had bought spare parts there years ago to keep his mother's old Ford running. "Does Mac Jardin still own it?"

She nodded.

"He might want to call you to make sure it's okay if I look around, so stay close to the phone. I'll be back in an hour or two."

He had reached the utility room door when she suddenly spoke. "Wait. I'll go with you."

Turning, he gave her a long look. She was still pale, and she acted almost as if she were in a trance. Seeing the truck, seeing the extent of the damage caused by the bomb and imagining what it had done to her father, might be more than she could handle. "You don't need to."

She gave a shake of her head, making her long hair shimmer. "Technically, what's left belongs to me. If there's a problem, I can deal with it."

"Can you deal with seeing the truck?" he asked more sharply than he'd intended. "Can you deal with knowing how your precious daddy died?"

His harsh questions made her pull herself together. Color returned to her cheeks as she gave him the haughty look that came so naturally to her. "I said I'll go with you. I want to know what you're looking for, and if you find something, I want to know what it is."

He didn't argue with her. It was just as well that she came along, he thought as he waited at the back door for her. Mac Jardin wasn't likely to let him look around without her permission, and it might help prepare her for his afternoon plans: more questions about her father's death. He'd let her put him off a few nights ago when he'd tried to question her because he'd felt sorry for her, but today he would get the answers—all of them.

When she joined him, they left for a silent drive to the salvage yard. Rory parked in front of the ramshackle building that housed both a garage and the office. His shiny black pickup looked strangely out of place, surrounded by rusted and smashed-up car bodies, ten-foot-high piles of parts and junk and small mountains of old tires.

"Can I help you?" a young man asked, stepping out of the garage as he wiped his hands on a rag. He looked from Rory to Shanna, nodded in greeting, then looked back to Rory.

"I understand Joseph Cassidy's truck was brought here a couple of weeks ago. We want to see it."

"It's around back." He looked at Shanna again. "You're his daughter, aren't you?"

"Yes, I'm Shanna Cassidy." She extended her hand, then let it drop back to her side when the young man held up his greasy hands. "You're Mr. Jardin's son-in-law, aren't you? Troy?"

"Yeah, that's me. I guess you can go on around and look at the truck. There's not much there to see."

"Thanks." Rory waited until Shanna fell in step beside him, and they circled the small building. There were more vehicles back here, some standing alone, others stacked precariously one on top of another. Joseph's truck sat alone in the middle of a clearing a hundred yards back.

The closer they got, the slower Shanna's steps became. Finally Rory left her standing motionlessly some fifty feet away and approached the burned out hulk alone. He walked in a slow circle around it, then moved in closer.

The cab of the truck had been blown apart, the windows shattered, the doors ripped off. The left front fender was gone, too, and the hood was grotesquely twisted on the left side. There was nothing recognizable inside, just lumps of charred rubber and chunks of misshapen metal. Rory crouched in front of the door on the driver's side and sifted through a pile of ash that had collected on the floor, sorting out a few metal fragments. After a moment he repeated the process on the other side, then stood up, his gaze catching on Shanna.

She had that sad, vulnerable look again that tore at his heart. She had been so close to her father, had shared a very special relationship with him. Damn it, this wasn't right. Joseph Cassidy may have been a bastard, but he hadn't deserved this. *She* hadn't deserved this.

A cloud of dust in the sky behind the garage drew his attention from her. Someone was coming into the salvage yard, apparently in quite a hurry, and he had a pretty strong hunch who it was. Someone who wouldn't want them coming around here. Someone with a vested interest in *not* solving Joseph's murder. Someone who'd already harassed them once today.

The sheriff's car came to a stop only a few yards from Shanna, and Hart climbed out of the passenger seat. "What are you doing over there, boy?" he called.

Rory folded his fingers over the metal fragments he'd found and slid them into his jacket pocket before he walked around the truck and started toward them. "Just looking."

"At what?" the sheriff demanded.

"I wanted to see how the old man bought it." He saw Shanna's stunned look, heard her swift intake and ignored it.

"That's evidence in an official investigation. You can't go snooping around it."

Shanna's head swiveled back around from Rory to the sheriff. "Evidence?" she echoed. "In what investigation? The only 'investigation' you've conducted was to have the truck brought out here."

"Now what else would you have us do, Shanna?" Hart asked.

Rory didn't like the condescension that colored the man's voice every time he spoke to Shanna. He remembered what she'd told him about Hart's attitude on the night of the break-in: *He patted me on the head like I was a silly little girl.* Yes, that was exactly the way he treated her—as if she were a dim-witted child whose whims had to be indulged.

"How about reporting the bomb to the ATF the way you're supposed to?" she responded hotly.

Hart looked incredulous. "A bomb? Now, Shanna, we don't have any reason to believe that this was caused by a bomb. Where in the world did you get an idea like that?"

"*You* told me." Her voice was strained by anger. "The day after the explosion, you told me that the bomb had been wired to the ignition or the brakes. You *told* me that."

"Layton, do you remember me telling her anything like that?" Hart asked the deputy who'd driven him out.

"No, sir, I don't."

"Damn it, Sheriff—"

He interrupted her with a pat on the arm. "Now, Shanna, you know you took a pretty good bump on the head that day. The doctor said there were things you couldn't remember, things you might never remember. Maybe that explains, too, why you're remembering things that didn't happen." With another pat on the arm, he walked away from her and went to stand beside Rory. "According to the neighbors, she was outside when it happened," he said in a low, confidential tone. "She saw the explosion, saw the body, too, though the doc says she doesn't remember it. Now there's no reason for you to encourage this crazy notion of hers that it was a bomb. . . ."

The sheriff continued talking, but Rory quit listening. He struggled to keep his expression blank as he looked at Shanna, who was staring furiously at the sheriff's back. He'd known from her injuries that she'd been somewhere nearby when the bomb detonated, but it hadn't occurred to him that she could have been outside, that she could have actually seen her father die.

He knew what explosions like this one could do to a fragile human body. The thought that Shanna had witnessed it, too—and that the victim had been her father!—sickened him. Dear God, no wonder she had nightmares. No wonder she'd turned to the Scotch for peace. And no wonder her mind had tried to protect itself by refusing to acknowledge those memories.

"So why don't you take her home where she belongs?" the sheriff finished up. "And both of you stay away from here. Don't nose around in department business, boy."

Rory didn't speak, but simply turned away, took hold of Shanna's arm and led her back to his truck. She waited only until the doors were closed and he'd started the engine before she blurted angrily, "That bastard! He's lying, Rory. I swear he is. He told me—"

"I believe you." He turned out of the driveway and onto the highway, then glanced at her. "What he said about the concussion—is that true?"

She refused to meet his eyes. "Yes," she said grudgingly. "But I didn't imagine him telling me that it was a bomb. Is it possible to wire a bomb to the brakes?"

"Yes."

"So you see, that proves it. How would I know that if someone hadn't told me? All you ever see on TV or read about is bombs wired to the ignition. They never talk about the brakes. He *told* me!"

"Shanna, I said I believe you."

His quiet assurance seemed to deflate her. She slumped back against the seat and closed her eyes. "God, I am tired," she whispered. Then, drawing from some inner reserve of strength, she drew herself upright again and asked, "What was the purpose of that remark back there?"

I wanted to see how the old man bought it. Rory winced at the memory of the shock that had clouded her face when he'd spoken. It hadn't been an easy thing to say, not only because Shanna was listening but also because of the sheriff. Experience had taught him long ago that the best course of action when confronted by a law officer was to keep his mouth shut. When he was a kid, innocent or careless words had often provoked violence that he'd been unable to handle. But the sheriff had wanted an answer, and that one had seemed most appropriate.

"What should I have told him? That we're trying to pin your father's murder on Channing? Or maybe that I'd picked a rather bizarre place to pay my respects to Joseph?'' He shook his head. ''Everyone in town knows how your father and I felt about each other. They've got to figure that I was overjoyed when he died, because it meant no more sneaking around. It meant I could move into town, right into Joseph's house, and flaunt our affair in front of them all.''

He turned onto her block, drove past the house and the scorched area, then pulled into the driveway. After he shut off the engine, he rested both arms on the steering wheel and looked at her. ''And *you* know how I felt about him. I'll help you, I'll protect you, and I'll pretend to be involved with you, but don't ask me to pretend to feel any grief over his death. The only way it affects me is through you. I'm sorry your father is dead. I know how that hurts. But I don't particularly care that District Attorney Joseph Cassidy is dead.''

He waited for her to turn away, angered by his animosity or insulted by his insensitivity. And she did turn away, but only to get out of the truck. She waited for him on the brick walk that led to the back door. ''I won't expect you to pretend to care about him,'' she said quietly. ''Particularly in light of what you told me this morning. I just wasn't prepared for that remark. It seemed so . . . callous.''

''It was meant to.'' He took the steps to the porch two at a time, unlocked the door and went inside. He flipped on the kitchen lights, then went to the table where he emptied his pocket of the pieces of metal he'd gathered from Joseph's truck.

''What are those?'' Shanna touched one with the tip of her finger, turning it end over jagged end.

''Metal fragments.''

''They're all the same kind of . . . what? Iron?'' she commented, comparing the color and the thickness and texture of several pieces. ''Why did you want them?''

''They're all that's left of the pipe bomb that killed your father.''

She jerked her hand back as if the cool gray chunks had burned, and she raised her eyes, dark and frightened, to his face. "Are you sure?"

He sat down in the nearest chair and pushed the fragments into a rough-edged circle. "I'm sure." He had put together enough bombs and had seen enough remains of detonated bombs to have no doubt.

But in another moment or so, Shanna would have doubts—not about the bomb, not about the information he was going to give her, but about *him*. In another moment, she was going to get over the shock that these few pieces of scrap metal had been responsible for her father's death, and she was going to realize that Rory, more than anyone else in Sandy Spring, was the most likely candidate to kill a man in this particular way.

"Judging from the extent of the damage, this bomb was about eight, maybe ten, inches long. It was probably placed underneath the seat on the driver's side, since that was where their target would sit. The worst damage was on the left side of the truck. The wires were run under the seat and the dashboard to tie into the electrical system." He looked up to see how she was dealing with his little speech. She was pale again and gripping the back of the chair in front of her for support. "Sit down, princess," he softly advised. "There's more."

Shanna slowly pulled the chair away from the table and sank into it. Her knees bumped his as she scooted the chair in.

"You were right about the brakes. The bomb could have been wired to the ignition and blown up when the key was turned, or it could have been hooked up to the brakes. The engine would start just fine, but the instant the brake pedal was pushed down and the brake lights came on, the bomb would detonate."

"Is there any way of finding out?" she asked numbly.

Other than the person who had wired it, he suspected that she was the only one who could tell them. If what the sheriff had said was true, if she had been outside when the blast happened, she might have other answers for them, too. But the sheriff had also said she didn't remember, and she admitted to having suffered a concussion. The answers might be locked up in her head—and she might insist on keeping them there. "It's not really important. It's just a matter of personal choice."

She was staring at the fragments with a sort of fascinated horror. "Is there any way to trace this pipe and whatever else was used?"

"No. The blasting cap could have been, but it was probably destroyed in the explosion. The rest of it—the pipe, the caps to seal the ends, the gunpowder, the wire—can't be traced."

Finally she looked at him again. "Why not? All those things had to be bought somewhere, and there aren't too many stores in this part of the state to choose from. We could check—" She broke off when he shook his head.

"This is standard, everyday plumbing pipe. It's sold in every hardware or building supply store in the country. So are the wire and the metal caps. The powder could have been bought at a gun store, or it could have been mixed up at home, with ingredients as harmless as sugar." He shook his head again. "Without the blasting cap, this kind of bomb is virtually untraceable."

For a long time they sat in silence. Rory listened to the ticking of the wall clock behind him and watched Shanna. She was assimilating everything he'd told her, and soon she was going to reach the one inescapable conclusion: that *he* might have killed her father.

Would she call off their agreement and order him out of her house? Would she call the sheriff and confide her suspicions in him? Would she be angry or shocked, or God help him, would it be fear and revulsion in her eyes when she looked at him?

He could handle her throwing him out, and he could deal with her setting the sheriff on him. But knowing that she feared him would be too much to endure.

Shanna couldn't stop her gaze from returning to those small pieces of metal lying on the table between her and Rory. They looked so innocent, so harmless, but they had killed her father. They were obscene in their innocence, deadly in their harmlessness.

Then she looked at Rory. He appeared neither innocent nor harmless. He knew so much about the making of bombs. Too much for the average soldier? She wanted to believe the answer was no. Bombs were an instrument of war, and soldiers were trained to fight wars. But in spite of her deplorable lack of knowledge about the Army, she knew the answer. She knew the average soldier was no more capable of building a bomb than she was. The Army had experts for that. And Rory had been one of those experts.

"Last Wednesday you took one look at the street outside, and you knew without a doubt that a bomb had gone off there," she said quietly. "The next night you told me that all bombings have to be reported to the ATF. Now you're telling me that you can put one of these together with sugar and plumbing pipe and a piece or two of wire. That's what you did in the Army, isn't it? You were a . . . what do they call it?"

"Explosive ordnance disposal specialist. A demolitions expert." His voice was hard and tough. "A door, safe, bridge, vehicle, building, plane, runway, ship, harbor entrance, on the ground, in the air or under the water—whatever you want, I can take it out for you. And it will be precise. Nothing but the target will be damaged. No one but the intended victim will be killed. I take pride in my work."

His boasting sounded defensive, she thought. Because he knew what she was thinking and he was guilty? Or because he knew that guilty or not, he would be *found* guilty, the way everyone in Sandy Spring had always found him guilty? He expected her to believe the worst of him the way everyone always had. No one had ever shown any faith in him, and he knew better than to expect it now.

Could he have killed her father? Logically she admitted the possibility. Some would say he had the motive, and there was no doubt he had the training. But immediately she rejected that possibility. Maybe it was her lawyer's instinct insisting that he wasn't guilty, that no matter what his training, Rory Hawkes wasn't a murderer. Maybe it was a woman's emotional defense of a man she was attracted to. Or maybe it was a girl's memories of a boy whose life had been harsh but who had managed to be gentle and caring in spite of it all.

No matter what line of reasoning she followed, she reached the same conclusion: she simply couldn't believe it was Rory who had placed the bomb in Joseph's truck. She knew that as surely as she knew she hadn't done it herself.

He was staring at the shrapnel, his head lowered, when she spoke. "When you told me the other night that your job in the Army had included picking locks, rappeling from aircraft and speaking exotic languages, you could have told me that it also included demolitions. I wouldn't have run screaming the other way."

His head jerked up, and his eyes met hers. Their expression was unguarded—surprise and confusion and relief so sharp that she knew beyond a doubt she'd been right. This man was no murderer. Then wariness replaced the other emotions, and he asked cautiously, "Are you sure you understand what I said? What I used to do?"

"What you *used* to do," she repeated. "I think it's safe to say that you haven't built any bombs since you came back to Sandy Spring." When the wariness remained, she smiled faintly. "This morning in my office I said that you were a good, decent and honorable man. That wasn't just talk, Rory. I believe it."

She paused to let the import of her words sink in, then gestured to the fragments. "What are you going to do with those?"

"Keep them for now. Do you have a plastic bag I can put them in?"

She got one from the pantry and handed it to him, then watched him seal the pieces inside and slip it into his pocket. "We're going to catch them, aren't we, Rory?" she asked quietly.

He looked up and smiled faintly. "Yeah," he agreed. Then his half of the bargain would be completed. She would pay her half, and he would go back to his lonely life and never be with her again. As futures went, it wasn't much.

But it was all he had.

Sundays had always been lazy days for Shanna, with no work, errands or housework to claim her time. Today, though, she sat on the floor in Joseph's office, sorting through the piles of papers she and Rory had gathered. She knew it would be easier to simply set aside anything that didn't pertain to Lawrence Channing, but she preferred to reorganize all the files as she went. It made a tedious job more so.

With a sigh she leaned against the wall and rolled her head in a slow circle. "Want to take a break?"

Rory, also seated on the floor and surrounded by stacks of paper, shook his head. "You aren't too anxious to work on this, are you?"

"Putting thousands of loose pages back into their proper folders? No. It bores me."

"I mean the investigation." He set down the handful of papers he held and picked up his cigarettes, drawing one out of the package and lighting it. Shanna wordlessly slid her empty coffee cup over to him for an ashtray. "Have you figured out a course of action? How are you going to proceed? Where are you going to start?"

"I have my father's personal phone directory. It includes numbers for some people I don't know—people whose only possible connection to him must be business. I thought I would compare our long-distance charges for the last couple of months to those numbers to find out if he'd called them recently. If he did, maybe they'll talk to me. Maybe they'll tell me what he wanted from them." She shrugged uneasily. "After all, it worked with you."

"Okay. What else?"

"Well, we know that the mayor, the town council members and the sheriff are on Channing's payroll, so—"

"We suspect," he interrupted.

"We *know* it. Come on, Rory, the people in power in this town are so corrupt that it's frightening."

"Do you have proof?"

She stared at him in annoyed silence.

"You're a lawyer, Shanna. I shouldn't have to explain the concept of slander to you."

"All right," she agreed with a scowl. "We *suspect* that these people are on Channing's payroll, so I thought they would be a good place to start—see if we can find proof connecting them to Channing."

"What else?"

"Channing himself. I want to know where he lived before he came to Sandy Spring, how he made his money, if he'd ever been arrested."

"Have you started any of this?"

She rose to her knees, then leaned forward and took the cigarette away from him, stubbing it out in the cup. "If I can give up the Scotch, you can give up those horrid things."

"If you'd told me it bothered you, I would have stopped," he said coolly. "You're changing the subject. Have you put any of these plans into motion?"

With a sigh she dropped back to the floor. "No, I haven't."

"Why not?"

"Because I'm afraid." She knew right now that the danger facing them, if any, was minimal. There'd been no more incidents since the break-in. Either Channing's men had found what they wanted or they believed, as she did, that it must have been destroyed in the explosion. She was safe, and so was Rory.

But the minute she began actively looking into Lawrence Channing's activities, she would place both their lives in danger—hers because Channing wouldn't tolerate her snooping any more than her father's, and Rory's because he was protecting her. She could be setting in motion the events that would lead not only to her own death, but also to Rory's, and she wasn't certain she could face that possibility.

"Afraid of dying? Or of failing?"

She smiled. "I'm used to failure. That wouldn't be anything new. No, I believe we can find the proof we need if we just look in the right places. But I don't want to die, and I don't want to be responsible for your death. I don't want to live with the fear of dying. I don't want to be afraid to go to the store or to be alone in my office in the afternoons while Susan picks up her daughter. I don't want to spend every day wondering if this is the day they're going to try to kill us."

"So you have two choices. You can forget this and remain safe and know that Channing got away with murdering your father. Or you can get this investigation over with as quickly as possible so you don't have to spend every day wondering if it's going to be your last."

"I can't forget it."

"I know."

"So . . . I'll get started tomorrow. I promise."

He shook his head. "We started yesterday, when we went out to look at your father's truck. Did you ever wonder why the sheriff showed up at that particular moment?"

She hadn't really given it any thought, she realized, probably because she had been too numbed by the sight of her father's pickup. Now she made the most logical guess. "Because Jardin's son-in-law called him?"

"Right. Do you suppose the kid calls the sheriff every time someone comes out to look at one of their vehicles?"

She moved from the floor to sit in one of the two leather chairs, feet drawn into the seat, disregarding the damage done in last week's search. "You're saying that the sheriff told Jardin and Troy to call him if we showed up?"

Rory shook his head. "He couldn't know that it would be you and me. You could have hired a private detective to look into it, or you could have reported it to the ATF, who would have sent a couple of agents out, or maybe one of your brothers could have gone out there. He probably told them to let him know if *anyone* showed up to look at your father's truck."

"So you think they may already suspect that we're up to something."

"I think we can't afford to underestimate them. Your father did, and look what it got him."

She was silent for a moment, then she asked in a slightly unsteady voice, "Do you have any suggestions?"

"A couple." He got easily to his feet and turned the second chair to face hers before sitting down. He braced one foot on the seat of hers, his leather tennis shoe big and clunky beside her slender, socked feet. "First, can you get me the full names and social security numbers of the sheriff and all his deputies?"

"The names are no problem. For the social security numbers I'll have to check with voter registration. That's in the courthouse. So is Hart's office. I'm not sure it's a very good idea to go over there asking questions about him and his men."

"No," he agreed. "Just the names, then. If I have to have the social security numbers, I can get them."

"What are you going to do?"

"See if any of them were in the military and what their specialties were."

"You think the person who set the bomb might have been an explosive ordnance...." She'd forgotten the rest of the title he'd given her yesterday and improvised. "A demolitions expert?"

"Not everyone who builds pipe bombs has a military background, but it can't hurt to check."

"All right. And your other suggestion?"

He sat in silence for a moment, studying her. She looked stronger today, better rested, although there were still faint shadows beneath her eyes. She had been up in the middle of the night again, but she'd slept until nine this morning, and the few extra hours' rest showed on her face.

He took a deep breath and let it out. He had tried to question her about this once before and had let the subject drop because she'd been so vulnerable at the time. Yesterday he had promised himself he would talk to her after their visit to the salvage yard, but that promise had been broken, too. Between his revelations about Joseph in her office yesterday morning, the two run-ins with the sheriff, seeing all that was left of her father's truck and the bomb that had destroyed it, and finding out about his own expertise with bombs, she'd had enough stress for one day, he'd decided.

But he couldn't put it off anymore. "I want you to tell me everything you can remember about the day your father died."

He saw the rigidity spread through her. Within moments she was so stiff that he could move her, and she wouldn't bend—but she might break. He stifled the familiar urge to tell her to forget it, to avoid anything that might cause her further distress.

"I don't want to talk about that," she said, her voice unnaturally taut.

"You have to. You might remember something important."

"Didn't you hear the sheriff yesterday?" she asked flippantly. "There are things about that day I don't remember. Things I will probably never remember."

"Because of the concussion? Or because they're too horrible to remember?"

She fixed a cold and angry glare on him. "I'm not going to talk about this. You want all the gruesome details, go ask the neighbors. But you're not getting them from me."

She started to stand up, but he was quicker, leaning forward, blocking her way, forcing her back into the chair. He bent toward her, his hands braced on the chair arms. "You're going to tell me, princess, because you want the man responsible for your precious daddy's death brought to justice. It may be difficult, but you're going to sit here and tell me everything."

"Sometimes I hate you," she whispered fiercely.

He hid the stab of pain her words caused behind a mocking grin. "You're a Cassidy, and I'm a Hawkes. So what's new?"

"Get out of my face." When he didn't move, she sat back in the chair, putting as much distance between them as possible. "What do you want to know?"

"Everything."

She stared at him a moment longer, her expression mutinous; then everything went blank. There was no emotion in her eyes, on her face, in her voice. "I'd had company the night before, so I'd gotten to bed late and overslept that morning. I got dressed—everything but my shoes. I was still wearing slippers. When I came downstairs, Dad was already on his way out. He kissed me, said he would see me at noon—we had lunch together whenever we could—and he left. Then..." She clasped her hands together tightly. "I heard the explosion. It was loud, and it made the ground shake. And the smells... Gasoline and burning rubber. They were awful. The neighbors came out of their houses, and someone called the sheriff and the ambulance, and everyone was shouting, and someone was screaming." Her voice trembled then. "It—it was me."

Rory considered her recitation for a moment. It had raised more questions and answered none. "Where were you when your father kissed you goodbye?"

"In the hall at the bottom of the stairs."

"Did he leave through the front door?"

"Yes."

"Where did he normally park his truck?"

"In the driveway where yours is. But my friend's car was there when he came home the night before, so he parked in the street. He was already in bed by the time she left, so it stayed there all night."

"So you came downstairs as he was leaving. He kissed you and went out. Did he close the door behind him?"

"Yes."

"And the next thing you remember is the explosion."

She turned her head sharply to avoid looking at him.

"What did you see when the bomb exploded?"

"Flames," she whispered.

"Where were you?"

"On the sidewalk."

"Why?"

She said nothing.

"Why did you go outside after your father left? Was there something you wanted to tell him? Something he'd forgotten?"

She met his eyes then and smiled sickly. "That's one of those things I don't remember."

"How did you get hurt?"

She shrugged.

"You said you'd gotten dressed. What were you wearing?"

"A beige skirt, a red blouse and yellow slippers. I don't have them anymore. The nurse at the hospital threw them away."

"Why?"

She lifted her hand to her throat, her fingertips tracing the almost-healed laceration there. "They were dirty and bloody. I didn't want them anymore."

"Was it cold that morning?"

"Yes."

"You went outside on a cold February morning wearing a skirt, blouse and slippers—no jacket, no coat, no shoes. Your reason must have been important."

"I suppose it was." She gestured impatiently. "But I don't remember, and no matter how many times you ask, I'm not *going* to remember."

"You don't want to, do you?" he asked quietly.

"What a brilliant deduction," she said sarcastically. "And here I thought all Hawkeses were stupid."

He forced himself to ignore her insult and to concentrate on the issue. "When the bomb exploded, the blast knocked you to the ground, and you hit your head. Do you remember that?"

"No."

"Do you remember feeling any pain in your face?" He touched the scrape on her cheek, then her jaw where the bruise had faded to a pale shadow.

"No."

"You don't know if you lost consciousness."

She shook her head.

He drew his hand away and, for the first time since beginning the conversation, settled back in the chair. "Would you consider talking to a psychologist?"

"No," she said flatly.

"He could help you deal with this."

"I'm dealing with this just fine."

"No, you're not. You're not sleeping well. You were drinking too much. You still have nightmares. I hear you in the middle of the night when you're trying to fall asleep again."

"I'll be quieter in the future."

"Damn it, I'm not complaining!" he snapped, surging forward again to trap her in her seat. "I'm trying to help you, Shanna!"

"*Help?* How? By forcing me to remember the things that my brain has chosen to forget?" She leaned forward, too, until they were so close that he could see the tears forming in her eyes. "I'm not stupid, Rory! I realize that I was outside when the truck blew up! I *saw* it happen! I *saw* my father die! And I *won't* remember it! Do you understand? There's nothing anyone can do that will make me remember what I saw that morning!"

Grimly he left his chair and went to look out the window. She was wrong. He knew from his Army training that there were several things that could be done to make her remember: an injection of sodium amytal, a barbiturate used as a sedative or hypnotic, or possibly simple hypnosis. The problem was getting her permission for the first, her cooperation for the second. No ethical doctor would conduct a sodium amytal interview on an unwilling patient, and he wasn't sure how successful hypnosis would be with a hostile one.

And he couldn't even argue with her. He knew what she had seen, knew the ugliness and the horror. Finding out exactly what had happened that morning wasn't worth making her live with those memories for the rest of her life.

"I'm not trying to be obstructive," she said quietly from some point close behind him. "From the time my father walked out the door until after the explosion, there are a lot of things I simply don't remember. I don't know why I went outside. I don't know when. Logically I know that I got hurt when the blast knocked me down, but I don't remember that."

He saw her come to stand beside him, leaning against the window frame to face him.

"During that blank, I have only images—the flames, the smells, the noise. It's like a bad dream. Like a movie out of focus. Then, starting about ten or fifteen minutes after the explosion, I can remember everything."

"How did you get to the hospital?"

"A friend who lives on the next block and her husband took me."

"What did the doctor say?"

"That I had a mild concussion. That none of the other injuries were serious and that they wouldn't leave any scars." Her voice quavered.

"He was wrong, wasn't he?" Rory asked quietly. "The scars are inside. No one can see them, but you can feel them, and they're worse than any he could imagine." He touched her hair in a light caress that ended on her shoulder. "But the hurting will go away in time. You'll be able to remember your father and the way he lived without remembering the way he died."

She looked up at him solemnly. He was speaking from his own experience. He understood how she felt in a way that her mother and her brothers couldn't, because he'd seen people he cared for die violent deaths.

She wished he would use his hand on her shoulder to pull her close, wished he would offer the comfort she needed. It would ease the growing need within her to simply be held, to feel someone's arms around her—to feel *his* arms around her—and know that for those precious moments, he would take care of her.

It would be so easy, he thought, still gazing out the window, to draw her against him, to wrap his arms around her and simply hold her slender, fragile body against his. It would fill a need he'd had since he was a kid, a need that he had buried for twenty-one years under anger and bitterness and hatred for her family, for her town, for the injustice in life that had let a poor, worthless nobody like him fall for a beautiful, privileged princess like her. Entire years had passed when he hadn't thought of her, but she had always been a part of him, a part of who and what he was.

But if he held her, if he allowed himself that innocent contact with her, how would she respond? Worse, how would *he* respond? Wanting her the way he did, holding her close would result in a need so powerful that it couldn't be hidden or denied.

How would she view his arousal? With fear? Disgust? Would she assume that her grace period had run out, that it was time for him to take what he'd demanded, what she had promised? Would she be reluctant to share such intimacy with him, or would she be resolute, determined to get it over with as quickly and as painlessly as possible?

Or would she enjoy it? Would she be as eager to have him for a lover as she'd been at fifteen?

He frowned harshly at the scene outside. Shouldn't he have said as eager as she had *pretended* to be at fifteen? It had all been part of her game, hadn't it—leading him on, making him think she liked him, that she wanted him? But her responses to his kisses and caresses had been real. He'd been with enough women in his life to know that. As virginal and naive as she'd been, she couldn't have faked them.

But that didn't make sense. If she'd really wanted him, if her husky, passionate pleas for him to make love to her had been sincere, why had she been so cruel the day he'd confronted her at school? Why had she publicly shamed him for daring to want her?

What did it matter? he wondered wearily. It had happened more than twenty years ago. They were different people now, both responsible, mature adults. An unpleasant incident from their teens shouldn't affect the business between them now.

But it did. That bitterly hurt boy still lived inside him and still wondered in the dark, lonely nights why she'd done it.

He withdrew his hand from her shoulder, denying her even that small contact. Aware of the despair it might reveal, Shanna kept her sigh inside. Maybe, because she was trying to deal with the loss of her father, she was vulnerable to any man right now. Maybe she had always been vulnerable to *this* man. Whatever the reason, this affair was going to cost her a great deal. When it ended, when he walked away without a single look back, she was going to have to deal with another loss.

This time she was going to lose her heart.

Chapter 6

In her office Monday morning Shanna pulled her father's appointment calendar from her briefcase and laid a stack of telephone bills on top of it. Rory had found them last night, just as they were getting ready to call it a day. Even though she'd known she should compare the numbers right away, she had put it off until today, and he had let her.

But now, while Susan was gone and the answering machine was turned on for any calls, she copied the numbers from her father's calendar and began comparing them to the phone bills. They had made a lot of long-distance calls in the last four months—to her mother in Dallas, Jody in Austin and Alex in Oklahoma City, to her friends from college and her mother's parents in Fort Worth, and to her father's fellow lawyers and friends all over the state of Texas.

A half hour later she studied the list she'd made from the bills. There had been no calls to the FBI agent in El Paso, but in the six weeks preceding Joseph's death, he'd made four calls to the private detective in Odessa and three to the accountant in Midland. And they had been lengthy calls, each lasting twenty minutes or more. Had they been about Lawrence Channing?

She picked up the phone and started to dial the accountant's number, but halfway through she hung up again. What would she say to him? How would she convince him to confide the nature of his business with her father to a stranger over the telephone?

Maybe she should go see him, and the private detective, too. A short stretch of interstate connected the two cities. She could leave early in the morning and be back that night.

Or maybe she should wait and ask Rory's opinion. He was due anytime now to take her to lunch. She didn't know if he'd offered because she had told him that she'd always had lunch with her father, or if it was just another part of their act for the town, but she had gratefully accepted. Now she was looking forward to his arrival, even though he'd dropped her off at work less than four hours ago.

"Every time I come in here, you're sitting there so lost in thought that you don't hear me. Don't you ever work?"

She turned to look at Rory and smiled. "Both times I was thinking about you."

"Where is your secretary?"

"Gone to lunch. She'll be back in about fifteen minutes. Come on in and sit down."

He did as she suggested, slouching down in one of the chairs facing her desk. "Find any matches on the phone bills?" he asked, gesturing with a nod to the papers spread across her desk.

"Yeah, I did—the private detective and the accountant." She handed him the notes she'd made. "I thought it would be best if I talk to them in person. I can drive to Odessa, then go on to Midland, talk to them both and be back the same day."

He studied the list for a moment, then leaned forward for the phone. While Shanna listened, he called the accountant and made an appointment for Wednesday morning in his name. He chose not to call the private detective, though.

When Shanna asked him why, he responded with a shrug. "You said last week that your father didn't tell you anything about his investigation. So how did you know to come to me for help?"

She opened the appointment calendar to the last week in February and slid it across the desk. He read the five-word note she had memorized. *See Rory Hawkes about L.C.* "How did *he* know I could help?"

"He told me once that he'd checked into your background."

"How?"

"My father was a powerful man. He had friends everywhere. I'm sure one of them is somehow connected to the Army."

"Or?"

She frowned. There was obviously a point he wanted to make—no, wanted to make her discover—but she must be dense because she certainly wasn't finding it. What did the method her father had used to check out Rory's background have to do with his refusal to make an appointment with the private invest—

"Or he might have hired the P.I. to find out for him." Her groan was heavy with self-disgust. She *was* dense not to have seen it.

"Right. So we'll drop in on him after we see the accountant Wednesday. There's no sense in giving him advance warning."

"We?" she echoed. "You don't think it's okay for me to drive that far alone?"

"I don't think it's okay to take any unnecessary chances." Then he changed the subject. "I was in your father's office again this morning. Where are the disks to the computer?"

She thought of the computer that lay on the floor at home, not just moved aside during the search but deliberately destroyed. "I don't know where he kept them—somewhere in the office, I'm sure. Maybe they're buried underneath the papers or the books."

He shook his head. "I put all the books back on the shelf, and we cleaned up most of the papers last night. I couldn't find them anywhere."

"Maybe he didn't have any. Some computers don't require them for everyday use, do they?"

Again he shook his head. "To work without floppies requires a hard disk drive, and that computer doesn't have one. He had to have some disks somewhere, but they're not in that office."

"Maybe Channing's men took them."

"Maybe." He glanced at the door, becoming still and quiet moments before Shanna heard movement in the outer office.

"You must have exceptional hearing," she commented as she stood up and walked toward the door. "Susan?"

"Yeah, it's me." The secretary reached the door about the same time Shanna did. "You can head out for lunch as soon as your date— Oh, he's here." She smiled uneasily. "Hello, Rory."

His only response was a curt nod. He rarely spoke to anyone, Shanna noticed—not to Susan or the people in the café Saturday, and he'd said only a few words to the sheriff. She wondered if he had always been so quiet or if it was a learned response—if he didn't speak, he didn't draw attention to himself. She wondered if he ever got lonely for someone to talk to, someone to share his thoughts with.

She did. She'd paid little attention to the empty space in her life because there had always been others around—her mother and grandparents and friends in Dallas, her father, family and friends here. But as close as she was to all those people, none of them could take the place of someone special in her life. Someone she could tell that being a lawyer wasn't enough, that she wanted more from life. Someone who would understand that she wanted to be a mother, that she worried because she was thirty-six years old and there was no potential husband, no potential marriage, no potential father for her child.

She wanted someone to share her thoughts with, some-one to share her life with. She wanted someone to love. She wanted to matter to someone.

She wanted to matter to Rory.

Suddenly she became aware that her secretary was watching her with an amused expression. "Did I miss something?" she asked, shaking her head to clear it.

"I said you'd better go if you're going to get back in time for your one-thirty appointment. And the special at the café is meat loaf, so be prepared."

"Thanks for the warning." She gathered the papers on her desk, put them into her briefcase, then picked up her purse. Leaving the jacket to her pale blue suit on the back of her chair, she left the office with Rory, achingly aware of the light touch of his hand in the center of her back as they walked.

After a few steps toward the café, she stopped walking. "Remember the drive-in over by the school?"

He nodded.

"Let's go there for lunch instead. The kids should be back in class by now, and the hamburgers are still good, and we can sit outside at one of the tables."

He didn't question why she wanted to avoid the café, but simply gestured toward his truck parked at the curb.

When they arrived at the drive-in, there were few customers, all teenagers gathered at one end. Rory parked at the opposite end, shut off the engine and rolled down the window.

"See the flashy sports car?" Shanna asked. "That belongs to Darren Webster. Counting Dad, there were three lawyers in town. One, Channing's right-hand man, is the new district attorney. The other is Bert Webster, Darren's father. He works for Channing, too. The Websters have a big gorgeous house a couple of blocks from ours, and they gave Darren that car to replace the Mustang he got for his sixteenth birthday. The Mustang was totaled in a drunk driving accident. Several people were injured, but the sheriff didn't even give him a slap on the wrist. My father and Hart had a serious argument about it."

"When was this?"

"Last month."

"Channing apparently pays well. Maybe you should court a little of his business yourself," Rory remarked idly. "What do you want to eat?"

She told him, and he placed the order through the speaker mounted outside his window. When he finished, she gave him a slight smile. "I gather you're not impressed with my law practice."

"It's not my place to approve or disapprove."

"It's not thriving—I'll be the first to admit that. The only reason I can afford to have Susan full-time is that I don't pay rent. The building belongs to my fath—to my family. Fortunately I have enough money of my own that I don't have to worry about it."

"Why are you here? It seems like you'd fit in better in some big fancy firm with a couple dozen names on the letterhead."

She gazed out the window for a moment, watching the kids, wondering if she'd ever been that young, knowing she hadn't been that carefree—at least, not for long. One brief, springtime romance had made sure of that.

Then she looked back at her partner in that springtime romance—her partner in something far more serious, more dangerous, this time. "I tried that route. After graduation from law school, I got a job, with my father's help, I think, at one of the most prestigious law firms in Dallas. It was okay—not what I had hoped to do with my degree, but all right as jobs went. I'd been there four years when the partners called me in one day. They felt it was only fair to tell me that I was never going to make partner myself. It wasn't my education or my grasp of the law, they said, but me personally. I wasn't aggressive enough or tough enough. I didn't have the killer instinct. I didn't want to win at any cost."

She broke off to watch the carhop, a young girl not more than eighteen and about five months pregnant, carry their food out. She balanced the tray on the partially raised window on Rory's side, took his money and made change, then returned to the kitchen, moving as if she were worn-out.

"Hell of a job for a pregnant kid," Rory commented. "Do you still want to sit at one of the tables?"

She glanced at the tables situated between the two rows of parking, then at the kids again. They were a rowdy bunch, always looking for trouble or fun and often finding both. The less she and Rory did to attract their attention, the better. "Let's stay here."

He handed her lunch to her and passed out napkins, catsup and small packets of salt and pepper. "So you didn't have the killer instinct. You couldn't have been incompetent. I heard that trait was bred out of the Cassidys a few generations back."

What would have been a stinging insult last week was merely a mild jibe today. She managed not to smile at it. "No, I wasn't incompetent. I only lacked in the area that mattered most to them: money. Billable hours. The big bucks come from winning the big cases, and I didn't win the few I handled. The kind of cases I was good at were the occasional *pro bono*. Of course, rather than bringing money into the firm, those took it out. Not only were my services free to the client, but also those of the staff who helped me prepare. So... I quit."

"Why didn't you go into practice for yourself and handle nothing but *pro bono* cases? You couldn't make much less than you're making here."

"I thought about it," she replied with a smile. "A friend of mine from law school has a little storefront practice in one of the rougher neighborhoods in Dallas. He's so busy that he needs all the help he can get. But... Dad wanted me to come back here, and considering everything that went bad in Dallas, I thought it would be best."

Did she know her smile was wistful? Rory wondered. Who ever would have believed that Shanna Cassidy had a burning desire to donate her services to people who needed them? She must be the first Cassidy in at least a hundred years to develop a social conscience.

He finished his hamburger and wadded the foil-backed wrapper, tossing it onto the tray. "Everything that went bad?" he repeated. "You quit your job. That hardly constitutes a major disaster. What else happened?"

While she delayed, he finished his French fries and took a few of hers. By the time they were gone, too, she was ready to continue.

"I was engaged at the time. My fiancé was a state senator with big plans for the future. A wife who was an up-and-coming hotshot lawyer with one of the biggest firms in Dallas would be an asset to his political career. When he realized that I *wasn't* a hotshot lawyer..." She sighed. "It was nothing personal, you know, but he had to consider his future."

Rory stared at her, the muscles in his jaw clenched tightly. Nothing personal? The bastard called off their engagement because she wasn't successful enough, and it was *nothing personal?*

She wrapped her leftovers in a tight ball, stuffed them inside the soft drink cup and handed it to him. "He really was a son of a bitch," she said, her tone almost pleasant.

He removed the tray from the window, leaving it on the post beneath the speaker, then settled back in the seat. Had she been in love with the man? he wondered. The possibility made him uneasy... because he was jealous? Because even though he couldn't have her for his own, he didn't want any other man to have her?

Maybe her feelings for the senator had had no more depth, no more permanence, than his for her. Maybe her reasons for accepting his marriage proposal had included everything but love. She certainly didn't sound like a woman jilted by the man she'd loved.

But it had happened a long time ago, and time, so the saying went, healed all wounds.

Except his.

"I didn't mean to talk so much about myself," she said apologetically. "Now it's your turn."

He gave her a silent glance.

"Don't forget—I'm a lawyer. I know how to ask questions," she teased.

"And I've been trained not to answer them." Then he relented. "What do you want to know?"

"Well...have you ever been married?"

"No."

"Ever come close?"

He thought about the women he'd known in the past twenty years—the affairs and the one-night stands, the relationships, the friendships, the warm bodies whose names he'd never known. "I lived with a woman for five years, but I never wanted to marry her."

"Why not?"

He shrugged. He wasn't going to talk of love—the love he'd never felt, had never even come close to except with Shanna all those years ago. Not to her.

"What was her name?"

"Melanie." He hadn't seen her in a long time, not since he'd come home from a training operation that had taken him out of the country for a week without warning. Her plans had been made, her bags packed. All she'd waited for was to tell him goodbye. She didn't want to live with a man who did what he did for a living. She was tired of the secrecy his job required, tired of his frequent absences, tired of his brooding silences when he was home. All in all, except for the sex, she was tired of *him*.

He had carried her bags to the car, given her some money and watched her drive away. And when he had returned to the empty apartment, he'd hardly missed her. For five years she had been the only woman he'd gone out with, the only one he'd spent time with, the only one he'd slept with, and her leaving hadn't caused more than a minor disruption in his life. It had made him wonder why she'd waited so long to go.

"Did you like the Army?"

"Would I have stayed in more than twenty years if I didn't?"

"People have been known to stay in jobs they dislike."

He smiled faintly. "Yes, I liked the Army. But I could have done without Vietnam."

"It must have been horrible," she said softly.

"It was a war, princess. Wars are always horrible."

"Does it . . ." She chose her words carefully. "Does it bother you?"

He gave her a long, hard look. "You mean, do I have flashbacks? Do I see Viet Cong around every corner? Do I wake up in a cold sweat believing I'm back in the jungle? Am I liable to creep across the hall some night believing you're the enemy and slit your throat?" Slowly he shook his head. "It was a job, and it was terrible, but it's been over for years. I don't think about it much. It doesn't affect my life today, any more than fighting in Europe in World War II affected your father's life twenty years later."

"Some people who were in Vietnam still have a lot of trouble dealing with what they saw and did there," she said quietly.

"Some people do. But the majority of men who fought in Vietnam are leading normal, productive lives, just like the majority of veterans of other wars. Just like the majority of men who didn't fight."

He glanced at his watch, then started the engine. "Question time is up. You've got an appointment in ten minutes."

They drove back downtown in silence. As they approached the block where her office was located, Shanna said, "You can just let me out in front since there aren't any parking spaces nearby."

He stopped in front of her office as she'd suggested, then quietly remarked, "Since we have four of Sandy Spring's finest watching us from across the street—including your friend and mine, Sheriff Hart—why don't you lean over here and give me a kiss?"

His request startled and embarrassed her, he saw. Well, she couldn't be any more reluctant than he was. He'd had some foolish notion that their first kiss ought to be a prelude to something more intimate, not a public display for the sheriff's benefit. But things had rarely worked out the way he would have liked, so why should this be any different? "Just a quick goodbye kiss, princess," he murmured. "It won't hurt too much."

She touched the tip of her tongue to her lips, swallowed hard and slid across the seat. "This is going to make it hard to concentrate on Benny Wallace's will," she said before her mouth brushed across his.

It was perfectly acceptable for a public kiss—brief and impersonal. There was no reason it should make him think of passion. No reason it should call up images of what a real kiss with heat and need and hunger would be like. No reason it should make him think about tangling his hands in her soft black hair and holding her still for a leisurely exploration of her mouth. There was no reason at all this simple dispassionate kiss should make him hard with desire.

But it did.

Shanna slid back across the seat and opened the door. "Thanks for taking me to lunch," she said, avoiding his gaze. "I . . . I'll see you later."

He watched until she was safely inside the office, then drove away. This is going to make it hard to concentrate, she'd said.

God, she had been right.

When Rory returned to the office with Shanna after lunch Tuesday afternoon, she gave him a list of every employee of the sheriff's department, including dispatchers. Every name on the list included a middle name, and each one was followed by a number.

"Where did you get this information?"

"The library has the commencement programs from every graduation ever held at Sandy Spring High, and they list full names for each graduate. The numbers are the years each of them graduated. That gives us some idea of how old they are." She watched him fold the paper and slide it into his hip pocket. "The program for 1970 listed you. Rory Joseph Hawkes."

The look he gave her was measuring. "So?"

"You're named after your father."

"Joseph was his name, the name his family called him—just like your father. Only folks in town decided that name was pretentious for poor trash like him, so they called him Joe. Crazy Joe." For a moment he was silent, looking at her but not seeing her. Then he added quietly, bitterly, "They wouldn't even let him have the dignity of his own name."

Shanna felt the weight of his sorrow as if it were her own. She remembered some of the taunts, the insults, the spiteful tricks people had pulled on his father. Joe had never seemed to care—he'd been too gentle, too simple, to even recognize malice in others. But Rory... God, how it must have hurt him! She touched him, her fingers resting lightly on the sleeve of his jean jacket. "I'm sorry. I didn't mean to resurrect bad memories."

He looked at her hand, then took a step away. "Bad memories are the only kind I have, princess."

"That's not true," she quietly disagreed. "I know your life was hard, but you were lucky in some respects. Your parents loved you a great deal. Your mother taught you to be responsible and honest—in spite of all the trouble you got into—and your father taught you to be gentle and kind."

Gentle and kind. He smiled humorlessly. He'd never thought of himself as a gentle or kind man. He was too selfish, too intent on looking out for himself, on keeping anyone from getting close enough to matter, close enough to hurt him. Even Melanie, the woman he'd been most deeply involved with, hadn't been able to hurt him. Even she would agree there was little gentleness or kindness in him.

"I need to make some long-distance calls," he said. "Is it okay if I do it from your house?"

The subject of his past had been closed, and she had been shut out along with it. She tried not to let the hurt show on her face or in her voice. "Of course. Or you could do it here if you want."

He shook his head. There were things he was planning to discuss that would be best done in private. "I'll do it from the house. See you later."

A sheriff's department car was parked a few spaces down from Rory's pickup, and the driver, the deputy named Layton who'd been with Hart at the salvage yard Saturday, was standing beside it. He climbed into his car as Rory walked by and backed into the street after Rory drove past. He remained a couple of car lengths back all the way to the Cassidy house. There he drove past, made a U-turn at the intersection and came back for a second slower look.

The sheriff had claimed Saturday that the increased patrols in the neighborhood were for their own protection because of the break-in, but Rory knew better. He'd been under close scrutiny from the sheriff's department often enough in his life to know that he and Shanna were being watched. They weren't even trying to be subtle about it.

He let himself in the back door and automatically locked it behind him. The house was quiet during the day, empty when Shanna wasn't in it. It made him uncomfortable, as if he didn't belong here—and, of course, he didn't. This was Joseph Cassidy's house, and no Hawkes had ever earned the right or been offered an invitation to enter it. *He* hadn't been invited, either. He had forced his way in, and Shanna, because she was alone, because she was afraid, had let him stay.

He climbed the half dozen steps to Joseph's office, seated himself at the desk and reached for the phone. Within moments he was talking to Rick Montoya, the Delta staff sergeant in charge of personnel. After a few moments of idle conversation, he said, "I have a favor to ask of you, Rick. Can you run some names through the computer for me and see if you can find any record of past military service?"

"Sure thing, Rory. Give me the names."

He read each name from the list, finishing with Charley Mangrum. "I don't have social security numbers on them, but if it's necessary, I can probably get them."

"Unless you're in a real hurry, don't bother yet. Some of them may not even show up. It may be a couple of days before I can get back to you. I'll have to call the National Personnel Records Center in St. Louis and see what they can turn up."

"I appreciate it." He gave him Shanna's phone number, then added, "If you can't reach me here, call this number and leave a message for me to get in touch with you. Don't mention what it's about." He followed that with her office number. "Listen, is Doc Saxon still with the unit?"

"Yeah, he is," the sergeant replied. "You want to talk to him? I think I can switch you."

"Please. Thanks a lot, Rick." He waited a moment, listening to the soft hum on the wire before the psychologist came on.

"How's retirement treating you, master sergeant? Miss the job much?"

"No, sir. I kind of enjoy the quiet life." He paused for a moment, debating what he wanted to say. Somehow it seemed like a betrayal of Shanna—a necessary betrayal, but a betrayal all the same. "I'd like your professional opinion on something, sir. I have a friend whose father was recently killed—murdered," he amended, "in an explosion that she witnessed. She was slightly injured herself—some cuts and bruises—and was diagnosed as suffering a mild concussion. Her memory of the explosion is pretty sketchy. She's clear on some points and totally blank on others."

He paused and cleared his throat. "She was always extraordinarily close to him, so I'm guessing that the shock of seeing him die triggered some type of amnesia. If she were your patient, sir, what course of treatment would you recommend?"

"It sounds like psychogenic amnesia in the selective form. Does all the memory loss focus around her father's death?"

"Yes, sir."

The psychologist considered it for a moment, then said, "Frankly, I don't know that I would recommend treatment. If it's not affecting other areas of her life and she seems to be dealing with her grief... Is she?"

"Reasonably, although she's not sleeping well. She's had nightmares about the explosion ever since it happened." He swiveled around in the chair and opened the blinds so he could see the burned area out front. "But that's not really the problem. You see, it's possible that she saw or heard or knows something about the last few minutes just prior to the explosion that could help catch the man responsible."

"So you need to know what she can't remember. In that case you'd have the choice between an amytal interview and hypnosis. Any good psychologist can hypnotize her, but she would have to see a psychiatrist as an inpatient for the amytal."

"How long would she have to be hospitalized?"

"Is there someone who could stay with her and take care of her?" Dr. Saxon asked.

Rory's mouth thinned into a bleak smile. Taking care of her was *his* job...although if he convinced her to go through with this, she might not want him around afterward. "Yes, sir, that's no problem."

"Then she could probably check into the hospital in the morning and be discharged that afternoon. That's the route I would take. Hypnosis, on the other hand, could be done just about anywhere at anytime, but you probably wouldn't have the same degree of success."

"One more question, sir. Once the interview or the hypnosis is finished and she's awake again, will she have complete recall, or will there be no change?"

"She'll be the same. Some things she'll remember, and others will be blank. You don't *want* a patient to remember something that traumatic. That would create a whole new set of problems." The doctor became silent for a moment, and Rory heard the shuffling of papers. Then he asked, "You were here when Dr. Holloway was, weren't you?"

"Yes, sir."

"And you're someplace in Texas, right?"

"Yes, sir. West Texas."

"Well, Holloway's on staff at Brooke now, over in San Antonio. Of course, he can't treat your friend if she's not entitled to care in the military system, but he can explain this further and help you find a civilian psychiatrist. Why don't you give him a call?"

"I'll do that, sir. Thank you for your time." Rory hung up and leaned back in the chair, propping his feet on the battered desk. Getting Shanna to see any kind of doctor was going to present a challenge, but he was afraid he was going to have to force it.

The fact that she'd been outside the morning her father had died bothered him. Joseph had already told her goodbye, and she was going to be late to work, yet she had gone out on a cold winter morning wearing slippers and no jacket. Why? The only newspaper delivered in Sandy Spring was a small weekly that came out on Thursdays. There was no milk delivery, no mail that early. He couldn't think of a single reason for her to be outside that particular morning.

It might be something totally innocent...or it could be an important piece of the puzzle. Whatever, he wanted to know. He couldn't shake the feeling that, somewhere down the line, they might *need* to know.

So he would talk to her again, and this time he would tell her what Dr. Saxon had said: she wouldn't remember what she had seen. She wouldn't have to add images to the terror that disturbed her sleep every night. He would try to convince her because their plans might depend on it.

Maybe even their lives.

"Shanna?" Susan opened the door between their offices barely wide enough to slip through, closed it again and went to stand in front of her boss's desk.

Shanna shifted a heavy law book from her lap to the desktop. "What's up?"

"Your aunt is here. She wants to talk to you about Rory." Susan checked her watch. "And if he sticks to his schedule, he'll be here in about fifteen minutes. You know you're not going to be able to get rid of her in fifteen minutes. Do you want me to have him wait in his truck until you're ready to leave?"

Dear Aunt Eugenie, Shanna thought with a sigh. She was a Cassidy only by marriage and not by birth, but no one would know it from the way she acted. She was proud of the Cassidy name, proud of their position on the highest level of Sandy Spring society. "Actually I expected to hear from the family sooner. After all, Rory and I have been the prime topic of gossip for a week now," she said, rubbing her temples. "This means Mother will be calling soon. Eugenie likes to keep her informed."

"What can you expect? A Cassidy taking up with a Hawkes in this town is big news." Susan's smile took the sting from her comment. "Do you want me to waylay him?"

The secretary's suggestion held a certain appeal, but Shanna shook her head reluctantly. He was so defensive at times. He wouldn't see that she was trying to protect him from Eugenie's censure, but would probably assume that she was ashamed to acknowledge him in front of her family. "No, don't do that. Just ask him to wait out there with you—and warn him, would you?"

Susan nodded and left, leaving the door open for Eugenie Cassidy. Shanna waited, fixing a smile on her face that hid her dismay.

Her aunt was an impressive woman—or perhaps formidable was a better word. She swept into the room, hardly noticing when Susan closed the door behind her, and seated herself in front of the desk. Her gray hair was fashionably styled, and her dress was better suited to an elegant afternoon tea in Dallas than a visit to a slightly shabby law office in tiny Sandy Spring. Her features were arranged in a suitably stern expression—not a frown, of course. One mustn't do anything to encourage wrinkles, particularly at her age.

"Well, young lady, what do you have to say for yourself?"

Shanna stifled a smile, managing to look appropriately serious. "You look lovely today, Aunt Eugenie, and it's so good to see you, although I am a little busy." She tapped the open book on her desk. "So how have you been? And how is Uncle—"

"Shanna."

The quiet, commanding tone stopped her short. That was the voice that had allowed Eugenie to control all the rowdy Cassidy children without anything so coarse as a shout.

"I've been hearing rumors about you."

Shanna remained silent, her hands folded over on the book.

"I don't like it when members of the family are the subject of rumors."

Shanna started to open her mouth, thought better and closed it.

"You realize, of course, that Sandy Spring is a small town. Behavior that might be perfectly acceptable in a place like Dallas or Houston isn't always tolerable here. And, of course, being a Cassidy puts even more restraints on what you can and cannot do."

Her aunt paused to take a breath, and Shanna spoke quickly. "If you want to ask me about Rory, Aunt Eugenie, then please do so. I don't want to hear a lecture about my behavior."

"So you don't deny the rumors."

"I haven't heard the rumors, so I can hardly deny them. People in this town excel at talking behind your back, but they rarely find the nerve to say the same things to your face." She sneaked a glance at her watch. In less than ten minutes Rory would be here. Twenty years in the Army had made him unfailingly punctual. She would really prefer not to subject him to her aunt.

"If you've escaped hearing the rumors, then you're fortunate. The rest of your family hasn't been so lucky. They're saying that you're having an affair with that Hawkes boy, that you've even moved him into your poor father's house."

"Then there's nothing to deny," Shanna said evenly. "I *am* involved with Rory, and he *is* living with me. In fact, he'll be here to pick me up in a few more minutes. I'll introduce you to him, if you'd like."

Eugenie stared at her in dismay. "You're *living* with that Hawkes boy?"

"'That Hawkes boy' is almost forty years old, Aunt Eugenie," she said patiently. "He spent more than twenty years in the Army. He's respectable. He's intelligent. He's sweet and kind and considerate and—"

"And he's a Hawkes," Eugenie interrupted. "His father was unstable, and his mother was your grandmother's servant!"

"Mrs. Hawkes was Grandmother's housekeeper," Shanna corrected. "There's no shame in that. *I* clean and mop and scrub toilets, and it wouldn't hurt you to do it once in a while." She left her desk, went to sit in the empty chair and took her aunt's hands. "Aunt Eugenie, I don't want to argue with you, please. It would create hard feelings between us, and it wouldn't change anything. I *like* Rory. I like having him in my life. I'm not going to live alone and unhappy because the family doesn't approve of my taste in men.''

But the older woman wouldn't relent. "You know I'm going to have to call your mother. I'm sure you remember the distress you caused her all those years ago with your ridiculous involvement with him then. How much worse do you think it's going to be now when she finds out that he's living with you?''

Shanna drew back. "The only reason Mother was distressed all those years ago was because Dad was, and Grandmother and you and Uncle Mike and everyone else. She trusted me then, and she trusts me now.''

"She was distressed because she knew exactly what he wanted. We all knew, Shanna—except you. You were too protected, too trusting. You were foolish enough to believe that he actually liked you when all he cared about was having his way with Joseph Cassidy's daughter. He was using you to punish your father. He didn't care about you.'' Leaning forward, Eugenie patted Shanna's arm comfortingly. "And he doesn't care about you now, honey. It's just your name. He wants to be able to claim that he's seduced Joseph Cassidy's daughter. That's all.''

Her words hit too close to home and made Shanna wince uncomfortably. Hadn't she acknowledged all along that Rory wanted her because twenty-one years ago, he'd been told she was too good for him? Hadn't she accepted that it was only her name and the fact that she was the only daughter of the man who'd made his life miserable that attracted him?

No. She'd thought she had—had thought she could accept anything in exchange for his help. But she'd been wrong. She wanted him to look at her and forget her name, to see only a woman. She wanted him to want her. She wanted him to care for her. She wanted him to feel as if his life was incomplete without her, because her life was certainly going to be empty without him.

She stood up and walked to the door, resting her hand on the knob. "Maybe you know what you're talking about, Aunt Eugenie," she said quietly. "After all, it seems that the only thing *you* care about is the name." She opened the door, then folded her arms over her chest. "Please leave my office now."

"You're upset, Shanna. Your grief over your father's death has caused you to behave foolishly and irresponsibly. You've made a serious mistake taking in that Hawkes boy, and the sooner it's set right, the better—for your sake, for the family's sake and for your father's sake." The old lady left the way she came in, sweeping imperiously through the outer office without so much as a glance for Susan at her desk or Rory, leaning against the wall.

The silence in the office was heavy. Susan was clumsily shuffling papers, and Rory was staring at the floor. Their refusal to look at her made it difficult for Shanna to tell if they'd heard any of her conversation with Eugenie other than her aunt's parting shot.

Leaning against the door frame, she sighed. "The last time I was in Dallas, I ran into an old friend from college. She's been married and divorced four times. She said the best advice she could give a woman contemplating matrimony would be to choose a man without a family. It'll save you a lot of grief." She smiled tautly. "There are times I wish my mother had taken that advice."

Susan glanced at Rory, still staring at the floor, then Shanna. "I think I'll go on home now. See you tomorrow."

"Okay." Shanna waited until the door closed behind Susan, then went to stand in front of Rory, moving into his line of vision. "Being a Cassidy isn't always—" Abruptly she broke off, unable to complete the sentence as she'd intended.

Rory lifted his gaze to her face. "Fun and games?" he finished for her.

Last week he'd taunted her with those words, but this evening they simply sounded weary. He looked weary, and she, Shanna thought, felt it.

"No matter what I do, these people are never going to change the way they feel about me, are they?"

That Hawkes boy. Though the words had been loaded with derision, Shanna knew she should be grateful that her aunt hadn't said something even more insulting. But looking at the bleak acceptance on Rory's face, she found gratitude hard to come by. "I doubt it," she admitted softly.

He nodded solemnly, as if he'd expected her answer. Then he reached out, wrapping her long black hair around his hand, burying his fingers in it. He moved away from the wall, closer to her, bent until his mouth was almost touching hers...

Then abruptly he released her and walked away. "Are you ready to go home?"

"Let me get my things," she said, disappointment barely noticeable in her voice. But for a moment, she simply stood there, staring at the wall. She had thought he was going to kiss her, had wanted him to, more than she'd ever wanted anything. But, as was the case more often than not these days, she was left wanting.

Always wanting.

Chapter 7

"You want to take my car?" Shanna asked as they left the house Wednesday morning. "It's nice on the highway—has all the luxuries."

He recognized the teasing note in her voice as he studied her car with a critical eye. It definitely was a luxury car, expensive and fancy and small—too small to provide any measure of protection if they ran into trouble on the road. A crash would leave it crumpled like a tin can. His pickup, on the other hand, was nothing more than comfortable, but it was big and built for heavy-duty work. With a well-trained driver behind the wheel—as *he* was—it would be difficult for anyone to run them off the road or worse.

"We'd better stick with the truck," he decided without offering reasons why. Making her aware of possible danger was one thing, but he didn't want to frighten her needlessly.

It was a long drive to Midland, and they made it mostly in silence. Shanna was uneasy—he read the signs in her frequent shifting and the taut lines of her body. Was she afraid that what they found out on today's trip wouldn't help? he wondered with a sidelong glance. Or that it would?

Shanna turned to face him and caught his glance. She smiled a little nervously in response. "Where are some of the places you went in the Army?"

"Fort Ord, California. Fort Bragg, North Carolina. Fort Benning, Georgia. Panama City, Florida. The Defense Language Institute at Monterey, California." He paused and looked her way again. "And Quang Tri, Hue and Da Nang, Vietnam."

She ignored the last three places and focused on the one before. "What made you decide to study Farsi? It's such an obscure language. It seems Spanish or German or French would be more useful."

"That depends on your reason for learning it. If you want to understand communications and message transmissions from the Iranian military or if you want to be prepared for the possibility, however remote, of having to enter Iran and not stand out like a sore thumb, Farsi comes in pretty handy. On the other hand, if you're interested in traveling to Mexico or Europe, obviously Spanish, German or French would be more helpful."

She studied him for a long time. He was darkly tanned, but his hair, with its various shadings of brown, and those clear blue eyes would give him away. "You couldn't pass as an Iranian."

"In the right clothes, with the right help and a flawless accent, you'd be surprised by what I could do. Fortunately, though, I never had to try."

"What exactly did you do in Special Forces?" she asked curiously. She had asked him before, and he'd told her a little, but not enough. The more she learned about his background, the more she wanted to know. She wanted to know it all.

"I told you."

"Not everything."

"Everything," he repeated. "We would be halfway to Dallas before I could tell you everything."

"Try."

"I learned to pick locks and operate heavy machinery. I became proficient on every weapon we used—rifles, pistols, submachine guns, grenade launchers, everything. I learned to skydive—made over three thousand jumps over the course of my career—and also got certified in scuba for open- and closed-circuit dives. Closed-circuit dives are the kind where you don't leave any telltale bubbles, when you don't want anyone to know you're there. I could repair an elevator, survey a city block and memorize the contents of any room. I could ski down a mountain and climb back up it. I could run a forty-mile land-navigation course in rugged mountain terrain carrying a seventy-pound pack in under twenty hours. I could clear a jammed weapon while on the run and under fire, and with the rest of my team, I could clear a room of bad guys without injuring the good guys in less than five seconds."

"And you could build a bomb from practically nothing," Shanna added, "and blow up practically anything."

"Not *practically* anything. I was good. I always took out my target."

"But you still haven't told me what you *did*. Surely you had a title to cover all this."

He smiled tautly. "That's classified, princess."

She looked away with a sigh and realized that they were in Midland. "Do you know where we're going?"

"No." He pulled into the right lane and left the interstate. "We'll ask up here."

The gas station attendant gave them directions to the building that housed the accountant's office. They arrived with ten minutes to spare.

Jeffrey Walsh was a handsome man in his late twenties for whom the description "stuffed shirt" must have been coined, Shanna thought when the secretary escorted them into his office. Everything about him was meticulously just so—not a hair out of place on his head and not a paper out of place on his desk. His movements were precise, as was his speech, each word properly enunciated. "Mr. Hawkes. Ma'am." He shook Rory's hand, nodded politely to Shanna and gestured to the chairs behind them. "Please be seated. How can I help you?"

Shanna exchanged glances with Rory, then crossed her legs, smoothed her skirt, swallowed hard and spoke. "Mr. Walsh, my name is Shanna Cassidy. My father was Joseph Cassidy. I believe you did some work for him."

The blandly polite expression on the man's face faded, to be replaced by wariness. "The business I conducted with Mr. Cassidy is confidential. Naturally I can't discuss it with anyone without his express permission."

She hated this part—had hated it with Rory and hated it even more now. She took a deep breath, searching for the proper words, but couldn't find them. Finally Rory did.

"Joseph Cassidy is dead, Mr. Walsh," he said quietly. "He was murdered two weeks ago. We're trying to find out why. We would appreciate anything you could tell us that might help."

"Murdered..." The accountant settled back in his chair, momentarily stunned. Then he straightened once again, resuming his oh-so-perfect posture. "My condolences, Ms. Cassidy. However, before I discuss this with you, I would like to see some identification."

She drew her wallet from her purse and flipped it open to her driver's license. Walsh studied it for a moment, then turned to Rory. "And you, Mr. Hawkes?"

He shifted to remove a small black ID case from his hip pocket and opened it to reveal two photographs, the first on a Texas driver's license, the second on a military ID card. Shanna caught a glimpse of both photos, his expression stern and uncompromising.

"Thank you." Walsh folded his hands on a doodle-free blotter. "Mr. Cassidy brought me computer printouts of bank records, credit histories, ledger entries and other financial information for a number of people. He was hoping I would find something to tie one of them, a man named Channing, to the others.''

"Did you?" Shanna asked.

"Yes. I gave him my findings over the phone on February twentieth and followed it up with a written report mailed the next day.''

Rory called up a mental calendar. The twentieth was a Wednesday, exactly one week before Joseph had died. He had probably received the written report by Saturday, and he'd come to see *him* the following Monday. Joseph had realized that he was getting close to catching Lawrence Channing, and he had known there was some risk. That was why he'd asked for Rory's help.

And he'd turned him down. Without listening to him, without even hearing what he had to say, Rory had told him no. Two days later he'd been dead.

He was smart enough to know he probably couldn't have prevented Joseph's death. The man had come to him for help, not protection. The terms he would have negotiated would have differed greatly from the arrangement with Shanna. Rory wouldn't have been allowed to move into the house, wouldn't have been asked to keep Joseph safe…but he could have given him advice, wanted or not, on security. He could have told him not to leave his truck parked on the street, so accessible, all night. He could have wired Joseph's truck with an alarm identical to the one he'd installed in Shanna's car. He could have—

He cut off the thought. He could run lists of "could haves" through his head until he went nuts, and it wouldn't change anything. He'd made a decision based on years of anger and bitter rejection, and because of it a man was dead. Maybe he could have prevented it; maybe he couldn't have. There was no second-guessing. All he could do now was make sure that the same thing didn't happen to Shanna.

"What exactly did you find, Mr. Walsh?" Shanna asked.

"An elaborate system of payoffs and bribes. It seems that when Mr. Channing wants something, he's in the habit of buying it. You live in a very corrupt town, Ms. Cassidy. Your father was probably the first man Channing tried to buy who turned him down."

"Do you still have the records?"

"No, I returned them to your father with the report."

"Do you have a copy of that?"

"Yes, I do. I'll make a copy of it for you. Excuse me." He went into the adjoining file room, then returned a few minutes later with a copy of the report. "There's a man mentioned in there who provided Mr. Cassidy with some assistance. He may do the same for you. His name is Singleton, I believe."

"Wayne Singleton?"

The dismay in Shanna's voice drew Rory's attention. "Do you know him?"

"Yes. He used to work for Channing."

"Used to?" He didn't like the sound of that, and her next words proved why.

"Yes. He—he disappeared about a month ago."

"What's wrong?" Shanna asked when they left the office building a short while later. She rolled the papers Jeffrey Walsh had given her into a tube, then slid them into her purse.

Rory stopped on the sidewalk and looked around. "I should have listened to him."

"To whom?"

"Your father. The day he came to see me, I should have listened to what he had to say."

Shanna knew what he was thinking: that if he had listened, Joseph might still be alive. That if he hadn't been so quick to turn him down for the simple pleasure of telling a Cassidy no, he might have saved her father's life. "That's not a very productive line of thinking," she said quietly. "You didn't owe my father anything, not even the time to listen. Considering everything he put you through, he showed incredible arrogance in going to see you."

"But—"

Impulsively she laid her fingers over his mouth. "Don't, Rory. Don't blame yourself. The only person responsible for my father's death is Lawrence Channing. *You* didn't do it, and you probably couldn't have prevented it. No guarantees, remember?" Pulling her hand back, she smiled gently. "Now . . . how about some lunch before we see Nick Langley?"

Nick Langley's office was even shabbier than Shanna's. It was located on the fifth floor of a low-rent building in one of Odessa's seedier neighborhoods, and the only elevator, she noticed with a grimace, was out of order. "I don't suppose you could repair *this* elevator."

Rory grinned. "Not without the tools, the parts and the inclination. Come on, five flights of stairs won't kill you."

"Says he who runs, lifts weights and has—what kind of belt do you have in taekwondo?"

"Black."

"Figures. Do you excel at everything you try?"

His grin faded as he took her arm and started up the stairs. He had failures, too. The first eighteen years of his life had been nothing but one disappointment after another. He had failed in his relationships with women. Even now he was failing in dealing with Shanna.

When he should remember how cruelly she had treated him twenty-one years ago, he thought of how gentle and warm she was. When he should remember the pain and shame and how deeply he should hate her, he thought of how desperately he wanted to make love to her. When he should curse her for everything she had cost him, his mind was on everything she could give him.

She had already offered him kindness and friendship. She had made him remember how to dream and how to hope.

She had given him respect. And someday soon, whenever he asked, she would offer him her body.

She had also taught him to be greedy. All those things were more than any one person had ever given him in his life, yet he wanted still more. He wanted permanence. He didn't want to face the fact every day that as soon as their business together was finished, she would expect him to get out of her house and out of her life. He wanted...

He substituted "affection" for the word he'd been about to use. After living a lifetime without any woman's love but his mother's, he knew that was too much to ask for, too much even to dream about. None of the women he'd known in the past twenty years, even Melanie, had ever come close to loving him—women who had enjoyed his company, women who had liked sex with him, women who had never understood what it meant to be a Hawkes. How could he even dream about love from Shanna Cassidy, who understood better than all of them exactly who and what he was?

On the fourth-floor landing, Shanna stopped, leaning against the rail, drawing in a deep breath. "This is ridiculous," she said, her voice thin and insubstantial. "I don't care if I'm clumsy or awkward or lazy. I've *got* to get in better shape. That course you were talking about in the truck—what did you call it?"

"Land navigation."

"Yeah. Forty miles in twenty hours with a seventy-pound pack. I don't think I could even *lift* seventy pounds, much less carry it. Even the thought exhausts me."

"That's the idea behind the course. To push you past the point of exhaustion, then see if you've got the determination to keep going."

"Why?"

"Because there are situations when you can't take time out to rest, when stopping or giving up means dying." He leaned against the opposite rail, folding his arms across his chest. "It was an interesting course. They gave me a map, a compass and coordinates and told me that I had to get to each rendezvous, where I would get new coordinates, within a certain time frame—but they never told me what that time frame was. It could have been one hour, five or ten.''

Shanna was breathing easier now, and her heart rate had slowed to normal, but she made no move away from the rail. "So, in effect, you were racing against a clock you couldn't see. And the fact that you successfully completed the course showed them that you were willing to push yourself to the limit and beyond.''

"Right.''

She was silent, thoughtful for a moment, then asked, "Was it worth it?''

His grin came quickly. "You bet.''

And she knew why, she thought as they started up the last flight of stairs. She knew why he'd spent over twenty years in the Army, why he had not only learned but excelled at all those unusual skills, why he had tested his endurance on that mountain course: because he'd been driven. He had wanted to prove that all Hawkeses weren't worthless, poor, stupid, crazy or trash. He'd wanted to prove that Rory Hawkes was as good as, maybe even better than, everyone else.

And he had proven it with a vengeance...only to come home to Sandy Spring and find that it didn't change anything. No one cared. He was still a Hawkes, and he was still no good.

She ached at the injustice of it all. She, who had never accomplished anything except becoming a mediocre lawyer, was treated with respect and deference by practically everyone in town, while Rory received only scorn or rejection tinged with fear. For his own sake, for his self-esteem, he needed to leave Sandy Spring for good. Maybe when this was over she would encourage him to go.

Maybe she would go herself.

Nick Langley's office was at the end of the hallway. The door opened into a tiny reception room crowded with worn furniture and lit by a naked bulb overhead. The secretary's desk was stacked with folders, newspapers and empty fast-food wrappers, and the rolling chair behind it held a box of trophies and old high school yearbooks. A heavy layer of dust lay over it all.

The whole room spoke of neglect and misfortune. If the office was anything to judge by, Nick Langley was as much a failure in his chosen profession as *she* was, Shanna thought. What had her father been thinking when he'd come to this man?

"Are you waiting for an invitation, or are you going to come on in?" a voice called through the open doorway.

Shanna entered the private office first, with Rory close behind her. The detective sat at a desk similar in condition to the one outside, although minus most of the dust. A portable black-and-white television balanced precariously on top of a file cabinet was tuned to a cable sports channel, but he wasn't watching it. His attention was focused on them.

"Hawkes and Cassidy, right?" He didn't wait for an answer. "Have a seat, and we'll get down to business."

There was only one other chair in the office. Rory gestured for Shanna to take it. She did so as she asked, "How do you know who we are?"

"My brother called me after you left his office. He told me about your father. Too bad."

"Your brother?" she repeated. She looked at Rory and saw the surprise barely noticeable in his blue eyes. "Who— You mean Jeffrey Walsh? He's your *brother*?"

He grinned. "Half brother. You never would have guessed it, would you? Jeff's the one who sent your father to me."

She compared the stuffy accountant—blond haired, blue-eyed, impeccably dressed and well mannered—to this scruffy man with dark brown hair and hazy green eyes who hadn't shaved in several days. He wore jeans faded nearly white with a rip across one knee, a lemon-yellow T-shirt that would have contrasted nicely against his dark skin if not for the black skull, underscored by the name of some heavy metal band, that adorned it and a pair of disreputable tennis shoes that were propped right on the middle of the desk.

Langley's grin disappeared abruptly as his feet hit the floor. "Your father had the same response. Tell me, do you Cassidys always judge everyone you meet based on how they're dressed or how their offices are decorated?"

Shanna felt a blush burn her cheeks. "I'm sorry if I offended you, Mr. Langley—"

"Nick. Or just plain Langley. No 'mister.'" He turned his attention suddenly to Rory. "There's a chair under those boxes behind you...but you probably already noticed that, didn't you?"

So his suspicion had been right, Rory thought. Joseph *had* used the private detective to check him out. He moved the boxes and pulled the chair over beside Shanna's, then settled back to study the man.

"I had the impression when Cassidy came in here that he was planning to hire you, not invite you to associate with his daughter," Langley said brashly.

"What do you know about that?" Shanna asked.

His grin returned, brighter and broader than before. "I know just about everything, honey. I know you're here to find out why your father hired me. I know Hawkes has already made at least part of the connection."

"How much did you find out?" Rory asked.

"I found out about Delta," he replied with a boastful smile.

Not so much as a flicker of emotion crossed Rory's face. He knew the man was guessing, and he neither denied nor confirmed the guess. "You *think* you found out about Delta."

"I think," Langley agreed. "They're pretty secretive about their men. Operators—that's what they sometimes call them, isn't it?"

Rory didn't respond to the question. "Let me guess," he began in a low, almost amused drawl. "You used to be in the Army yourself, and you've got buddies still in who help you out from time to time when a case calls for it. That's illegal, you know.''

The other man smiled and replied with identical amusement, ''It was the Navy for me. Tell me you haven't done it yourself at one time or another.''

Shanna was looking from man to man, understanding little of their conversation, bewildered even by the sense that Rory liked the detective. ''What are you talking about? What is Delta?''

''You want to tell her?'' Langley asked. ''Or should I?''

''Tell her what you know for a fact. Leave the speculation out of it.''

''Okay.'' Langley settled back in his chair, his hands clasped behind his head. ''What I know for a fact is that Joseph Cassidy was interested in a lot of people in his hometown. He brought me a list of names and asked me to find out what I could about them. Hawkes was at the top of the list.''

''Who else was on it?'' Shanna asked.

Leaning forward, he opened the bottom drawer, drew out a single sheet of paper and tossed it onto the desk. It landed in a flutter in front of her. ''See for yourself.''

She picked it up and scanned the typewritten list. Rory was, indeed, at the top, followed by Channing, Sheriff Hart, Judge Rhodes, Mayor Larkin and each of the council members. She replaced it on the desk. ''What did you find out?''

From the same drawer he removed a file folder. ''Most of them are harmless—small-time corrupt officials. The dangerous ones on the list are Channing, Hart and Hawkes.''

Shanna smiled uneasily at Rory. ''They seem to have us outnumbered two to one.''

''Odds are meaningless when dealing with someone like him,'' Langley said with a nod toward Rory.

''What did you get on Channing?'' Rory asked, ignoring the comment about him.

"It's all in here. You can take a copy with you." Langley tapped the edge of the manila folder on the desk. "Channing's dirty—there's no question of that. His legitimate businesses are just fronts for the real money-makers—primarily drugs, but he also dabbles in stolen cars, gambling, prostitution. His real operations are set up in El Paso. Sandy Spring is just his base—close enough to keep an eye on things, far enough away to provide him with a safety buffer if something goes wrong. The first thing he did when he moved to Sandy Spring was find out who could and couldn't be bought. Those who couldn't be—a judge, a deputy, one of the council members—got moved out of the way and were replaced by people more amenable to Channing's needs."

Shanna remembered the surprise when Judge Rhodes's predecessor, a kindly old man named Brown, had unexpectedly resigned for health reasons and moved away from Sandy Spring. At the time, she had attributed his decision to his age—he must have been nearly seventy—but Langley's information cast a different light on it.

"The only one he didn't replace in his first year in Sandy Spring was Joseph Cassidy," the detective continued. "I think he was held off by your family's position in the town. He figured that messing with the great Cassidys would bring him more trouble than he could handle at that time. But as his power grew and as he controlled more and more of the county, he got more confident. At the same time, your father got more concerned and finally decided to stop him. So Channing had to stop *him*." He paused. "I don't mean to sound morbid, but how did Cassidy die?"

"A pipe bomb was placed in his truck," Rory replied.

Langley held his gaze for a moment, then glanced at Shanna. "Interesting choice of weapon, under the circumstances."

She stiffened, and her eyes turned cool and defensive. "I already know about Rory's background in demolitions," she said icily. "You said Channing got rid of Judge Brown, a deputy and a council member. Is that speculation, or can you prove it?"

"I went to Florida and talked to the judge, and he confirmed that he resigned from his position because of threats made against him by Channing's people. Channing himself wasn't directly involved. Same with the council member. He's living in Albuquerque now."

"And the deputy?"

"He moved to El Paso, got a job with the police department, and two months later was killed in the line of duty."

El Paso, Shanna thought grimly, where Channing's influence was probably as powerful as it was in Sandy Spring.

"Now, the interesting thing about Lawrence Channing—"

She interrupted. "Interesting? You don't consider the fact that the man is scum, a criminal and a murderer interesting?"

His grin came quickly. "Not as much as the rest of this. You see, until he moved to Sandy Spring six years ago, Lawrence Channing didn't exist."

The silence in the truck on the way home was broken by Shanna's sigh. Rory glanced at her for a moment before returning his gaze to the road. She hadn't said more than a dozen words since leaving Nick Langley's office two hours ago, but had simply sat across the seat from him, clutching the two reports they'd gotten. She hadn't read either one, hadn't even sneaked a peek at the pages headed with his name.

She looked tired. He wished she would put all this behind her, would forget about Channing and her father's murder, get out of Sandy Spring so she wouldn't be reminded of it daily and get on with her life. But he knew what her response would be if he asked her to do that, what it had been all along. She couldn't forget. She couldn't let Lawrence Channing go unpunished.

"We're not going to get home until after eight," he said, his voice low and soft in the darkening cab. "Why don't you try to get some rest?"

She glanced at him, then at the width of seat separating them. "I can't sleep sitting up, and there's not quite enough room to lie down."

"Put your head on my lap." His smile was rusty and uneven. "I promise, I won't molest you while you're asleep."

She smiled unevenly, too, and laid her purse and the reports in the floorboard. "You'd have better luck trying it when I'm completely awake," she murmured to herself as she stretched out as comfortably as she could, pillowing her head on his muscular thigh, drawing her knees up to fit her long legs onto the seat.

You'd have better luck... Rory stared straight ahead, forcing himself to ignore the innocent intimacy of their positions. She'd sounded almost as if she *wanted* him to claim his payment. Because she'd been celibate too long? Or because she'd learned that the sooner she got something distasteful over with, the better?

Or maybe because she wanted *him?*

He shied away from the thought. He'd believed that once long ago, and it had brought him nothing but pain and trouble. How could he let himself believe it again?

It wasn't long before the rhythmic vibrations of the road lulled her to sleep. Rory shifted restlessly as he stroked the softness of her hair from her face. If life were perfect, when they got home, he would carry her, still sleeping, to her bedroom, where he would undress her and put her to bed before lying down next to her. He would sleep beside her through the night, would be there to offer her comfort when the dream awoke her, would be there to make love to her when the morning awoke her.

But life wasn't perfect, and the only way to make it so was to become somebody else. To deny who he was and become someone he wasn't. Maybe that wasn't such a bad deal, he thought bleakly, if it meant getting Shanna in return.

But he knew that was wishful thinking. He was proud of who he was, proud of what he'd accomplished. He was proud of the generations of Hawkeses that had gone before him. He couldn't deny his family and his name.

Not even for Shanna.

Shanna woke up earlier than usual Thursday morning. For a long time she lay in bed, watching the sky grow lighter and thinking about yesterday's trip. She and Rory had gone over the accountant's report when they'd gotten home last night and had learned a great deal about Channing's method of payoffs—and none of it was admissible in court, she had glumly pointed out. The information had come from various financial records, mostly credit histories and bank records. She didn't know how her father had gotten the credit histories, but she did know a court order was needed to obtain bank records, and Channing's judge would never issue such an order on himself and all the others. She'd seen from Rory's expression that she'd didn't need to explain how Joseph had gotten those records: the bank involved was Sandy Spring Federal, the only bank in town. The bank where her uncle Mike had been president for the past thirty years.

With a sigh, she pushed the covers back and reached for her robe. She wanted to look over the private detective's reports before she left for work, and for that she needed a clear head and several cups of strong coffee.

The house was silent as she started down the stairs, but it was a different kind of silence than the one that had haunted her after Joseph's death. That had been empty, lonely, bleak. This was peaceful. It was because of Rory. Even with him asleep in his bed, she could feel his presence, could draw strength and security from him.

Except that he wasn't asleep in bed.

She paused on the landing, her hand resting on the stair rail, and watched him in the living room. The furniture had been pushed aside, leaving a clearing in the center of the room, and he was using the space to work out. He wore nothing but a pair of white cotton trousers with a black stripe down each leg. They were cut full to accommodate the wide range of motion, and their loose fit, instead of simply looking baggy, served to accentuate his leanness and narrow hips.

His movements—kicks, punches, blocks—were both graceful and menacing, tightly controlled and full of raw power. She knew nothing about taekwondo, but even she could see that he was good. Even she could see that if circumstances required it, he could be deadly.

Slowly she continued her way down the stairs and came to a stop in the wide doorway. He was aware of her, although she wasn't sure how she knew that. He didn't focus on her, didn't break his concentration to greet her, didn't acknowledge her in any way, but continued his workout, and she watched.

There was beauty in the exercise that seemed so alien in her all-American living room. The disciplined movements flowed one into another, smooth but taut, full of grace and danger and power. Intense. Potent. Erotic.

She pushed her hands into her pockets to hide the fists caused by the tightness building inside her. Swallowing was difficult, and she had no success at slowing her heart rate or controlling her ragged breathing. Wonderful, she thought dryly. *His* exercise was giving *her* system a workout. But she couldn't bring herself to leave, to turn and walk away. She wanted to stay. Wanted to watch. Wanted to *feel*.

Rory *was* aware of her, a dim figure at the edge of consciousness, sending ripples through his concentration, faint disturbances that, like a crack, spread and widened until it threatened to shatter. He focused his attention more narrowly on his form, a set of movements done in precise order, similar to compulsories for ice skaters. Unfortunately he'd done it so many hundreds of times that his mind managed to wander anyway, right across the room to Shanna.

Why was she up so early? After yesterday's long trip to Odessa and Midland and the middle-of-the-night dream that had had her walking the floor, he'd expected her to sleep in, giving him time to work off a little excess energy, shower and fix a pot of coffee before she got up.

Her curiosity as she watched blended with something else, something he couldn't quite put a name to. Interest? Fascination? That was usual. People unfamiliar with martial arts were often fascinated the first time they got a close-up view. He'd seen it many times when he'd been part of his school's demonstration team and at tournaments.

But it was more than that. More intense. More emotional. More personal.

It was arousal.

The sudden recognition made him falter, made his mind go blank, form forgotten. His heart rate, only slightly elevated after nearly two hours of practice, shot upward, and his skin, covered with a light sheen of perspiration but cool, rapidly grew warm. His concentration shot, he ended his workout with a kick, swinging his right leg around, his bare foot slicing through the air only millimeters in front of her face.

He turned his back on her and reached for the towel he'd left on the sofa, drying his face, breathing heavily into the lemon-scented terry. Then he faced her, approached her, stopping directly in front of her.

He was too close, Shanna thought, swallowing hard. In spite of the early-morning chill, she could feel the heat radiating from him, could see the sweat beaded on his throat, could chart each movement of his chest as his shallow breathing slowed and deepened. Much too close... yet not close enough. "You're good," she murmured, leaning back against the door frame.

"Yes," he agreed without conceit. "I am."

"Can you..." She cleared her throat of hoarseness. "Can you break boards like they do on TV?"

"Yes."

"Why?" She wet her lips. "What's the purpose...?"

"If you can break three boards stacked together, you can break any bone in the body." He paused. "I can do four."

She started to speak again, but the words died forgotten as he raised the towel, drying his throat, then drew it down his chest. Her gaze followed it over brown skin and finely molded muscles, pausing when it stopped at the elastic waist of his trousers, then moving lower still to where the soft white fabric had grown less baggy. She swallowed hard, then forced her gaze back to the safety of his face, handsome and hard and unsmiling.

Most women would be flattered, Rory thought, to know they could arouse a man with no more than a look, by doing nothing more than simply existing. Was Shanna? Or was she merely nervous? Uneasy? After all, she wasn't most women. She was the only woman he'd ever wanted this way—fiercely, desperately, permanently. She was the one woman he could never have, not permanently.

He watched her touch her tongue to her lips again and wondered what her response would be if *he* did that, if he wet her lips with his tongue before kissing her, long and hard, with every bit of passion and hunger and need he'd saved for twenty-one years. Would she accept it because they had an agreement? Would she endure it because she'd given him the right to do that and so much more?

Or would she welcome it, enjoy it, return it?

This was a good time to find out.

The towel slid from his fingers to the floor as he leaned forward, eliminating the distance between them, close enough now to smell her exotic scent, to hear her uneven breaths, to feel her delicate shiver when his body brushed hers. When he touched his tongue to her lips, she trembled. When he coaxed her teeth apart, she let him. When he probed inside with his tongue, she responded with her own.

This wasn't acceptance or endurance. It was welcome. He had his answer.

But it wasn't enough.

He suspected that it'd been a long while since she'd been with a man. Long enough to make her amenable to any reasonably decent man's overtures? Long enough to let her body's needs override her head and her heart? Long enough to make any man the right man?

Simply being wanted wasn't enough. He wanted—*needed* to be wanted for himself. He wanted to know that both her head and her heart were involved. He wanted to know that she knew who he was, that she understood he was *Rory Hawkes* and wanted him anyway.

He wanted too much. Everything. For always.

She could go on like this forever, Shanna thought dazedly, with Rory's body pressed to hers, his mouth on hers, his tongue hungrily stroking. She felt wired, every nerve in her body tingling and sparking and demanding more—more contact, more heat, more passion, more everything. No one else had ever kissed her this way. No one else had ever made her feel, want, need and throb this way. No one but Rory.

As a boy, his kiss had been potent, making her long for pleasures only imagined, for satisfaction unknown. As a man, hard and strong and powerfully aroused, his kiss was devastating, for the pleasures were no longer imagined, the satisfaction no longer unknown. She knew now what intimacy between a man and a woman meant, knew it could be wonderful, knew that with *this* man, it could be exquisite.

She wrapped her arms around him, slid her fingers into his hair, wriggled even closer as if she were trying to become a part of him. She had accomplished that a lifetime ago, he thought. She had manipulated her way right into his heart, and he'd never managed to get her out again, to become whole again.

Maybe he'd never wanted to.

He ended the kiss but didn't release her or step away. He stroked his palm over her hair and, for a long time, simply looked at her. Maybe he'd kept her in his heart all these years because that was where she belonged. Maybe he had never loved another woman because he'd already loved *this* one.

But that was silly. What did a teenager know of love? How could a boy's love survive her betrayal, the war her father sent him to fight, growing up, the women in his life and the men in hers? How could he look at her now, twenty-one years later, and feel the same hunger, the same desperate need, the same incredible awe that, for this moment, she was *his* to hold and to love?

For this moment. Whether he'd loved her then, whether he loved her now, didn't matter. Nothing changed the fact that they'd made a bargain. As soon as they caught Channing, he would no longer be part of her life. She would no longer need him, would no longer want him, would no longer tolerate his presence. There was no chance of developing a permanent relationship between them, no chance that the desire they felt right now could ever be strong enough to survive the reality that she was a Cassidy, privileged and respected and admired, and he was a Hawkes. He could love her until the day he died, but she would never love him back.

Never.

Abruptly he released her and walked away. Perplexed, Shanna turned and called his name, bringing him to a halt on the landing. He offered her a bleak smile. "I've got to take a shower, princess." A long one.

A cold one.

Shanna sat at her office desk that afternoon, listening to the phone at her house ring over and over. After fifteen rings, she hung up, then walked to the window to stare out at the street. It was already five o'clock, and there was no sign of Rory. He'd been picking her up at work every night for a week now, and he'd never arrived later than four-forty-five. Susan had even joked about how punctual he was.

So where was he?

Granted, he'd been acting funny this morning when he'd come downstairs after his shower, sort of aloof and troubled, but that didn't explain his tardiness. Besides, he'd behaved perfectly normally at noon, when they'd eaten lunch together before going to see Wayne Singleton's wife.

For a moment she let Rhonda Singleton distract her. The woman worked at the bank and had been leaving for lunch when they arrived, but she'd been willing to give a few minutes to the boss's niece. She was distressed over her husband's disappearance and frustrated by the sheriff's failure to turn up any clues. Wayne had simply run off, according to Hart. It wasn't that unusual when men reached middle age for them to turn their backs on their families, jobs and homes and simply walk away from all responsibility, the sheriff had claimed.

Not Wayne, Rhonda had insisted. He'd been a good husband and an even better father. His family had been the most important thing in his life. And if he had simply run away, she had asked Shanna, wouldn't he have taken clothing or money? He had disappeared with only the clothes on his back and a twenty-dollar bill in his pocket.

Shanna turned her back on the street outside and leaned against the windowsill. Although it was possible that, for once, Hart was right and Wayne Singleton really had run out on his family, she didn't believe it any more than Rhonda did. It was more likely that Channing had found out Wayne was helping Joseph and had killed him. It was also likely that Channing's discovery had led to Joseph's death, too. When they had discussed it privately on the way back to the office, Rory had agreed with her.

"Hey, boss, it's quitting time." Susan appeared in the doorway, leaning against the frame. "Did you get hold of Rory?"

Rhonda Singleton's concerns faded away, replaced once more by her own. "No."

"Well, everyone's entitled to be late once in a while. Don't fret over it. He's a big boy now."

Shanna smiled unwillingly at the emphasis Susan placed on "big." "He's so dependable. If he says he's going to meet me at twelve-thirty, he may come a little early, but he's never one minute late. I can't help but worry a little."

"Hey, come on, what could happen? We're not talking about the wild kid he used to be. He grew into a perfectly responsible, reliable man. It's not like the folks in town or the sheriff's deputies are going to harass him the way they used to." Susan smiled confidently. "I think almost everyone is afraid of him, except you and me."

Shanna returned to her desk and placed the files she needed to take home in her briefcase, then pushed her hands deep into the pockets of her dress to still them. "You're not uncomfortable with him?" she asked curiously.

"I know he's tough, and I know a little of that wild kid still lives inside him, but I've seen how he is with you. I think he's probably capable of causing great harm, but I also think he has an incredible capacity for gentleness." She finished with a shrug and an easy smile. "Want a ride home? You could leave a note for him on the door."

"No, thanks. I'll wait here. I'm sure he'll show up soon."

"With a perfectly harmless excuse like a flat tire," Susan added reassuringly. "Then I'll see you tomorrow. Take care."

Shanna smiled tautly, then returned to the window once more. A moment later, she waved as Susan walked past. She watched a little longer, searching the street in both directions for some sign of Rory's big black pickup, then started for her desk, intending to try the house once more.

Just as she reached for it, the phone rang. Startled, she jerked her hand back, then picked it up on the second ring.

"Shanna?"

She gave a sigh of relief as she sank into the chair. "Rory, where are you? I was getting concern—"

He interrupted her. "I'm in jail."

"Oh, God." She swallowed hard, imagining the worst. "I'll be right over."

* * *

Rory stood motionless, his back to the bars of the cell, and waited while the deputy removed the cuffs that bound his wrists behind his back. They were taking no chances—handcuffing him for the brief walk to the phone in the next room, chaining him to an iron ring in the wall while he made his call, then cuffing him again for the return to the cell. Hell, they had even restrained him while they'd beaten him.

The deputy gave him a shove, then closed the cell door. "Tell me something, Hawkes," he said, resting his hands on the bars. "Is Shanna Cassidy always so prim and proper? Even in bed?"

Rory stared at the back wall, focusing his thoughts inward. Control had been an important part of his training—controlling his temper, his impulses, his needs. Now he concentrated on controlling the rage the deputy's question sent rippling through him.

"No answer, huh? Maybe I'll have to find out for myself."

Slowly Rory turned to face the man. His mouth was twisted in a macabre parody of a smile, and his voice was deadly soft. "If you ever lay a hand on her, I'll kill you."

It wasn't an idle threat, meaningless, made in anger, but a promise, plain and simple. It chased away the deputy's leer and, in spite of the steel bars that separated them, replaced it with fear. Without another word, he backed away until he reached the door, then left.

Rory moved awkwardly to the sink on one wall. There was no mirror above, but he didn't need one to know he looked bad. His left eye was puffy and tender. It hadn't swollen shut yet, but he'd had enough black eyes to know it was just a matter of time. His left temple was sore, too, scraped raw, bleeding and bruised from a blow with a flashlight, and his cheek and jaw were in similar condition.

He turned on the cold water and got a rusty, tepid flow. Using both hands, he splashed water over his face, rinsing away the blood. Finding no towel in the cell, he blotted it dry with his T-shirt, then used his fingertips to probe his swollen lip and the cut that had split it.

All in all, considering the odds, he hadn't come out of it too badly. Nothing was broken, although his face, ribs and wrists hurt like hell. Nothing was even seriously damaged except his pride.

God, he hated having to call Shanna! He would have given anything to keep this hidden from her, to be able to crawl off alone like a whipped dog and lick his wounds. He didn't want her to come here, didn't want her to see him like this, battered and behind bars.

He had spent a lot of time in this jail. The first time, thirteen years old, he had curled up in a ball on the cot, terrified and humiliated at being locked up like an animal when he hadn't done anything wrong. Soon, though, he had learned to hide his shame behind a teenage boy's bravado.

But how could he hide it now from Shanna?

By the time she reached the sheriff's department four blocks from her office, Shanna was trembling, although she couldn't say whether it was from anger or fear. She knew Rory couldn't possibly have done anything wrong, so the charges against him were trumped up—and that meant his arrest was the harassment Susan had innocently mentioned a short while ago. If they had hurt him, if they had committed even the most minor violation of the law, she would see that they all paid, she swore as she approached the duty sergeant's desk. "I want to see Rory."

The overweight officer looked at her and grinned. "You do, huh?"

Another deputy, one she had disliked all through school, came over to stand beside him. "You have to give the guy credit, Grady. He found himself someone to support him, a woman to sleep with and a lawyer for when he's in trouble, all in the same package."

She gave him a cold stare. "You are obscene, Charley," she said derisively. "I want Rory released now. Fill out whatever paperwork is necessary."

Neither man moved. "You see, Miss Cassidy," the sergeant said in a kindly voice, "Sheriff Hart is the only one who can authorize his release, and he's out of touch until 9:00 a.m. tomorrow. Until then, our hands are tied. Now, if you'll come back in the morning—"

"Are you denying me an opportunity to speak with my client?"

Charley poked the sergeant with his elbow. "See, she's not like her old man. She's a real bright lady. She understood exactly what you said."

Shanna stared at both men for a long frustrated moment, then walked determinedly to the pay phone in the corner. Opening her purse, she removed a notebook and pen, then dropped a coin in the slot and dialed information. "Yes," she said clearly when the operator came on the line. "I'd like the number of the FBI office in El Paso."

She scrawled the number she was given, then asked, "Is there a number for after-hours or emergenc—"

From behind a freckled hand reached out and disconnected the call. When she turned, she saw Layton standing there, his expression dark and hostile. "What can I help you with, Miss Cassidy?"

She felt a strong urge to back away from him, but defiantly she stood her ground. "What are the charges against Rory Hawkes?"

"I don't know that any have been filed just yet. The officers have been kind of busy, you know."

"I want him released now."

"And what if I say no?"

"Then I *will* call the FBI. They handle civil rights violations, you know, and I understand that they take great pleasure in investigating allegations of police brutality."

He stared at her, considering whether she was serious about the threat, she thought. He must have decided that she was, for after a moment, he turned away. "I'll see what I can do. Mangrum, take her back to the holding cells."

Muttering belligerently, Charley led her through a double-locked door and into a wide hallway bordered by three cells. Rory was in the first cell, leaning one shoulder against the concrete wall, his back to her, his head lowered. There was something so forlorn about his stance, Shanna thought, swallowing over the sudden lump in her throat. This must bring back unpleasant memories of other times in jail coupled with visits from another Cassidy.

Clearing her throat, she ordered the deputy to leave. When he protested, she cut him off coldly. "I have the right to speak to my client in private. Get out of here, Charley."

She waited until the door closed behind him, then walked to the cell, moving as close to the bars as she could, wrapping her fingers tightly around the crossbar. "Rory?"

He flinched at her whisper.

"Rory, are you all right?"

His head still bowed, he closed his eyes on the anguish and helplessness inside him. In a taut voice he asked, "Can you get me out of here?"

She heard the faint plea that crept into his voice in spite of his rigid control. It made her ache. "Yes."

His chuckle was bitter. "Are you sure of that?"

"I promise, you won't have to spend the night here." She clenched the bar tighter. "Rory, what happened?"

"Don't you mean, what did I do *this* time?" he asked sharply, then shook his head. "I'm sorry. Being in here tends to put me on the defensive."

"What did they do to you?"

Slowly he turned, first showing her the undamaged side of his face, then finally facing her head-on. Shanna pressed her fingers to her mouth, sickened by the injuries he'd suffered.

"They'll call it resisting arrest," he said in a flat, empty tone. "And there's not a damn thing I can do about it, except be grateful that they didn't kill me."

"My God, Rory, I'm sorry," she whispered. She reached out to him through the bars, but he refused to come closer, refused to let her touch him. "We'll file a complaint. We'll—"

"No." He came to the bars then, laying his hands next to but not touching hers. "Get me out of here. Just concentrate on getting me out."

She started to leave and met Deputy Layton at the door. He was jingling a ring of keys in one hand. "I'm going to release him into your custody. But if the sheriff doesn't approve, you can expect to hear from him tomorrow."

She stepped back and watched him unlock the cell door. When Rory walked out, he moved so cautiously that she knew he must have other injuries. It was the only thing that kept her from throwing herself into his arms—that and the fear that he wouldn't welcome her.

The sergeant had filled out the necessary release forms. While she signed them, Charley Mangrum grudgingly returned Rory's possessions to him: the black identification case, his keys, some money and his pistol. Shanna watched as Mangrum handed the gun to him grips first, then rested his hands on the desktop. For a moment she stared at them; then she followed Rory outside.

"Charley Mangrum was the one who hit you, wasn't he?" she asked quietly.

Rory stopped on the sidewalk. "What makes you think that?"

"His knuckles were swollen and skinned."

Only the right side of his mouth formed a smile. It was bleak. "You're getting pretty observant, princess. My truck's in the parking lot out back. Wait here while I get it."

He made it only a few feet before she caught up with him. "I'll take my chances with you."

He stopped again and glared down at her. "It's been in the sheriff's custody for the past hour," he said darkly. "Maybe they left it alone, or maybe they wired it with enough explosives to make your father's bomb look like a firecracker in comparison. Whatever, you're going to stay the hell away from it until I find out."

When he began walking again, she caught his wrist to stop him, then quickly released it when he swore. Looking down, she saw the bruises that encircled it. "Then forget the truck. We have my car at home. Don't risk your life for a pickup."

He was trying hard to hold on to his temper. "Look, the past few hours have not been particularly pleasant for me," he said in a voice so tense that it vibrated. "Just leave me alone, stay out of the way and do what you're told. Can you manage that just this once?"

Tears stung her eyes, but she blinked them away and nodded. She watched him walk to the corner, then called his name. He looked back at her questioningly.

"Don't die," she pleaded.

He looked at her for a moment, then relented enough to offer another painful half smile. "I won't, princess."

Chapter 8

Rory completed a thorough inspection of his truck, both inside and out, then climbed in, wincing as the action jarred his ribs. He fastened his seat belt, then slid the key into the ignition. This was the moment of truth, he thought with a humorless smile as he started to turn the key. He had searched everywhere, but there was always the possibility, however remote, that he'd missed something. He would know in the next few moments.

Glancing up, he saw Shanna standing at the gate that led into the parking lot. She hadn't been able to wait around front the way he'd told her to, he thought grimly. If he'd been harsher, more blunt, he could have made her stay there. *If my truck explodes and parts of my body come raining down with the debris, I don't think you want to see it.* That probably would have convinced her.

Almost as if she'd read his mind, she walked away, back around the building and out of sight. Grateful that she was gone, Rory turned the key and listened to the powerful engine roar. Tentatively he tested the brakes and said a silent prayer of thanks when nothing happened.

He drove out of the parking lot and around the corner, stopping in the street in front of Shanna. She looked up, her expression a mix of overwhelming relief and sickening fear. "Come on," he said softly through the open window. "Let's go home."

She sat beside him in silence all the way to her house. There she snapped out of it, though, ordering him to take a seat at the table while she set a handful of soft cloths, a dish of ice cubes, antiseptic soap and a basin of warm water on the table. He didn't need her nursing—would, in fact, prefer that she somehow pretend not to notice his injuries—but there was something comforting about her fussing. He had received little enough of it in his life.

She removed his T-shirt and tossed it across the back of the nearest chair, gently washed each injury on his face, then filled a soft cotton cloth with ice cubes and pressed it to his swollen eye. "I'd like to take you to the doctor," she suggested quietly. "Your ribs . . ."

Replacing her hand on the ice pack with his own, he looked down at his chest. There were two bruises, nasty and painful, one on each side of his rib cage. With a shake of his head, he looked back at Shanna. "Now you know why some of those deputies wear pointed-toe boots," he teased.

She didn't smile. Her expression hadn't changed since they'd gotten home. She looked somber as hell, as if nothing would ever make her smile or laugh again. He watched her clear the table of everything but a small vase of flowers and the yellow-and-white plaid napkins they left there after each meal. When she returned to the table, she picked up his shirt and turned it right-side out. The back was filthy where he'd crawled under the truck to inspect it, and the front was stained with blood and dirt. "Do you want to try to get the stains out?" she asked in that grim voice.

"Throw it away."

She nodded and laid it on the chair again, then sat down across from him. "What happened, Rory?"

"After I took you back to work after lunch, I went out to check on things at the house. I was on my way back to town when four of the county's finest pulled me over."

"Why?"

"No reason." He removed the ice pack and leaned forward to frown at her. "That's part of the problem your father was trying to correct, Shanna. They don't *have* to have a reason to do this to somebody."

"Why didn't you stop them?" Her voice trembled, but she ignored it and rushed right on. "You said this morning that if you can break three boards, you can break any bone in the body. You said that *you* can break four boards. So why didn't you stop them? Why did you let them hurt you like this?"

"Because if I had fought them, they would have killed me." He attempted a bleak smile. "Then who would take care of you?"

She stared at him a moment, then dropped her gaze to the tabletop where his hands rested. Both wrists were ringed with bruises from the handcuffs. "I—I want you to move out."

Rory was stunned. For a moment he felt nothing, then the unfairness of it all filled him with anger. She was cutting him loose, forgetting their deal, breaking her promise, simply because he hadn't stood up to *four* deputies.

The ice pack hit the table with a thump. "What's wrong, princess?" he demanded, a mean note in his voice. "Are you disappointed to find out that I'm no more infallible than your precious father was? You thought you'd hired yourself a *dangerous* man, and the first time there was trouble, they beat the hell out of me. This must be a real relief for you. Now you don't have to worry about keeping your end of our bargain. I didn't perform the way you expected, so you have a perfect excuse to kick me out—"

"I don't want you hurt anymore."

Her interruption stopped him cold.

"They did this to you—you *let* them do this to you—because of me. Punishing Channing isn't worth seeing you like this. *I'm* not worth it." She refused to look up at him. "If you move out, if you go back to your house and forget about Channing and me and our agreement, then they'll leave you alone. They won't have any reason to bother you anymore. They won't have any reason to hurt you anymore."

"The hell they won't," he disagreed. "*I'm* not going to leave *them* alone. And I'm not going to let them have a chance at you next time, and I'm not going to forget our agreement. You owe me, princess."

"Then I'll pay—right now, tonight, whenever. But I won't let you risk your life again." She clasped his hands tightly. "Rory, I can't live with that. I can't stand knowing that I'm responsible for this. I couldn't live the rest of my life knowing that I was responsible for your death."

"I knew the risks when I signed on," he said flatly.

"But *I* didn't. Logically I knew when I asked for your help that there would be some danger, but emotionally... I wasn't prepared for this."

"*I* was." He pressed her hands together, sandwiching them between the warmth of his. "You aren't responsible, Shanna. There are plenty of people to lay the blame on, but you're not one of them." He forced an awkward, puffy grin. "Remember what you told me yesterday? 'That's not a very productive line of thinking.' That applies to you too, princess."

"But, Rory—"

He cut her off. "It's not your fault," he repeated firmly.

Shanna sat in silence for a moment, then wearily asked, "So what do we do now?"

"About what?"

"About *this!* We can't let them get away with it."

"What do you suggest?"

"File a civil rights complaint with the FBI. Let them investigate Mangrum and the others."

Rory shook his head. "We can't do that for the same reason you wouldn't report the explosion to the ATF. The last thing we need right now is a bunch of federal agents around here."

Her expression grew mutinous. "So they get away with it?"

"For the time being, yes. If we can take down Channing, Shanna, the sheriff and his deputies will fall, too. I know it offends your lawyer's belief in swift justice, but don't do anything now. Just let it slide."

Let it slide. She slouched back in the chair and lifted her gaze to the ceiling. Let that bastard Hart and his deputies get off scot-free. Rory was right: the very idea offended her sense of justice. But he was also right that if they could get enough evidence to charge Channing in her father's murder, the sheriff's department would get caught in the fallout.

But how could she look at him, see what they'd done to him and do nothing? she wondered despairingly. Just the sight of his face—one side so perfect and handsome, the other swollen and battered—made her want to forget about Channing and her father's murder and take action *now*. She wanted the men who did this to pay dearly.

"What about dinner? Do you think you could eat something?"

Shanna looked at him and forced a smile. "Sure. Do you think *you* can?"

"As long as I'm careful."

"Let me change clothes, and I'll get it started."

She'd been gone only a moment when the phone rang. "Will you get that?" she called from the upstairs hallway.

Rory stretched back to reach the phone mounted on the wall just inside the door. When he said hello, he received a response in a very cultured, faintly familiar voice.

"This is Judith Cassidy. Who am I speaking to?"

"Rory Hawkes." He heard the guarded tone in his voice and shook his head in dismay. He'd rarely had any contact with Shanna's mother when he was a kid, so there was little reason he should be wary of her now—beyond the fact that she *was* Shanna's mother. It would be nice, he thought, if just one Cassidy didn't recoil in horror at the idea of their precious Shanna with *him*—nice, but unlikely.

"So Eugenie's tale wasn't as off-the-wall as it sounded. With her, you can never quite tell how much is truth, how much is exaggeration and how much is pure imagination." Judith laughed softly. "Joseph had told me you came back to Sandy Spring after retiring from the Army. I have to admit, I wondered at the time if you and Shanna would get together."

"Does it bother you that we have?" he asked cautiously.

The laughter, soft and reminiscent of Shanna's, came again. "In case you've forgotten, my daughter is thirty-six years old—old enough to be the mother of a young adult herself. And in case you somehow haven't noticed, she's quite headstrong, too. She hasn't wanted my mothering since she was sixteen and hasn't needed it since she was twenty. We have a nice little arrangement—she doesn't question me about the men in my life, and I don't advise her about the ones in hers. Is she somewhere close by? I'd like to say hello."

"She's upstairs changing. I'll call her—"

"No, don't bother. Now I can tell Eugenie I called and to mind her own business. Give Shanna a kiss for me. And Rory?"

"Yes, ma'am?"

"She may be all grown-up and stubborn, but she's still my little girl. Don't hurt her."

The admonition made him go still. *Don't hurt her.* That was why he'd come here, to make her experience firsthand the wide range of emotions—shame, embarrassment, humiliation, pain—she'd subjected him to. To use her the way she had used him, to make her suffer the way he had suffered.

Wasn't it?

No.

He had come here because he couldn't bear the thought of anything bad happening to her. Because he had wanted to see her, be with her, touch her, take care of her. Because in his entire life, only three people had ever really mattered to him: his mother, his father and Shanna.

"Rory? You won't hurt her, will you?"

"No, ma'am, I won't." As if he could. She didn't care enough about him to be hurt in the way her mother meant. He wasn't that important to her.

He murmured a response to Judith's goodbye, then sat there staring at nothing. Everyone's concern was for Shanna, but *he* was the one who was going to lose the most. He was the one who would be hurt.

Life as usual in Sandy Spring. The Cassidys would win, and the Hawkeses would lose. Shanna would have everything she wanted, and he would have nothing.

"Who's on the phone?" Shanna asked, stepping over the cord to enter the room. She had changed to jeans and a royal-blue sweater and carried a black shirt in her hands.

He glanced at her, then at the receiver, buzzing softly now. "It was your mother," he said, rising to hang it up.

"What did she want?"

"To confirm what your aunt had told her."

"She didn't want to talk to me?"

He shook his head. "She said not to bother calling you to the phone and to give you a kiss for her."

Her gaze went to his mouth, and she thought about this morning's kiss. She certainly wouldn't mind another one like that, but the lower left side of his mouth was puffy and red and showed a nasty cut that extended from the edge of his lip into the soft flesh inside his mouth. It would be a few days at least before he could kiss like that again. "I don't think you're going to be kissing anything for a while," she said, her matter-of-fact tone softened by regret.

"Kisses will keep."

She smiled, then held up the black shirt she held. "I looked for a shirt with buttons so we wouldn't have to pull it over your head, but you don't have one up there."

"I lived in starched and pressed uniforms and shoes and boots polished to a high gloss for over twenty years. I'm a little more casual now."

She gathered the crew neck in both hands, stretching it so it wouldn't touch any of his injuries when she slid it over his head. When that was accomplished, she guided his arms into the sleeves, then gently smoothed the fabric over his chest and stomach, covering the ugly bruises. "Did Mom say anything else?"

"That you're old enough to be the mother of a young adult, you're stubborn and you're still her little girl. She doesn't want to see you hurt."

She tried a careless smile, but she knew it merely looked sad. It already hurt to think of the days ahead when he would no longer be a part of her life. If only he could miraculously fall in love with her . . . But that would require so many other miracles. First he would have to forgive her for the past, would have to give up his bitterness and resentment against the Cassidys in general and her and her father in particular. He would have to learn to trust her, would have to learn to accept her as just a woman and not as the cause of so many of his problems.

And he would have to accept himself, too, as an admirable, responsible, intelligent man who mattered, who was important, who was as good and deserving as anyone else, and better than most. He would have to quit letting the people of this town get to him. He would have to learn to love himself.

Maybe she could teach him. Maybe he could learn by example. He was quick to master new skills—his Army record proved that. Maybe if she loved him well enough and long enough...

With a shake of her head, she moved away from the table. At this rate, dinner wouldn't be ready until bedtime. She had better things to do than dreaming hopeless dreams.

"Have you read the private detective's reports?" Rory asked as he sat down again.

"Some of them." She gave him a sidelong glance. "Not yours. It's interesting, you know. I've known most of those people all my life, and after reading those reports, I'm beginning to think I don't really know them at all."

"How well do you know your uncle's employees?"

Her frown was puzzled. "What are you thinking?"

"It's safe to assume that this—" he gestured toward his face "—has something to do with our snooping. I know Hawkeses have always been fair game to the sheriff's department, but I've been back two months. If it's just the usual harassment, why wait until now?"

She got a handful of potatoes from the pantry and began peeling them. "So they beat you because they know we're investigating Channing. It was a warning meant to scare you away. But what does that have to do with Uncle Mike's..." With the sudden realization, a stricken look crossed her face. "Because we went to the bank to see Rhonda Singleton, and practically everyone who works there saw us with her. If her husband's disappearance is tied into my dad's death... Oh, how could I be so stupid?"

"Not stupid," Rory corrected. "Careless. You're not used to distrusting people you've known all your life. *I* was the stupid one. I should have known better." He gingerly touched his lip. "I won't make the same mistake again."

He settled back in his chair and watched her for a moment. She had once commented on his own gracefulness, but compared to her he felt awkward. Her natural grace complemented by years of ballet made even such mundane tasks as fixing dinner a pleasure to watch.

He leaned his head back and closed his eyes. He felt battered and achy and wanted nothing more than a hot bath and a long night's sleep. He could manage the bath with a little help from Shanna, but the sleep might not be so easy, not when the slightest sound from her room across the hall woke him. It would be easier if they were sharing a bed, if he could lie beside her and know that she was all right instead of worrying twenty feet and two doors away.

Maybe he should tell her he wanted to move into her room. She couldn't feel too threatened, not with the condition he was in. But, as if to make a liar of him, his body responded powerfully to the image of Shanna in bed, curled next to him, her long hair falling over him.

What did he expect? he wondered with a humorless grin. He was hurt, not dead. He could still want her more than life itself. He could still take her.

He could still love her.

Friday was a slow day at work, leaving Shanna far too much time to worry about Rory. Finally she'd given in to the concern and called him at home less than two hours after he'd dropped her off this morning. She called again less than two hours after they'd had lunch together. He had understood her fear and had been patient with her, but she didn't want to push him too far by calling once again, especially when he was due to pick her up in half an hour.

She busied herself with clearing her desk for the weekend. She had no work to take home; her briefcase, when she closed it and set it on the floor, contained a legal pad, three ink pens, a microcassette recorder, her father's appointment calendar and the reports from Nick Langley and Jeffrey Walsh.

She was swiveling from side to side in her chair and taking frequent glances at the clock when she heard voices in the outer office. Susan was expressing her sympathy and indignation over his run-in with the deputies, and Rory typically brushed it off with an insistent, ''I'm okay.'' She'd heard that from him more than a few times in the past twenty-four hours, and she was no more convinced than Susan. How could he look so awful and not feel that way, too?

A moment later, there was a tap at the door, then he came in. She couldn't help but smile stupidly with relief that he'd made it here without further incident. "You're early."

He sprawled comfortably in one of the chairs in front of her desk. "Looks like you're through for the day."

"I rarely have enough business to justify eight-to-five office hours," she said with a shrug. "I keep those hours out of habit."

"When this is over, you should get in touch with that friend of yours in Dallas and see if he still needs help."

Her gaze locked with his. "I've thought about it," she admitted.

Rory slowly shifted his eyes away. That wasn't the answer he'd wanted to hear. He'd wanted her to say no, Sandy Spring is my home; this is where I belong, where my roots are. He'd wanted to know that, wherever he went, whatever he did, she was still living in her big white house and working in this shabby office. He'd wanted to know that if he ever came back, he would know where to find her. He had wanted to know that, whatever happened, she would be *here*.

What would Sandy Spring be like without Shanna? he wondered. Different. Less…home. It had always been home and, because of his parents, always would be, but it had felt less like it after his mother had died and he'd put his father in the institution. It would feel even less so if Shanna left.

"What will you do when it's over?"

He was too busy contemplating a future with absolutely no trace of her in it to hear the hesitancy in her voice, the uneasiness that meant the question was unimportant but the answer wasn't. "I haven't had time to think about it."

"You should move, too. To someplace where you don't have a reputation to live down. You know so much, and you have so many skills. You could have a second career in just about anything." She smiled to soften her next chastising words. "Thirty-nine is entirely too young to be retired and living all alone off in the back of beyond."

"Maybe." Of course he knew she was right. He was too young to retire, and as far as a career, he knew his options. He could go into the security business. He could go to work for the Army as a civilian consultant. Or he could open his own taekwondo school. Like most of the senior black belts he'd studied with, he was a certified instructor. With his background there were a dozen jobs he could do and a thousand places he could do them.

A thousand places without Shanna.

Susan interrupted before Shanna could offer any convincing arguments. "It's five minutes past quitting time, boss. Let's get out of here."

"Go on, Susan. I'll see you Monday." Shanna stood up and lifted her jacket from the back of the chair. Rory stood, too, and took it from her, holding it while she slipped her arms into the sleeves. Then he turned her to face him and slid his hands underneath her hair, pulling it free, cradling its weight for a moment before letting it float down her back.

He saw the surprise in her dark eyes and gave her a crooked smile. "I like touching your hair," he admitted as he unfastened the gold clips that held it back on each side, combed his fingers through it, then watched it fall naturally into place.

She tried to swallow and found it difficult. "I keep meaning to get it all cut off sometime."

"Don't do that." He took one last caress, then handed her purse to her. "We'd better go."

In the outer office, she stopped to turn on the answering machine on Susan's desk. Watching her, he warned, "When I came in, Layton and a couple of the other deputies were across the street, watching. If they're still there, ignore them. Don't let them know they make you nervous."

They *were* still there, three of them leaning against two patrol cars parked side by side. Rory locked the door, gave the keys to Shanna, then slipped his arm around her shoulders. "I'm parked down that way," he said with a nod of his head.

They walked unhurriedly to his truck and got in. As Rory backed into the street, so did one of the deputies with Layton.

"You know, a person ought to feel safe and maybe a little nervous with a deputy following him everywhere he goes," Shanna remarked, watching the car behind them in the outside mirror. "I just feel threatened."

"That's what they want."

The deputy stayed behind them all the way to the house, then made a U-turn and parked across the street. He didn't get out of the car but simply sat there and watched.

So they wanted her to feel threatened, she thought with a scowl as they followed the stone path to the tiny back porch. Well, they had certainly succeeded. After seeing what they could do to a man like Rory, she had never felt so threatened in her life.

Shanna had just started dinner when the phone rang. Rory answered it there in the kitchen, but when Rick Montoya identified himself, he stretched the cord into the hallway. "You're working late," he remarked with a glance at his watch, automatically adding on the time difference on the East Coast.

"I've been trying to get hold of you while I get caught up on some other stuff. I tried this number and got no answer, then called the other number you gave me and got no answer there, either."

Rory's features formed a frown as the memory of Shanna turning on the office answering machine appeared in his mind. "When was that?" he asked curiously.

"That I tried the other number? About ten minutes ago. Why? Is something wrong?"

"I don't know. Probably not."

"Well, listen, I ran those names you gave me, but I didn't have much luck. Four of the names are too common, so I'd need social security numbers to find out if one of them listed is the one you're interested in. The rest didn't show up, but I did get one definite match." He read off the information on that one, then said, "If you can get the social security numbers on the four, I'll try again and see what we get."

"No, that's okay. I think this is the one."

"Are you having some problems with this guy?" Montoya asked. "You want a couple of the guys to drop in for a little visit?"

The frown slowly turned into a grin. With "a couple of the guys" at his side, they would make the most formidable invasion force West Texas had ever seen. If things got worse—meaning if Channing threatened Shanna directly—he might accept a visit from a few old buddies, but not now. "Thanks, Rick, but I think I can handle it. And thanks for the information."

He returned to the kitchen and hung up the phone, then thoughtfully regarded Shanna. "How many times does the phone in your office ring before the machine picks it up?"

"Four when I'm there but Susan's gone, and two if we're both gone. Why?"

"What's the number?"

She told him, and he quickly dialed it. On the tenth ring he hung up. "It's not answering."

"Maybe it's broken."

"Maybe."

She set the heat on low underneath the skillet filled with chicken and turned her attention wholly on Rory. "Do you think something's wrong?"

"I don't—" The peal of the doorbell interrupted him. Gesturing to her to be quiet, he moved down the hallway and into the dimly lit living room. Maybe he was overreacting, but he had a gut feeling that something *was* wrong, and years of dangerous living had taught him to trust his gut feelings.

The instant he shifted the heavy drape at the window, a red glow flashed, faded, then flashed again. In addition to the car that had followed them home, there was another patrol unit parked out front, this one marked Sheriff on the door. The red glow came from its lights, rotating slowly and casting an eerie light in the night.

"What is it?" Shanna whispered at his elbow.

"Hart's out there. I'll answer the door. Stay beside me, okay?" He guided her back to the hallway with his hand on her arm. His other hand was behind his back, resting lightly on the pistol there. At the door he released her, opened the lock left-handed, then pulled the door open.

Sheriff Hart and Deputies Layton and Mangrum were on the porch. Hart's expression was smug, Layton's blank, and Mangrum's uneasy. Rory remembered the pleasure Mangrum had taken in hitting him while his hands were cuffed behind his back, while two other deputies had held him and a third had stood back, gun drawn, ready to shoot him if provided the proper incentive. He had been serious when he'd told Shanna last night that if he had fought back, they would have killed him. Dead serious.

But Mangrum didn't find anything pleasurable about facing him now, unrestrained. Smart of him. If Rory chose to demonstrate the proficiency that had won him the Army's ribbon for expert pistol shot, he could kill all three men in less than five seconds. Or, better still, he could put his years of training in taekwondo into use, disarm all three and cause some serious injuries, again in only seconds.

Hart gave Rory a long look, one that he withstood without a hint of anger or annoyance. "You look like you've been in some trouble, boy," he said with a broad smile. "You'd better be careful, or you might get hurt real bad."

"You might consider taking your own advice, Sheriff," he said coolly. "What do you want?"

The sheriff extended his hand to Shanna. "I'm going to have to ask you to come downtown with us, Shanna. There's been a bit of trouble at your office."

Rory extended his left arm, blocking Hart and moving her safely back out of his reach. "What kind of trouble?"

"I don't think that concerns you, boy, unless maybe you were the one behind it. Come on, Shanna, let's go."

Rory's cool, even tone turned ice-cold and hard. "If she goes anywhere, it will be with me. Now what happened to her office?"

Hart tried to appear somber and concerned, but he failed. "Why, it's not there anymore. Somebody blew it up."

They followed the sheriff back to the business district in Rory's pickup, parking more than a block away from Shanna's office. The street was roped off in both directions and was crowded with onlookers, but the deputies had no difficulty in clearing a path through the crowd and past the barriers for the sheriff, Shanna and Rory.

Shanna's footsteps slowed as they drew nearer. Finally Rory stopped and laid his hands on her shoulders, turning her to him. "You don't have to be here."

She stared at him as if she didn't recognize him. "I'm all right," she whispered. "It's my office. I have to see . . ."

Against his better judgment, when she turned and walked away, he let her go. But he stayed close, so close that no one could get near her—not the sheriff or the chief of the volunteer fire department or the editor of the weekly newspaper.

The scene had to be a gruesome reminder of her father's death, but he saw no sign of it in her face. He saw nothing but shock. No fear, no sorrow, no anger, no hatred—none of the emotions that were hiding inside *him*. Just shock with its protective, distancing numbness that prevented any of this from touching her now.

Finally they stood in the street in the middle of the block. The street was littered with chunks of wood and stone and misshapen metal, with broken pieces of burned furniture and thousands of shards of shattered glass. Where the walls of the office had stood, there was nothing, and the interior was filled with smoldering, blackened lumps that were unrecognizable.

Rory took a quick mental inventory of the important things in the office: her college and law degrees, the pictures of her family, the files of all her clients. The business that she had spent seven years of her life building was gone, literally up in smoke. No one would blame her if she sat down right here surrounded by destruction and cried, but her eyes were dry. Blank. Empty. Too empty.

They stood there in the middle of the street, watching as the firemen poked around inside the burned-out shell, extinguishing small fires that flared as fresh oxygen reached the embers. Rory's arms were around Shanna from behind, but she hardly seemed to notice him. When he leaned down once to whisper in her ear, she didn't instinctively shiver, didn't answer, didn't respond at all.

Dark clouds of smoke hung overhead, drifting away slowly on the still night air, intensifying the already overpowering odor of soggy ashes and burned leather and the noxious fumes of charred synthetics. It floated around them and clung to their clothing, slowly replacing the sweet scent of shampoo in Shanna's hair, where his chin rested. It filled every breath they took and would for a time even after they left, when they were breathing clean air again. One of the few things she had remembered clearly about her father's death, Rory recalled, was the smell. The awful smell.

Out of professional curiosity, he turned his attention to the surrounding offices. Windows were blown out, and there was bound to be structural damage in the ones closest to Shanna's, but the real destruction had been limited to her building. The man who had built and placed this bomb was good. Damn good.

And he was approaching them right now with Sheriff Hart.

"You can go on home whenever you want, Shanna," the sheriff said. "I don't guess it was really necessary for you to come down here after all."

She gave him no acknowledgment.

"Looks like you made some powerful enemies," Hart continued.

She placed her hand on Rory's wrist, her fingers clenching tightly at Hart's too-innocent comment. Rory ignored the stab of pain from the bruises beneath her fingers and responded to Hart's remark for her. "She's made some powerful friends, too."

"Maybe somebody intended this as some sort of warning. Maybe you're snooping around in something that doesn't concern you." Hart waited a moment for a response, then shrugged and walked away.

Rory shifted his gaze to the man who started to follow. "Nice job."

After a moment's hesitation, Deputy Layton looked from Rory to the rubble across the sidewalk, then back again. "I don't know what you're talking about, Hawkes."

"It was a damn smart idea to do it after-hours when you knew for sure that she wasn't there," Rory continued. "Because if you had hurt her, I would have killed you."

Layton remained expressionless, claiming no innocence, admitting no guilt. After a moment's hard stare, he said mildly, "It's not wise to threaten an officer of the law."

"It's not a threat, Deputy. It's a promise."

After another long stare, Layton turned on his heel and walked away.

Suddenly Shanna shivered, and Rory pulled her close to his side. "Let's go home, princess," he said gently. "There's nothing we can do here."

At home he threw out the oil-soaked chicken, made some sandwiches and heated canned soup, but he couldn't get Shanna to eat. He fixed a pot of the coffee she liked so much each morning, but after the first few sips, she wouldn't drink any more. For the first time since he'd poured the Scotch down the sink, he regretted it. She could probably use a stiff drink tonight, and heaven knows *he* could.

She sat at the table, her brown eyes soft and unfocused, her hands clasped tightly in front of her. Her thoughts were racing in about a hundred different directions, filled with disjointed ideas and horrible images, with sounds and smells and sights, with threats and promises, fear, helplessness, death.

Her mind had efficiently processed information over- heard there on the street even while she'd been too numb to understand any of it. Information about powerful enemies and powerful friends, about warnings and threats, about minding her own business.

Maybe Hart was right. Maybe she *should* mind her own business. Her father was dead, and Wayne Singleton most likely was. Rory had been beaten, and now her office had been destroyed. What if they had been in it? What if this investigation had caused not only her own death, but also Rory's and maybe even Susan's? It was a possibility too terrible to consider.

"Maybe we should stop," she murmured. She felt Rory's sharp look—because she had finally spoken for the first time since seeing her office? she wondered. Or because of what she'd said?

"No. We're not giving up."

"Maybe it's the only way to be safe. To stay alive."

He unfolded her fingers and grasped both hands in his. "Deputy Layton was in the Army for six years. His MOS was demolitions. He rigged the bomb in your father's truck. He set the one that blew up your office." He squeezed her hands tighter, urging her to look at him. "Shanna, he *mur- dered* your father, and he did it for Lawrence Channing. You can't let them get away with that."

She looked blankly at him.

"If people see that Channing can have the district attorney killed and go unpunished, his power will be absolute. No one in this town will ever be safe from him."

"If I don't leave him alone, *I* won't be safe," she pointed out in a calm, emotionless voice. "And if he kills me, he'll kill you, too. I won't be responsible for that, Rory. When my father died—" She broke off and closed her eyes. The memory she was reaching for was *right there*, close enough to feel but just outside her grasp. Something terrible. Something unendurable.

She opened her eyes again and shook her head. "I won't let that happen to you."

"The terms of our agreement are that *I* protect *you*," he reminded her. "Not the other way around."

"Oh, great. So I can just go on with whatever I'm doing and not care that they beat the hell out of you yesterday. I shouldn't care that they could have just as easily blown up my office with both of us in it, and I'm not supposed to care that you could end up dead because I asked you to protect me." She slowly stood up, drawing up to her full height, looking down on him with all the disdain Cassidys had always felt for Hawkeses. "I'm sorry, but I'm not that cold and I'm not that selfish. I don't want Channing punished at any cost. I don't want to live—or die—with you on my conscience. I won't go on with this, Rory. I can't."

She walked past him, down the hallway and up the stairs to her room. She knew he watched her until she was out of sight—she felt his gaze, strong and unwavering—but she didn't look back. She didn't relent. If it ended their relationship, fine. She could live without Rory in her life, as long as she knew he was alive and well.

But she couldn't live knowing she had caused his death.

When she hadn't come down again after half an hour, Rory went upstairs to check on her. She was in bed, still dressed, her head pillowed on her arms, her hair falling in a silken tumble around her. Her breathing was the slow, deep rhythm of sleep.

He carefully removed her shoes and folded the bed-spread over her. After switching off the bedside lamp, he started to leave. Instead, though, he knelt beside the bed and tenderly brushed her hair from her face. "Sleep well, princess," he whispered, the words a mere breath in the near silence of the room. He placed a kiss on her temple, watched her snuggle deeper into the covers, then left the room.

Sleep well. After all that she'd been through, God knew she needed a night of peaceful rest. He prayed she would get it tonight, to prepare her for what was to come.

At the stair landing, he turned right, into Joseph's office. It was dark and felt empty, abandoned—fitting, he acknowledged, since its owner would never be back. He sat down behind the desk and reached for the phone. It took several calls to reach the Administrative Officer of the Day at Brooke Army Medical Center. After a brief explanation, the captain agreed to contact Dr. Holloway and pass along a request that he call Rory as soon as possible.

The call was returned within ten minutes. Rory explained about Joseph's death, Shanna's memory loss and night-mares, and tonight's explosion. He told Dr. Holloway about Dr. Saxon's recommendation that she undergo hypnosis or a sodium amytal interview and asked for his assistance in setting it up.

"I have a friend on staff at one of the local hospitals. I can speak to him, if you like, and arrange an interview. I take it you're in a bit of a hurry, so how soon would you be able to come to San Antonio?"

"Tomorrow. She needs to get away for a few days any-way, so if you could set up something for the first part of the week . . ."

"All right. Why don't we meet Sunday afternoon? I can talk to your friend and give Mark—Dr. Berry—some idea of which way to go with this. Give me a call before noon Sunday, and we'll arrange a meeting place."

"Thanks, sir. I appreciate it."

After a moment of casual catching up, Rory hung up, tilted his head back and wearily closed his eyes. Getting Shanna to San Antonio wouldn't be much of a problem. She really did need to get away for a few days. If she balked, he would simply tell her that *he* needed a few days away. Given her degree of concern for him, she was sure to agree to that.

But talking her into the treatment would be a different matter altogether. She had been adamant about not wanting to do anything that might open up the part of her memory that was locked away. Even the doctor's assurance that she wouldn't remember anything new afterward might not change her mind.

It was a long drive to San Antonio, he thought with a sigh as he got to his feet. A long time to argue with her. A long time to convince her.

Chapter 9

San Antonio. When Rory had told her this morning that they were going to spend the next three or four days in San Antonio, Shanna had listlessly agreed. What reason did she have to stay in Sandy Spring? She certainly didn't have to go to work Monday. So she had recommended that he make reservations at a hotel on the river, then gone to her room to pack.

Now she'd been sitting beside him for the past seven hours, listening to him when he talked, saying little herself, mostly just being melancholy. She couldn't shake the sense of defeat that had fallen over her last night. She hated giving up, but what other choices were left? They had no hard evidence to tie Layton or Channing to the bombs. They had proof of the corruption in town, but most of it had been gained illegally. What they had mostly were suspicions, doubts, hunches and rumors. If they kept pushing to find hard evidence, something they could take to the FBI or the state attorney general's office, they were going to be killed, just like her father.

They had to give up.

And when they did, Rory would go back to his own life— a life that didn't include her. And she would have to learn to live with the knowledge of what it meant to love someone who didn't love her.

She had known there were risks from the beginning, but she had thought the physical ones were a bigger threat than the emotional ones. Stupid. She'd been just plain stupid.

Rory found the hotel with little trouble, and within minutes they were checked in and on the way up in the elevator. Had he booked adjoining rooms, she wondered, or one with two beds...or maybe a single? She would like to share a bed with him tonight, would like to have the intimacy and closeness of lovers. It would soothe all the hurts and ease all the worries. It would heal her.

The bellman opened the door, then stepped back so she could enter first. There *was* only one bed in the spacious room—king size, she noticed disparagingly, but still only one. She set her handbag on the dresser as she passed it, then went to the window to look down on the city below while Rory settled with the bellman.

The door closed, leaving them alone in the room. She waited for him to speak, and when he did, it was from clear across the room. "This is all they had on such short notice."

He sounded uneasy, she thought, seeing her smile reflected in the window glass. Did he expect her to complain or to insist that he find another room for himself or sleep on the love seat against the far wall or on the floor?

Then he cleared his throat and continued. "But even if it hadn't been, I would have taken it anyway. I'm tired of sleeping in separate rooms, Shanna. I want to sleep with you. I want to make love to you."

Her smile widened, but there was no hint of it in her response. "So you finally decided that, did you?"

"I've known all along."

"Then why have you waited? You could have moved into my room at any time."

His voice was quiet, unsteady with need and taut with longing. "Maybe I was waiting for an invitation. I don't want you to do this because you feel obligated. And I don't want you to do it because it's been a long time for you and I'm the only man around."

"What *do* you want?" she asked softly.

"I want you to know who I am. . . ."

He didn't finish, but she understood. He wanted her to go into this with her eyes open, to acknowledge up-front that he was a Hawkes, that Joseph Cassidy's daughter was going to share this most intimate of acts with a Hawkes. "All right." She heard her voice tremble and knew he must have, too. "I'll remember who you are . . . if you'll forget who I am."

"Forget?"

"That I'm a Cassidy. That I'm Joseph's daughter. Forget what I've done to you, what the Cassidys have done to you." She closed her eyes on the tears that burned. "You know what it's like to be hated for nothing more than your name. *I* know what it's like to be wanted for nothing more than *my* name."

After a long silence, he spoke again, his voice edged with a harsh bitterness. "I wanted you in spite of the name, Shanna, not because of it."

Slowly she turned to face him. "Then show me," she whispered.

He covered the distance between them in four long strides, then reached past her to close the drapes. The room grew darker, more private, cozy.

Then he touched her.

Her hair was soft and cool, her skin softer and warm. He stroked her face in slow, sensual caresses that moved down her throat, over her breasts in light brushes that circled around their sensitive peaks, and ending at her waist. With his fingers hooked over the waistband of her jeans, he pulled her to him, not stopping until her body was taut against his.

He wrapped his hands in her hair, using it as gentle leverage to tug her head back for his kiss. The first attempt was awkward due to the lingering tenderness in his lip, but he found that pleasure truly could overcome pain as his tongue slipped into the familiar heat and flavor of her mouth.

Years ago, Shanna remembered, as an inexperienced young girl in Rory's arms, she had felt this kind of need—mindless, relentless, endless—but she had lost it when she'd lost him. No other man had ever kissed her or touched her or aroused her like this. No other man had ever made her feel like this—not the boy who'd taken her virginity, not the numerous men she'd dated and certainly not the man she'd been engaged to marry. Only Rory.

Her skin tingled where it touched his. Her breasts were swollen, her nipples achy and hard, and lower, the dampness that made her throb gathered fiery hot between her thighs. She pressed closer to him, brushing her breasts over the hard muscles of his chest, rubbing her belly against the heavy, rigid length of his arousal.

He ended the kiss for a badly needed breath, then, intently watching her face, he freed his hands from her hair, letting it fall in a tangle. Slowly he followed it down, smoothing and caressing it, until each hand covered one small breast. He watched her eyes close and her mouth part in a breathless gasp as he rubbed his hands side to side, and he felt her nipples, already erect, harden even more against his palms.

He had once known her breasts intimately, had traced every delicate vein with his fingers and his tongue, had suckled her nipples until she arched her back and pleaded for a relief that she didn't understand. He had always stopped then, had always put her away from him, even though the desire to bury himself inside her had made him tremble with weakness, the way he trembled now. But this time he didn't have to stop. This time she understood what they were doing, understood how it would end, and she wanted him anyway.

She wanted him.

Knowing that was the most powerful thing he'd ever experienced.

He worked his hands beneath her T-shirt, then impatiently pulled it over her head and dropped it to the floor. Her breasts were small, her nipples a dark rosy brown and hard and eager for his kiss. He drew one into his mouth, capturing it gently between his teeth and drawing the rough tip of his tongue over it. Then he suckled it, making her groan, making his own flesh stiffen even more.

Shanna tangled her fingers in his hair, forcing him back. "Please," she whispered, leaving frantic kisses along his jaw. "I need you now, Rory." No more playing, no more knee-weakening caresses, no more delaying the satisfaction she so desperately needed.

They each removed their own clothes, then came together on the bed, Rory catching her in his arms and lowering her gently to her back. He knelt between her parted thighs, stroked through the soft black curls that shielded her, then slowly, surely filled his place inside her. He pressed until she had taken all of him, then for a moment adjusted to the feel of her, tight and hot and moist, around him.

He'd been with women before—more experienced ones, less experienced ones—but this was new, different. This was like coming home. This was where he belonged. Forever.

Or at least for the next few days.

He shut his mind on that thought, on all thought, and concentrated instead on feeling. On the need, heavy and sharp edged, that was building low in his belly. On the sensation, soft and erotic, of her breasts rubbing his chest. On the confinement, close and welcoming, of her legs wrapped around his hips. On the pleasure, powerful and addictive, that being inside her brought.

She shifted beneath him, drawing him closer. Her hands moved restlessly, kneading his shoulders, tenderly stroking his bruised chest, flicking across his nipples. When he bent to suckle her breast, she groaned and twined her fingers through his hair, pulling him closer, prolonging the intimate kiss, and at the same time arching her hips against his, drawing him in, pulling away, taking him deeper.

Her rhythm was simple and easy and sent shudders rocketing through him. Every muscle in his body was strained taut, struggling against the demands made by her body, to hold back, to draw out every moment of intense pleasure to its fullest. But his body's own demands were stronger than his will to make this dream, this fantasy, last. He took control from her, sliding his hands beneath her hips, thrusting deeper and longer and faster. Her ragged cries when she reached fulfillment and the tiny, tight clenching of her body around his drove him on, feeding his uncontrollable need, fueling his own completion. Muscles trembling, body shuddering, he held her tight, filling her. Loving her.

She was trembling beneath him, and he held her, whispered to her, stroked her. He wanted to tell her he loved her but didn't dare—maybe *she* could forget she was a Cassidy, but *he* couldn't—so he kept the words in his mind, his own private secret. His own private treasure.

When he left her body, Shanna shivered with the sudden chill as cool air touched her heated, sweat-slick skin. But the shiver went deeper, all the way into her soul. It was a sign of things to come, of the way she would feel when he left her for good. Of the emptiness and cold that would fill her life.

Then he drew her into his arms again, thigh to thigh, belly to belly, and the heat from his body warmed her again. This was no time to think of the future, of loving and losing and being alone, she silently chided herself. He was with her now, in the most special and most intimate way. She would think only of that.

She tilted her head back, then pressed a kiss to his jaw. "I've wanted for so long to touch you. Your body fascinates me. It's so powerful and strong and graceful." She drew her fingertips lightly over his chest and laughed delightedly at his swift response—nipples tightening, muscles rippling, breath catching unexpectedly.

"I can tell you about wanting, princess," he said, rubbing her nipple gently between two fingers and bringing the same swift response from her. "The first time I remember seeing you was at your grandmother's house. My mother had just started working there, and I was waiting for her to get off. I was eleven, so you must have been eight. You had this long black hair even then and eyes big enough to get lost in. You were wearing a blue dress with a frilly white apron over it and blue socks with white lace and little blue bows in your hair, and you looked like you hated it." His voice grew softer, and his eyes took on a distant expression, as if he was seeing it all again. "I thought you were the prettiest thing I'd ever seen. I wanted . . . I wanted to just look at you—like a china doll on a shelf, you know. I never would have touched you."

Then the softness faded, and his voice was normal again, maybe a little colder, maybe a little harder. "But your grandmother said I was too dirty to be around you—I'd been weeding her flower beds. She said I would make you dirty, and she sent me outside to wait until you were gone."

Shanna remembered not the day but the memory. There were photographs in the album at home of her best friend Elaine's eighth birthday party, of Shanna and Elaine wearing matching blue dresses and white pinafores, with silly party hats on their heads and sillier grins on their faces. Even though she *had* hated being all dressed up—she'd been in a faded-jeans-and-scuffed-sneaker stage that she'd never outgrown—it had been a happy day for her. That made her ache for Rory all the stronger.

"My grandmother lived her entire life in Sandy Spring," she said softly. "It was her own little kingdom. My grandfather was the king, and she was the queen."

"And you were the princess."

Sadly she nodded. "It was the only life she knew. She had always been taught that she was someone special, that she was better than everyone else. She had grown up watching her family look down on everyone else in town, and she learned to do it even better than they did.''

''You were always taught that you were special, too, but you don't look down on everyone else. Why not?''

Her smile came quickly. ''My mother lived all her life in Dallas until she went to college, where she met my father. She knew that the Cassidys might be the biggest fish in the small pond of Sandy Spring, but anywhere else they were nothing more than minnows. She never let us forget that.''

Then the smile disappeared, and the sadness returned. ''Grandmother was a product of her environment, and she couldn't have been any different than she was, but it doesn't make what she did all right. I know she did things like that in a misguided effort to protect me, but she was wrong. She was always wrong.''

Not that time, Rory thought bitterly. He *would* have made her dirty, both literally and figuratively. People would have turned away from her because of him. They would now, too. Hadn't her best friend's mother ordered her out of the shop last week simply because *he* had been with her?

He shut away the unpleasantness and concentrated only on Shanna, on arousing her, on pleasing her. Gathering a thick strand of her hair, he used it to tickle across her ribs, between her breasts, over her softening nipple, making it pucker into arousal again. Opening his hand, he watched her hair cascade down to completely cover her breast, then lazily caressed the small, sensitive mound through the soft black web. She gasped, and her eyes turned dark and hazy. Eyes big enough to get lost in, he'd told her, and he hadn't kidded. *He'd* been lost practically all his life.

''Make love to me, Rory,'' she whispered, reaching for him. He let her pull him into position, let her gentle fingers wrapped around his swollen manhood guide him into place, let her body draw him deep, deep inside hers.

And as he filled her, bleakness washed over him. He was in love with her. With the one woman he couldn't have. The

one woman he could never keep. The one woman who deserved, God help him, so much more than he could give.

He *was* lost. Completely. Irrevocably. Hopelessly.

While Shanna showered before dinner, Rory called Dr.
Holloway, and they arranged to meet in the hotel bar at
three o'clock the next afternoon.

"How does she feel about this?" the doctor asked.

"She doesn't know, sir," Rory admitted reluctantly.
"She's afraid of remembering. The only times we've talked
about it, she got so upset that I haven't brought it up again."

"We can make sure that she doesn't remember anything."

"You'll have to convince her of that."

"We will. Don't worry about it. See you tomorrow at
three, then."

Shanna came out of the bathroom, wearing a towel
around her hair and a short robe in deep coral satin. "Who
was that?"

"I called an old friend of mine who's stationed here in
San Antonio. We're getting together tomorrow afternoon if
you don't mind."

"Am I invited?"

"Of course."

She smiled so warmly that he felt doubly bad for deceiv-
ing her. "Good. I'd like to meet your friend."

He wished it was that innocent, simply introducing an old
buddy to a new lover. He had to tell her the truth...but not
now. Not when she was smiling so sweetly at him. Not when
his body was still slowly recovering from the heated pleasure of loving her. Not when he could love her again and
again.

Tomorrow. He would tell her sometime tomorrow.

They had dinner in one of the restaurants in the hotel.
Once they were fully dressed and out of the intimacy of their

room, Shanna felt a new shyness with Rory. Most of the time he looked as if nothing had changed between them— and maybe for him, she admitted, nothing had. Maybe he had simply collected his first payment.

But at times she felt his eyes on her and looked up to see pure, naked desire in their shadows. Something *had* changed. Everything had. She was even more in love with him now than before, and he... Well, he *wanted* her. It wasn't love. It wasn't even caring, but it was something. For now, it was enough.

When they left the restaurant, they passed a dimly lit club where couples swayed back and forth to the music of a live band. Shanna glanced inside, then at Rory. "Would you like to dance?"

"I don't know how."

"Oh, come on. Anyone who moves like you do has to be able to dance."

He pushed his hands into his pockets as they continued walking. "No. Someone was supposed to teach me how years ago... but she never did."

The memory raced into her mind, a clear, warm April day in her grandmother's backyard. *You asked me to the spring dance, and you can't dance?* She had teased him mercilessly until he'd begun his own addictive brand of teasing: lazy, hungry kisses and slow, make-her-burn caresses. He'd made her need, had made her plead, until she'd offered a trade. *Teach me to love, and I'll teach you to dance.* And he had agreed.

But the dance had been held without them.

"Why did you do it?" His voice was quiet and emotionless, as if he were asking something no more important than why she'd chosen to wear a skirt tonight or why she'd ordered scampi for dinner. As if her reasons really didn't matter.

Or maybe hiding how much they mattered? Shanna wondered.

She'd had plenty of time to prepare an explanation, but she hadn't because thinking about her actions so long ago still shamed her. She considered them now. Were there any words she could use that would make her seem less selfish, less contemptible? Any magical phrases that could erase the pain she knew she had caused him?

No. There was only the truth. While it couldn't make everything all right, maybe it would help.

"That dance was going to be my first date. Mom was so excited about it that she didn't even ask who I was going with until the weekend before, when she took me shopping for a new dress. When I told her, she took me straight to Grandmother's—Dad was over there, and Uncle Mike and Aunt Eugenie—and she told all of them."

She turned away, walking toward the fountain that gurgled nearby. Only Uncle Mike had remained quiet. Grandmother had been outraged, Aunt Eugenie nearly hysterical, Judith quietly disapproving, and her father... Her father had been coldly furious. And *she* had been in tears, trying desperately to tell them that they were wrong about Rory, that he was sweet and gentle and would never hurt or take advantage of her.

But no one had listened to her. She was told—no, *ordered*, under threat of punishment—to have no further contact with him. When she had pleaded for an opportunity to explain to him why she couldn't see him again, her father had exploded and slapped her. It was the first, and last, time he'd ever touched her in anger.

"Mom wasn't really angry with me," she continued when Rory joined her. "She just thought I had used poor judgment in choosing a boy that I knew Dad didn't like. But Dad..." She touched her fingers to her cheek, remembering the faint sting of his palm against her skin. "For the next week, he refused to speak to me or look at me or acknowledge me in any way. It was as if I no longer existed."

She broke off when two small children raced across the lobby to the fountain, crowding around them. After their parents collected them, she glanced apologetically at Rory and continued. "When you asked me about the dance that day at school, I guess I blamed you. If it hadn't been for you, my father wouldn't have been ignoring me. He wouldn't have stopped loving me. I was hurting because of you, and I wanted you to share the pain, so I said those awful things."

Then she had gone into the girls' room and had thrown up. She had skipped the rest of her classes, gone home and locked herself in her room and had cried well into the night. Her brothers had been all too eager to tell their mother what she'd done, and Judith had insisted that Joseph come home early and talk to her.

He had begun by trying to justify his opinion of Rory, then had progressed to meaningless assurances that what she'd done wasn't really so bad—he was just a Hawkes, after all; that in a few days everything would be all right; that in a few weeks she would forget all about Rory and meet somebody new.

She had spoken to him only once the entire evening. *I'll never forgive you for making me hurt him.*

Of course she eventually had, but she'd never forgiven herself, and she knew Rory would never forgive her, either. Still, she said softly, "I'm sorry. God, I am so sorry."

When a moment went by without a response from him, she risked a glance at him, steeling herself for the worst. But he seemed... She took a startled closer look and confirmed her first guess. Sheepish. Not angry, not condemning, but sheepish.

Her reasons really *hadn't* mattered to Rory. Somewhere deep inside, he supposed he must have known that her family, particularly her father, had been involved in her sudden change of heart toward him. One week she had been the sweet, carefree girl he'd fallen for, kissing him, teasing him, asking him to teach her about love, and the next she'd cut his heart out, along with his pride, with her bitter mocking words. Only her father, her dear beloved father, could have effected such a tremendous change.

"I don't guess there was a man alive who wouldn't have objected to my dating his daughter," he said with a crooked grin. "I was every father's nightmare."

"Don't do that," she chided. "Don't accept the blame for something that wasn't your fault."

"I knew how your father felt about me, Shanna," he pointed out in a reasonable voice. "He thought I was a wild punk who should be locked up in reform school instead of in Sandy Spring High School. And he was right. I *was* wild. I *was* a punk. By the time I was eighteen, I had an arrest record longer than practically any adult in the county. If I ever have a fifteen-year-old daughter, princess, I can guarantee that I'll be a lot stricter where boys are concerned than your father ever was."

"But he was wrong about you," she protested.

"Was he?" Rory shrugged. "I'd like to think all my intentions toward you then were honorable, but I honestly don't know. I do know that if you'd gone to that dance with me and taught me to dance, I was damn sure going to keep my end of the deal and teach you about making love. And I wasn't exactly responsible about sex in those days. What if you'd gotten pregnant? They would have tried to force you to have an abortion or give the baby up for adoption. I would have forced you to run away with me. Any of the choices would have destroyed you."

He linked his fingers through hers and started walking back the way they'd come. "In the end, it all worked out for the best. If your father hadn't found out about us, he wouldn't have made me join the Army the next time I got busted. And if I hadn't joined the Army, I would probably be in prison right now—or dead. I certainly wouldn't be here with you."

Shanna raised his hand and pressed a kiss to his knuckles. "My father *was* wrong about you," she repeated. "You're a good man, Rory."

The quiet compliment filled him with warmth that not even an unexpected thought of Dr. Holloway could diminish. He freed her hand and slid his arm around her shoulders instead, pulling her close to his side. When they passed the club once again, the music now seductively slow, he reminded her, "You still owe me dance lessons."

"How about now?"

He thought about holding her close in the dark, smoky room, of moving to the music in a lazy rhythm better suited for making love, and his body responded. "I have a better idea, princess," he said in a suddenly husky voice. "Come to the room with me, and we'll turn the radio on and the lights off and take our clothes off, and I'll show you a whole different kind of dance."

She gave him a long look, her gaze never wavering from his face, then smiled. She knew he was aching with desire for her—he could see it in the purely feminine satisfaction in her eyes—and it turned her on. He could see *that* in the sudden tightening of her nipples beneath her plain white blouse.

They had to share the elevator with a dozen other guests, stopping at virtually every floor. Rory stood at the back of the small car, with Shanna directly in front of him, and she tormented him all the way up, brushing against him first with her fingers, then her hip, then her very shapely bottom. When they finally reached their floor, he held her almost at arm's length as they went down the hall to their room.

"In a hurry?" she asked with an innocent smile as he unlocked the door and ushered her inside.

"You're dangerous," he said as he put the Do Not Disturb sign on the outer doorknob, then fastened all the locks. The door secured, he turned and gave her a smile that was as innocent as her own and sweetly threatening. "But so am I ... when aroused."

She took another long look, her gaze never reaching above his belt buckle this time. "You look pretty aroused to me. Of course, you're pretty when you're not aroused, too."

Then her teasing faded and was replaced by longing. "Make love to me, Rory."

He slowly shook his head. "We're going to dance first, remember?" He left her standing near the door and turned on the radio on the night table, then shut off the lights the maid had left burning when she'd come in while they were at dinner. He turned on the bathroom light, pulled the door half shut to soften it, then flipped off the last light at the door where Shanna still waited.

Leaning against the wall, he removed his shoes and socks, then took her hand and led her into the room, stopping near the bed. When she reached for him, he shook his head. "First the clothes—but not all at once. We've got all night."

Under his watchful gaze, she pulled her blouse free of her skirt and began unfastening the buttons, one by each slow one, all the way down the front, two on each fitted cuff. When she shrugged out of it, he caught it, wrapping his hands in the fabric. "What is this?" he asked.

"Silk."

He rubbed it between his fingers, then grinned. "The night I moved in with you, when I touched your cheek there in the living room, I thought your skin was as soft as silk. Now I know you're even softer."

Untangling the blouse, he let it fall on the bed behind her, then saw what she wore beneath it. All ribbons and lace and silk again, he thought, rubbing his hand over her midriff. It was pale ivory, disappearing beneath the black skirt she still wore, gleaming against her dark skin, covering her small breasts but revealing her nipples. He didn't know the name for the garment, but he liked it. Very much.

She guided his jacket down his arms and dropped it to the bed, then slid her arms around his waist. "Put your arms around me," she instructed, shivering when he did. "Most places where you can dance are so crowded that you don't have room to do anything fancy. For most people, dancing is just an excuse to get close, anyway, so all you have to do is put your arms around your partner and move in time to the music.''

''Hmm.'' He rested his cheek on her hair, closed his eyes and savored the sensuous sway of her body against his. He was so aroused that he was starting to ache, but he made no effort to speed the seduction along. He wanted to take his time, to absorb every feeling, every scent, every texture, every motion. He wanted it to last forever.

The music was soft and romantic, classics from their youth mixed with more recent hits. Slow dancing on a Saturday night, the female DJ with the sexy voice informed them between songs.

He'd never had much interest in dancing. He had invited Shanna to the spring dance all those years ago because it had seemed fitting that crazy old Joe's juvenile delinquent kid should make his relationship with the Cassidy princess known at the biggest event of the school year, at an event that kids like him never went to because they didn't fit in and wouldn't have been welcome anyway.

But her family had interfered, and he'd never gotten his lessons. Over the years he'd had other offers from other women, but none had tempted him. He was active enough on his job, he had claimed as an excuse. Getting out on the dance floor wasn't his idea of a pleasant way to spend the evening.

Maybe he'd been waiting for Shanna to teach him.

Her hands moved restlessly, tantalizingly brief touches on his spine, his waist, his chest, his shoulders. He responded with his own caress, a long, lazy stroke up her back, beneath her hair, down her sides, his fingertips brushing over the softly rounded curves of her breasts. In his explorations, he found the button and zipper that fastened her skirt and slowly released them. His hands slid down her hips, taking the skirt with them, letting it fall by itself when they reached the bare skin of her thighs.

Shanna stepped out of the skirt and kicked it aside, then moved close to him again. His fingers were stroking along the edges of her teddy. The legs were cut high, almost to her waist, and he started there, one hand on each side and followed the lace down, down, until his fingers met between her thighs.

"Nice," he murmured thickly when lace and silk gave way to heated flesh.

She trembled, muscles clenching involuntarily. He withdrew his hands, then tilted her head back for a kiss.

Being careful of his healing lip came naturally to her now. Their kisses were lopsided but no less potent. His tongue probed her mouth with strokes as smooth, practiced and deep as those yet to come, and she mimicked them, tasting him, experimenting with her power to make *him* tremble. That power increased when she tugged his shirt from his slacks and slid her hands underneath to rub across his belly and his ribs to his nipples, taking the fabric with them. She gently pinched them, then, when he groaned, broke off the kiss to bathe each small brown nub with her tongue.

Rory pulled his shirt over his head, then wrapped his hands in her hair, weaving a fine black web that trapped his fingers. When she rested her cheek against his chest, he continued to play with the long, heavy strands.

"I can feel your heartbeat," she whispered. "It's a little fast."

He found hers with one long, slender finger pressed to her throat. "Yours is throbbing."

Her laugh was soft and choked. "It's not the only thing, I bet."

"Find out for yourself."

His belt buckle opened easily beneath her questing fingers, and the button on his trousers slipped right out. His zipper glided silently down its track. Then Shanna stopped, forcing herself to take deeper breaths, to control the trembling that had spread from her hands to every other part of her body. "You're in better shape than I am," she said ruefully.

Releasing her hair, Rory brought his hands up to her breasts, covering them, gently caressing them. While one hand teased her nipples, the other slid down to cup her bottom. "There's nothing wrong with your shape, princess. It's perfect for me—soft where I'm hard."

She reached around to pull the holster from his waistband, fumbling with the metal clip, finally freeing it. She handed it to him, and he tossed it lightly in the center of the bed. Next she guided his slacks over his hips and down his long legs. Now he wore even less than she did: a pair of pale blue briefs that were just that. Brief. The soft cotton was stretched taut to accommodate his arousal.

She cradled him gently in her hands, first through the briefs, then flesh to satin-smooth, hot, swollen flesh. "Definitely throbbing," she announced with a caress that emphasized her point and made him suck in his breath.

His eyes were closed and his jaw clenched as she showed him at the same time the true meanings of the words pleasure and torture.

He fumbled with the thin ribbon straps, pushing them off her shoulders. For a moment the silk caught on her breast, the lace edging draped over her erect nipple, then fell to her waist, baring both breasts. Clumsily he drew it down, stopping when Shanna commanded, leaving her to unfasten her stockings. An instant later, the teddy slithered down her legs to the floor, and he pulled her to the bed.

He sat on the edge of the mattress, lifting her over him, pressing a kiss to her breast as he lowered her into place. He probed with fingers and stiffened flesh, then, with a groan, sheathed himself deep inside her.

She still wore her shoes—he felt cool leather and spiky heels pressed against his legs—and he'd given her no chance to remove her hose, he discovered when he stroked her legs and moved from silky, warm skin to silky, shimmering stockings. She discovered it, too, and weakly protested, but he quieted her. It felt different. Sensual. Erotic.

Slow dancing on a Saturday night continued on the radio, but in the room it had given way to slow dancing of another sort. To slow heat. Slow torment. Slow delight.

Slow loving.

"So tell me about this friend of yours."

Rory twisted his glass around in a slow, precise circle, using the movement as an excuse for not looking at Shanna right away. "What do you want to know?"

"The important things."

Briefly he glanced at her, then back at the glass. "You're an attorney, Ms. Cassidy. Surely you can question better than that."

She made a face at him, then leaned forward to pick up her own glass. "Okay. What is this man's name? What does he do? Where and how did you meet him? How long have you known him? Is he a close friend?" She paused. "Are those questions specific enough for you?"

"Yes, ma'am." But instead of answering, he reached for her free hand. "How about another dance lesson tonight?"

Her cheeks turned a delicate blush, as he'd known they would. Last evening's "lesson" had lasted well into the night and had left them both exhausted. They had slept until after eleven this morning and had awakened in a rumpled bed with articles of clothing, one high heel and one holstered .45 scattered around them.

"That would be—" Before she could finish, a slender, bespectacled, thinning-haired man stopped beside their table.

"Hey, master sergeant," he greeted, extending his hand to Rory. "Are you being all that you can be?"

"I'm trying." Rory stood up and shook hands with the man, then turned to Shanna. "Sir, this is Shanna Cassidy. Shanna, this is . . . Major Holloway."

The doctor exchanged handshakes with her, too, before sitting down. "Pleased to meet you, Shanna. My name's

Bryan.'' He signaled the waitress and ordered a drink, then gave Rory a long look. "My God, I'd hate to see the men who could do that to you."

He offered the half smile that was becoming second nature. Everything was healing nicely, and his vision was fine. The abrasions on his forehead and cheek were already fading, but the bruising around his eye, shades of purple and blue and murky yellow, still looked bad.

"How do you know it was more than one?" Shanna asked curiously.

"Because I know what he can do. It would take a half dozen or more to inflict that kind of damage."

"Only four," Rory corrected. "With handcuffs and guns."

Dr. Holloway grew serious. "Are you in trouble?"

Hesitating, he glanced at Shanna, and she answered for him. "*I* am. Rory's helping me, and the local sheriff's department doesn't like it too much."

"You know you have plenty of people to call on if you need help."

"Yes, sir, I know." That was why they were here. And first off, he needed help in explaining that to Shanna.

As it turned out, he didn't need to. Her very next question was, "What do you do in the Army, Major?"

Dr. Holloway turned to Rory first, caught his barely perceptible shrug, then smiled at Shanna and politely replied, "I'm a psychologist."

She stared at him so long that his smile slowly faded and he shifted uncomfortably in his seat. Then she transferred the hard, cold look to Rory. "You bastard."

If she had yelled or cried or jumped up and hurried away, he wouldn't have been surprised or even overly concerned. He would have gone after her, of course, and let her anger run its course, then brought her back. But she'd spoken in a deadly quiet voice and showed no intentions of rushing off in a temper, and *that* worried him.

"Well, what's my diagnosis, Doctor?" she asked sarcastically. "You two have obviously already discussed this between yourselves. I think it's only fair that *I* know what's wrong with me."

"All right," he said calmly. "Based on what I've been told, I believe you have psychogenic amnesia. There are four types—localized, generalized, selective and continuous. I would say you have the selective form. It's generally caused by severe stress, often dealing with physical injury or death, and is characterized by an inability to recall some, although not all, events during a specific period of time." He paused. "As the master sergeant has explained to me, your father was recently killed."

"Did the master sergeant—" she put particularly derisive emphasis on Rory's former rank "—explain to you that my father was blown to bits when a bomb went off in his truck? Did he tell you that I saw it happen?"

"Yes, he did."

"'Severe stress' doesn't even begin to cover what I went through," she said, speaking slowly and clearly to make sure they understood, to make sure she didn't lose control. "I won't relive that for *anyone*." She looked pointedly at Rory. "Not even you. So, Doctor, I wish I could say it's been a pleasure, but—"

"You don't have to relive it," Dr. Holloway interrupted as she got to her feet. "We can find out what the master—what Rory needs to know, and you won't have to remember a thing."

She stared at him for a long time, weighing his quick claim against her anger, Rory's desire to know what had happened that morning against her own desire to never think of it again. Slowly she sank into the chair again. "How can you do that?" she asked grudgingly.

"We have two options. Hypnosis or a sodium amytal interview. Hypnosis is pretty straightforward. Any psychologist can do it at anytime almost anywhere. Amytal would require a one-day stay in the hospital and would be done by a psychiatrist."

"But I can't remember what happened that morning. What makes you think either of these procedures will *make* me remember?"

"The memories weren't erased, Shanna. They're still there in your head," he explained gently. "You saw something so traumatic emotionally that your mind has chosen to lock it away. It refuses to remember so that you don't have to live with that shock. Both hypnosis and the amytal would allow us to get around the lock and find out what you know. But you'll be hypnotized or, in the case of the amytal, sedated, so when it's over and you wake up, you won't remember a thing."

She leaned back in her chair and shifted to stare across the bar, deliberately cutting both Rory and the doctor out of her line of vision. It sounded so easy. She would go to sleep for a while, and when she woke up, everything would be the same...except *they* would know all her secrets and *she* wouldn't.

"What if you're wrong?" she asked, turning back to Dr. Holloway. "What if I *do* remember? What am I supposed to do then? Learn to live with it? Accept the nightmares and the horror? Get used to never having any peace again as long as I live?"

"You won't remember. I promise."

There was something creepy about the idea, she thought with a shiver, that a total stranger could just reach into her mind and draw out memories that she herself couldn't touch. Even considering it created a sense of violation deep inside. It was repugnant. Frightful. Unthinkable.

Yet she *was* considering it. She *was* thinking about it. "If hypnosis could be done right now upstairs in my room, why should I wait until tomorrow and check into the hospital for this amytal stuff?"

"Each method has its drawbacks. Hypnosis is quick and involves no drugs. However, not everyone is a good candi-

date for it. Amytal, on the other hand, is likely to give better results. It would be my preference if I were your doctor."
He paused to see if she had any more questions, then offered, "I have a friend who's a psychiatrist here in town. He's offered to do the interview first thing in the morning if you want."

She stared down at her hands. They were trembling. It seemed that she'd spent the better part of the past few weeks trembling—from terror, fear, sorrow, desir—

She hastily cut off that last thought. It made her think of Rory and how badly she had wanted him last night, how desperately she loved him. And *that* made her think of how he had betrayed her.

Aware that both men were waiting for her answer, she finally met the doctor's even gaze again. "Tell your friend I'll see him in the morning."

Rory felt little of the overwhelming relief he had expected at her decision. He was too concerned about the emptiness in her eyes, the blankness in her voice. He had gotten what he'd come here for, what he'd hoped for.

But at what price?

Chapter 10

Rory came out of the bathroom, his hair damp and slicked back from his face, and began unbuttoning the jeans he'd just put on after his shower. Under better circumstances, he wouldn't be wearing anything at all, and he wouldn't be going to bed to sleep. But circumstances had been pretty bad, he admitted with a sigh, ever since Shanna had asked Dr. Holloway what he did in the Army.

She was sitting sideways on the love seat, wedged back into one corner, her knees drawn up to her chest and her chin resting on them. It was a defensive posture, he was sure—sitting like that, she could keep him from getting too close—because it sure as hell couldn't be a comfortable one. She'd been like that ever since they had finished picking at a room-service dinner. Just sitting there, staring at nothing, ignoring him.

She hadn't ignored him when they had first returned to the room. No, to the contrary, she'd had plenty to say then. About how he had lied to her. How he hadn't had any right to interfere in her personal life. How sleeping with her hadn't been necessary to get her to talk to Dr. Holloway. How he'd made her feel dirty.

That one had hurt the most. That one had made him wince, and she'd seen it. Her angry flow of words had stopped then, but their power was still in the air, still between them.

He turned off all the lights except the one on her side of the bed and folded the covers back. Then he circled the bed to the love seat and crouched in front of her. "Come to bed, Shanna."

Without bothering to look at him, she shook her head.

"Come on." He wrapped his hand around her bare foot and found it cool. "You need some rest."

Finally she focused her empty gaze on him. It made him feel cold all the way through. "You know what?" She paused. "You finally lived up to your reputation."

Worthless. No good. Trash.

He drew back as if she'd slapped him. If she had to punish him, he would have preferred a physical blow. It couldn't hurt as much as her deliberately offered insult. Nothing could.

Slowly he stood up and gazed down at her for a long time; then he bent and pressed a gentle kiss to her forehead. "Your father would be proud of you, princess," he whispered, then turned away. Returning to his side of the bed, he kicked off his jeans and slid naked beneath the covers. He closed his eyes and slowed his breathing and willed the pain to go away so sleep could come.

He lay awake all night.

Dr. Holloway picked them up early Monday morning and drove them to the hospital, only a few miles away, where Dr. Berry was waiting. It was a strained trip—Shanna had nothing to say to either man, and Rory was too concerned about her to engage in idle conversation.

At the hospital, she had to go through the admissions procedure even though she would be there less than twelve hours. Then she was escorted to a small room on the psychiatric ward, given a hospital gown to change into and subjected to a brief physical exam.

"What are the odds if I'd called you myself that you would have been able to see me this quickly?" she asked, wiggling her toes inside the socks that were all she wore besides the starched cotton gown. She'd decided that she was cold when she'd left them on, but now she didn't know if it was really cold or just nerves that made her shiver.

Dr. Berry smiled. "Not good."

"So why are you making an exception?"

"The Army takes care of its own."

"We're not in the Army," she pointed out.

"I used to be—I retired six months ago."

"Doing a favor for an old Army buddy, right?" She didn't really feel the faint disparagement that shaded her voice, though, but rather envy. This doctor who had never met her before was doing this favor for her simply because Rory had spent more than twenty years in the Army. *The Army takes care of its own.* Had she ever known that kind of camaraderie? Did lawyers look out for fellow lawyers? Friends? Even her family, at this point, was more interested in taking care of themselves than of each other.

"Are you ready, Shanna?"

She glanced around the room uneasily, her gaze skimming over Dr. Holloway at the foot of the bed and Rory, standing in the shadows near the door. "I guess."

"First I'm going to start the IV—I'll give you the amytal through that—then we'll hook up the cardiac monitor. Dr. Holloway and Mr. Hawkes are going to stay in here with us, but I'll be the only one asking you questions. The interview itself should take between thirty and forty-five minutes, but when it's over, you'll sleep probably four to six hours. When you wake up, I'll check you over, then you'll be free to go."

"And I won't remember anything." She tried to make it a statement, but doubt crept into her voice.

"Not a thing."

She swallowed hard, folded the covers back on the bed and climbed in.

The hospital room was exactly twelve feet wide and sixteen feet long. Rory knew because he'd paced it off probably a hundred times in the past five hours and twenty-seven minutes.

The interview had gone smoothly, according to Drs. Berry and Holloway. *He* thought it had been a real, living, breathing nightmare. No wonder Shanna had had such trouble sleeping. No wonder she had turned to the Scotch to dilute the horror.

He'd had some idea what to expect. He had witnessed explosions before, had seen people die that way. He had known what Shanna had seen, but he hadn't been prepared to hear her describe it in such vivid, heartrending detail. He hadn't been prepared to see the haunting images so clearly in his own mind. He hadn't been prepared for the pain.

Now she was asleep, as she'd been for the past four and a half hours, a deep, peaceful, drug-induced sleep. She would probably sleep another hour or two, Dr. Berry had said when he'd stopped in to check on her a few minutes ago, and she would feel better when she woke up.

Better? His smile was twisted. Anything had to be an improvement over what she'd gone through.

He looked out the window briefly, then returned to stand at the foot of the bed and looked at her instead. He wished he'd had two minutes alone with her while she was still under the influence of the sodium amytal. He wished he could have asked her if she'd meant everything she'd said yesterday. He wished he could have asked her—and known that her answer was the indisputable, undeniable truth—if she cared at all about him, if she thought she might ever love him.

But there had been no opportunity, and there had been no need. He knew the answers. Most of what she'd said yesterday had been influenced by anger and hurt and feelings of betrayal. She had been coldly furious with his deception regarding Dr. Holloway, and she had reacted blindly, hurting him because *he* had hurt her.

He knew, too, that she cared about him—in the way that any woman cared about the man she was having an affair with. Her caring was made up of a multitude of other feelings—shame, guilt, fear, relief, gratitude, desire and maybe a certain fondness.

But it wasn't the way he wanted her to care, and it certainly wasn't love.

Years ago he'd learned not to want something he couldn't have. When had that lesson been unlearned? When had he forgotten that he was a Hawkes and she was a Cassidy? That he could look at her, want her, need her, love her... but he could never have her for his own?

She stirred, drawing him out of his bleak thoughts and to the side of the bed. He had always thought she seemed delicate, but never more so than right now. She was pale against the coarse sheets, and her hair spread in a tangle across the pillow. Gently he combed his fingers through it, smoothing it, stroking it. He kissed her forehead, then took her hand, clasping it snugly between his.

"Rory?"

When he saw that she was awake, her brown eyes soft and hazy, their expression confused, he sat on the edge of the mattress and leaned over her. "I'm here, sweetheart."

"Sweetheart?" she echoed, then yawned. "What happened to princess?"

"You told me once you didn't like it, remember?"

"Things change, you know." She yawned again, then rubbed her eyes with her free hand. "Is it time to get up?"

"Not yet. Just lie here a little longer."

She rolled her head from one side to the other, stretching taut muscles, then turned onto her side, snuggling closer to him. "I'm sorry about yesterday, Rory. I didn't mean—"

He touched his fingers to her lips to silence her. "It's all right."

"No, it's not. I said some nasty things, and I didn't mean them. I know this whole weekend wasn't some elaborate plan to get me *here*." She gestured to the room around them. "And I know you wouldn't make love with me just to get me to agree to something else. I was hurt and upset, and I overreacted, and I said those awful things, and—"

"My God," Rory interrupted, sounding scandalized. "The princess is a mere mortal, after all. She feels and hurts and reacts just like any other human being."

She drew back and looked at him for a moment, then recognized his gentle teasing for what it was. Her smile was shyly self-conscious. "I missed you last night."

Spending the night on the sofa had been *her* idea, but he didn't remind her of that. Instead he honestly admitted, "I missed you, too." It had been a long night. A lonely one. The kind that would fill his future.

When she started to sit up, he helped her, his hand slipping inside the open back of the gown, grazing the warm, silk-soft skin at her waist. He allowed himself only a moment to enjoy it before pulling back and adjusting the bed so she would be comfortable.

She looked down at her hands for a moment, plucked at the too-long sleeves of the gown, smoothed a snag in the thermal blanket. Finally she raised her troubled gaze to Rory's. "Did you learn anything?"

"A little. I don't think any of it is very important. I'm sorry."

Disappointment surged through her, but she shrugged as if it didn't really matter. She had hoped that the secret to the case had been locked away with the bad memories, but apparently it hadn't. They would simply have to keep trying. "Did you find out why I was outside that morning?"

"Your father had forgotten his briefcase. You were taking it to him when the truck exploded."

Her face wrinkled into a frown of intense concentration for a moment, then the muscles relaxed and she gave a shake of her head. "I don't remember that. The doctors were right." While one part of her had believed them, the other part had been afraid that they were wrong. Afraid that she *would* remember, that she would be the exception to the rule. Thank God she wasn't! "What happened to the brief-case?"

"It was knocked from your hands in the blast. I imagine one of the sheriff's men took it." Rory leaned forward and kissed her, then stood up. "I'm going to let the nurse know you're awake so we can get out of here. We'll go back to the hotel for tonight so you can get a good night's rest, then we'll go home tomorrow, all right?"

She smile faintly and nodded, then watched him leave the room. As the door closed behind him, the smile faded. Home tomorrow. Back to Sandy Spring and her bombed-out office. Back to Lawrence Channing's domain, to Sheriff Hart's threats. Back to the danger.

All in all, she thought grimly, she'd rather stay here.

Tuesday's drive home was long and uneventful. They passed the time by talking—about Channing and Hart, about how to proceed with their investigation, about being a soldier and a lawyer. Rory even told her about his years with Delta, realizing as he did so that he was sharing one of his most closely guarded secrets with her, knowing that she would realize it, too, and would probably realize the impli-cation behind it: that he was telling her things a man would only tell someone he trusted. Someone special. Someone loved.

The only subjects they didn't discuss were the interview and the future. Shanna ventured only one question about the interview as they neared the town limits of Sandy Spring. "Sometime...will you tell me about it?"

Another mile passed before Rory gave her a long look and replied, "No, princess. I won't."

Neither of them mentioned their future.

It was already dark by the time he turned onto her street. "I wonder if the house is still standing," she remarked in a light, teasing voice. She didn't realize, Rory thought grimly, that it was entirely possible it wasn't. If Channing had decided another warning was in order, the house would be the perfect place to strike. Since he didn't want to kill but only to frighten—so far—their trip out of town would have provided him with the perfect opportunity.

What if her house *were* gone? What would she do then? he wondered, then answered his own question. She would leave Sandy Spring for good. He would turn the truck around and take her to Dallas himself, placing her in the safekeeping of Judith Cassidy and her family. They would make her forget about justice and punishing Channing. They would make her forget the explosions, the break-in, his beating, the threats. Soon she would even forget *him*.

He convinced himself so easily that leaving Sandy Spring, giving up on justice and forgetting him would be in Shanna's best interests that he was almost disappointed to see the house, dark and imposing but apparently undisturbed. *Almost*.

He carried their bags upstairs while Shanna searched through the refrigerator and pantry for something for dinner. She was weighing the merits of sandwiches and boxed macaroni and cheese—quick, easy and requiring no trip out—against dinner at the café on Main Street when he returned. "Which would you prefer?" she asked, giving the two choices.

Taking the box from her, he glanced at it, then tossed it on the counter and pulled her close. "That's all you have to offer?"

"Not by any means," she said loftily. "But I was speaking of food. I'm hungry."

He nipped at her ear, making her wriggle against him, then murmured, "There are different kinds of hunger, princess. Come upstairs with me, and I'll show you the kind I'm feeling."

She tilted her head to the side to dislodge him and pretended to consider it. "Umm...convince me," she said and waited for his sweet, hot kisses and his tender, tormenting caresses.

"All right." But for a moment, he did nothing. Then he smiled slowly, slyly, scooped her up over his shoulder and carried her off to bed.

It was much later when she snuggled close to him, her long hair spilling across his chest, and blew out her breath in a soft sigh that cooled his skin. "Convincing," she whispered sleepily. "*Very* convincing."

"What's the combination for the locks on your father's briefcase?"

Shanna groaned, rolled over in bed and pulled the covers to her nose.

"Come on, wake up, it's morning, and we've got things to do." Rory dropped onto the bed where they'd made love half the night and slept the rest... Slept? He poked her through the bedspread. "Hey, you haven't had any nightmares the last couple of nights."

She opened one eye, slipped one hand out to push her hair from her face and focused a cross stare on him. "*You're* a nightmare. It *isn't* morning—it isn't even light outside yet. Go away."

She retreated even deeper under the covers, but he didn't let that deter him. He simply caught a handful and stripped them away.

"Rory!"

She was awake now, naked and shivering and so damn beautiful that looking at her made him ache. He stared at her for a long moment, then closed his eyes and still saw her in his mind. He always would. "Sorry, sweetheart," he said in a subdued voice. He spread the covers over her again, tucking them around her shoulders, then stretched out beside her, adding the heat of his body to that of the blanket and spread. "Is that better?"

"It would be better if you'd take your clothes off and get under here with me, where you belong. It isn't even six o'clock yet. Why are you up?"

"I was working out. I haven't done it in almost a week, and I'm getting out of shape."

She wriggled her fingers out from beneath the covers for an intimate caress, than parroted one of his earlier statements to him in a sultry voice. "There's nothing wrong with your shape. It's perfect for me—hard where I'm soft."

His eyes closed, Rory let her talented fingers work their magic for a moment, then reluctantly forced them away. "Listen to me, will you? I was thinking about your interview and about Joseph's briefcase and the house and the explosion. You know, most people around here have to be satisfied with sandy yards and sparse grass, if any, but not the people on these few blocks. You can afford the expense of real yards—grass, trees, shrubs."

She was frowning at him. "Am I not awake enough to follow this conversation? What do yards have to do with the explosion?"

"The shrubs. Every house in this neighborhood has shrubbery planted across the front. When you told us at the hospital that the briefcase had been thrown out of your hand when the explosion knocked you down, I just assumed that it landed nearby, in plain sight. But after thinking about it this morning, I realized that you were relatively close to the house when it happened, because you hit your head on the bottom step. Considering that, along with the location of the truck, the likely place the briefcase would have landed is in the bushes west of the living-room window."

She was watching him wide-eyed. "Did you check?"

Rory rolled into a sitting position and retrieved the case from the floor beside the bed. He laid it on the mattress between them.

Slowly Shanna sat up, holding the covers to her chest with one hand and reaching out to touch the case with the other.

She drew her fingers over the scuffed leather, rubbed a scratch that made the *C* on the engraved nameplate look more like an *O* and brushed away a spot of dirt. "His father gave him this briefcase the year Dad became district attorney. Grandfather died the next year—I never even knew him. Even though the case was pretty badly worn, Dad never wanted a new one." She broke off, cleared the huskiness from her voice, then looked at him. "What's inside?"

Rory shook his head. "It's locked. Do you know the combination?"

This time she shook her head.

"Do you know any series of six numbers that would have been important to him? His birth date? His anniversary?"

She told him both dates, and he tried them but with no luck.

"When is your birthday?"

"It's not enough numbers. June sixth, nineteen fifty-four."

He twisted the left knob to zero six zero, then the right one to six five four. With a click, both locks popped open. He handed the case, still tightly closed, to Shanna.

After a long silence, she shook her head, then got up and walked naked to the closet. She took out her terry-cloth robe, put it on and tied the belt snugly around her waist, then tugged on a pair of thick, snuggly booties. She walked to the rocker and sat down to wait.

Rory turned the briefcase around again and raised the lid. Inside, each in its own special pocket, were an expensive gold pen and pencil set, a small stack of engraved business cards and a slim address book covered in the same brown leather as the case itself.

There were also a half dozen manila folders containing arrest reports, handwritten notes and occasionally photographs—Joseph's current cases, Rory assumed. Underneath those were two large envelopes, both addressed to his home. One bore a neatly typed label that was printed with

Jeffrey Walsh's return address in the corner. The other was written in a barely legible scrawl, and the return address— no name, simply street and city—was Nick Langley's. Those would be Joseph's copies of their reports, along with the financial records Walsh had returned.

He set everything aside, then simply looked at the briefcase.

"Is that everything?" Shanna asked.

Shaking his head, he reached inside and drew out two computer disks, holding them so she could see the fronts.

So she could see the labels marked *L.C.* in black ink.

It was over four hours to El Paso. She had traveled more in the past week than in the previous year, Shanna remarked as she shifted uncomfortably on the wide seat. With a somber expression, Rory had pointed out that it would be over soon. She didn't like the sound of that, she'd decided privately. Yes, she wanted this business with Channing over and done with, but how could she endure the end of her relationship, business or not, with Rory?

When they had stopped for gas, he had called yet another old Army buddy at Fort Bliss and arranged to meet him as soon as they got to the post. Once again she found herself envying the lasting, solid friendships he had formed in the Army.

Fort Bliss was the first military base she'd ever visited. It seemed an alien world to her—one she would have liked to experience, she realized with a smile. It certainly would have been a different life from the one she'd led.

"You know your way around," she commented as he turned off the broad thoroughfare onto a narrower street. "Were you ever stationed here?"

"I attended a school here, then did some training in the area."

"Do you miss the Army?"

He found the building he wanted, pulled into one of the few visitor spaces and shut off the engine. "Sometimes. It was the only place I ever belonged. For the first time in my life, people judged me based on my performance and capabilities rather than my name. That was something I'd needed."

"Why did you get out?"

"That's too complicated to explain right now, and Zeke is waiting. He's looking forward to meeting you."

It took Shanna about two seconds to decide that Zeke Monroe was as different from Rory as Dr. Holloway had been. He was a good-looking man, big and muscular, and showed no qualms about giving Rory an exuberant hug, practically lifting him off the floor, in front of a room full of people. She simply stared, never having imagined that anyone would have the nerve to give Rory such a greeting, nor that he would tolerate it. But he not only tolerated it; he enjoyed it. It was obvious in his grin.

As Dr. Holloway had done a few days earlier, Zeke waited only until the introductions were complete before commenting on Rory's face. "It's a good thing you retired when you did, my friend, because you must be really slowing down to let somebody actually land a blow."

"What can I say? It wasn't one of my better days."

"No kidding." To Shanna he said, "This guy can shoot better, run faster, throw farther and find cover quicker than anyone I ever saw. Over in 'Nam, I always stayed as close to him as I could, 'cause I figured if anyone was going home in one piece, it would be him. I was right, too. He got us both home in one piece. So...what brings you to Fort Bliss?"

"Do you have someplace quiet where we can talk?"

"Right this way." Zeke led them into a small office tucked into one corner. It wasn't much bigger than her bedroom closet, Shanna thought, and every available space was taken up with furniture or boxes. There was barely room for Zeke to squeeze between the desk and two metal file cabinets and reach his chair, and when she sat down in the only remaining chair, her knees bumped the battered metal desk.

Rory stood behind her, one hand on the chair, one on her shoulder. In a quiet voice he told his friend everything that had happened in the previous weeks, beginning with Joseph's visit to him at his house and ending with this morning's discovery of the briefcase. The only thing he left out was the terms of his arrangement with Shanna. She was grateful for that.

"You have the disks with you?" Zeke asked when Rory finished.

Shanna drew them out of her purse and handed them across the desk.

"Come on upstairs." He led them out of the office, down a narrow hallway and up a set of steep stairs. In the first room on the left, a young man who looked barely old enough to be out of high school was sitting at a computer, his fingers flying over the keys. Zeke settled on the corner of the desk and asked, "Specialist, can you take a break from that and call up whatever's on these disks?"

"Sure, master sergeant." The specialist exited his program and picked up the first disk. "What kind of program were they written with?"

Zeke looked to Rory for an answer, and he shook his head. "Don't know, son. That shouldn't slow you down much, should it?" With a grin, he patted the younger man's back. "Paul is our resident whiz kid. He knows everything there is to know about computers and then some. He'll have the information for you in a heartbeat."

It took a little longer than that, but not much, by Shanna's calculations. In a matter of minutes, a directory of files contained on the disk was listed on the screen.

"You want to look at anything in particular?" Paul asked.

Rory picked a file at random. It was a journal of daily activities, Shanna thought, reading it over Paul's shoulder. A moment later, she revised that: not daily activities, but *criminal* ones. It was a detailed list of Lawrence Channing's illegal business transactions over the last three months of last year. The next file was a record of payments to both local and state officials: names, dates, amounts, account numbers and how they were paid. The third contained a detailed list of Channing's associates, both in the U.S. and Mexico.

This was the help Wayne Singleton had provided her father, Shanna thought. This was the reason Wayne had disappeared, the reason her father had died. It was valuable stuff, no denying that, but had it been worth two lives?

No. There was no way it had been worth dying for.

After skimming through the remaining files, they moved on to the second disk. It contained another half dozen files, filled with Joseph's notes, presenting his suspicions, detailing his investigation, organizing the information provided on the first disk.

"Paul, will you print out copies of everything on both disks for us?" Zeke asked quietly as Shanna walked away after reading the last file.

She heard the printer click on, then listened to its loud, back-and-forth racket. Lawrence Channing had threatened her father and had all but admitted to killing Singleton, according to Joseph's notes. Oh, he'd been too smart to actually say it, but he'd made it clear that was what he'd meant. *Drop this investigation, or you might not come home some night, just like Wayne Singleton. What would happen to that pretty daughter of yours then, without Daddy there to take care of her?*

But Joseph hadn't been able to drop it, and it had cost him his life. Now Channing would pay. Now they had enough evidence to take to the FBI. Now they would have justice.

But sometimes justice could be bittersweet. Her father was dead, gone from her life forever. All she had left of him were memories and love.

And unless she did something, unless she found some way to hold on to him, Rory would soon be gone, too, and all she would have left of *him* were memories and love.

Her father was in the past, and she couldn't change that. But Rory was here, alive and well. No matter what happened today or tomorrow or the next day, as long as they lived, they could change their present. They could make their future.

She was damn well going to give it a try.

From the post, they went straight to the local FBI office, where Rory repeated their story once more to a couple of very interested agents. After the agents had exhausted every line of questioning possible, Shanna gave them the computer disks, the printout and copies of the financial records and the accountant's and private detective's reports.

When they left the building and stepped out into the bright afternoon sunlight, Rory slipped his arm around Shanna's shoulders and pulled her close. "It's a long drive home, and I'm tired. Let's spend the night here."

"But we didn't bring any clothes," she reminded him.

"So we'll wear these again. It won't kill us. We can pick up a couple of toothbrushes—that's all we really need."

She looked at him for a moment, her brow wrinkled. "You don't look tired," she decided.

"Okay. I'm aroused."

Her gaze dropped lower. "You don't look that, either."

He held her tighter and brushed his mouth across hers. "Find us some privacy, and I will."

Shanna laughed, but it quickly faded. "You're worried, aren't you?"

"Yeah."

"Why? They said they were going to move quickly. They think Channing changed his name when he appeared in Sandy Spring to avoid prosecution on some other charge, and they're afraid he might disappear again, so they're going to talk to him today, right away. Why are you worried?''

"You think, when the FBI shows up on his doorstep in a couple of hours, he's not going to know who's responsible?" he asked. "He'll know it's you, and he'll want revenge. He had Wayne Singleton killed for betraying him, and he had your father killed for coming too close to exposing him. He'll want you dead too, princess, so until he *and* his men are in custody, you're safer someplace where he can't find you.''

He expected her to show some concern for her immediate safety, but instead she gave him a pleased smile. "So you're going to have to stay with me until then, aren't you?''

"Of course. Do you think I'd walk away now?''

"No," she said with another easy smile. "I don't think you would. So let's go to your house. As much as we've been gone lately, they wouldn't expect us to be there. Besides, you can see or hear anyone coming from miles away.''

She was exaggerating, but not by much. He did have a long view from the front windows. And she was right, too, that no one would expect them to stay there. Everyone in Sandy Spring associated them with Shanna's house; his remote place wouldn't even enter their minds.

But did he want her to stay at his house? Did he want to make love to her in his bed? Did he want her scent on his sheets? Did he want the memory of her long hair spread across his pillow?

Just as everyone in town linked them with her house, so did he. His house was safe from her memories because he'd never seen her there, had never held her there, had never loved her there. Wouldn't that make it easier to stay there when he lost her?

No. Nothing would make it easier. So why not gather as many memories as he could?

"All right. We'll go to my house.''

* * *

The first time she'd seen his little house, she had thought it was shabby with its unpainted wood, sagging porch and rusted screens. The windows had been covered by faded yellow gingham, so she hadn't seen the interior, but it was shabby, too, she discovered. A few weeks ago she might have assumed that he couldn't afford anything better on his Army pension, but now she knew that wasn't true. He simply didn't care much about his surroundings. As long as he had the basics—a place to sit, a place to bathe, a place to sleep— what did it matter whether it was elegant and expensive or used and worn? He hadn't been impressed by her father's house with its gleaming woods, fine fabrics and costly rugs, and he wasn't ashamed of this place.

She loved him even more for that.

He had stopped the truck out front, unlocked the door and taken her inside, then left her there while he parked the truck out back in the barn. Now she took advantage of the few moments alone to look around.

Through the open doorways, she could see the kitchen and a portion of a bedroom. They were in the same condition as the living room: furnishings worn and tattered, wallpaper torn, peeling and faded, linoleum scuffed bare to reveal splintery wood underneath, and all impeccably neat, impeccably clean.

She was surprised to find no personal touches around her. Surely after over twenty years in the Army, living all over the United States, he had accumulated some possessions, some treasures that he would want to display, but she found nothing. No photographs of the friends she knew he had, no souvenirs of the places he'd seen, no keepsakes of those twenty years of his life.

After a moment she wandered into the kitchen, turning on the bare bulb overhead. There was a stove, a refrigerator and a rickety-legged table, all practically as old as she was, and in one small corner, a scratched-up washer and dryer were stacked precariously. One set of cabinets, open shelves with no doors, held dishes, pots and pans. The rest were filled with canned and packaged food. That was where she was heading as Rory came in the back door.

"Do you have any hamburger meat in the freezer?" she asked as she stretched to reach the boxes on the top shelf.

He opened the refrigerator, then pulled open the wide freezer door. He had to stoop low to see inside, she noticed with a grin and switched places with him. "I'll bend, you stretch." She sorted through the neatly wrapped and labeled packages in the freezer and found a small square marked ground beef.

"Want me to cook that?" he offered.

"No thanks. I think I can manage."

"Then I'm going to take a shower." He watched her for a moment longer before leaving the kitchen, trying to find something in her expression—some dismay or disdain for this place where he chose to live. All he saw was that same relaxed, easy smile she'd been smiling all evening.

Was she simply happy that the ordeal of the investigation was almost over, that she had succeeded in achieving Joseph's final goal and that Lawrence Channing was definitely going to prison? Or was she happy that *this* ordeal was almost over? Was she relieved that soon his claim on her would end and he would be out of her life?

He scowled as he walked through the back bedroom and into the tiny bathroom. He was scowling as he climbed into the shower, and he still scowled when he returned to the kitchen ten minutes later in clean jeans. There he stopped abruptly in the doorway.

Standing in front of the stove and singing softly to herself, she certainly didn't look as if she considered spending the night here with him an ordeal. She didn't seem unhappy that there would be yet another night in his bed. She didn't seem to be anticipating his departure from her life.

She just looked happy. Carefree. He hadn't seen her like that in more than twenty years.

He walked barefoot to the refrigerator and took out a carton of milk and two sodas. The milk, sour and thick, went down the sink. He opened both sodas and carried one to Shanna at the stove. She accepted it with a smile and continued to stir the pasta and ground beef mixture in the skillet.

"What do you think of the house?" he asked as he leaned back against the nearest counter.

Her smile broadened into a grin. "Why do I have the feeling that there's no right answer to that question?" she asked, then shook her head in warning. "Don't try to start a fight with me. I'm not in the mood."

He wondered if that had been his intention—to take offense at whatever she replied, to fuel an argument that they couldn't make up from, so they couldn't make love tonight or share his bed, so that tomorrow or the next day or whenever it was safe for her to leave, he could let her go.

Probably, he thought with a rueful smile.

"For a house this old, it's fine—a little worn around the edges, but so are we. It has everything you need—a kitchen, a bedroom, a bathroom and privacy. Solitude. Peace." She turned off the burner, then took two plates from the cabinet and divided the casserole between them. "Do you ever see your grandparents?"

"No."

"Hear from them? Talk to them?"

"No." He got silverware from the drawer behind him, then joined her at the table. "I was never close to them. The first time I ever talked to them—the only time—was after my mother's funeral. They wanted to leave Texas and needed some money. I gave it to them, and in exchange, they signed this place over to me."

"Oh. I thought maybe..."

"Maybe what? That I came back here because of family ties? Because I felt closer to my mother and my grandparents here? That it reminded me of better times when I had a family?" He shook his head. "My family died with my father. Whatever relatives I have on his side are so distant that they probably don't know I exist. The ones on my mother's side know I exist—they just don't care."

"I'm sorry."

He smiled faintly. "That's just one more difference between you and me, princess. You can't imagine life without your family, even nosy old Aunt Eugenie, and I can't imagine it with them."

"Differences are healthy. People who are too alike become bored with each other."

"And people who are too different become dissatisfied." She made a face at him. "You're a pessimist."

"No, I'm a realist." Realistically he knew that whatever she felt for him wouldn't last. In the long run, she needed a man with the same background, the same upbringing, the same experiences, as she'd had. She needed someone who would fit into her life, someone acceptable both socially and financially. She *didn't* need someone like him.

With a weary sigh, he pushed his dinner plate away. "Let's clean up and go to bed, princess, okay?"

Thursday morning, wrapped in a thin blanket, Shanna left Rory in bed to study his room. All the photographs, souvenirs and keepsakes she had missed in the living room last night were in here, and she wanted to examine every one of them.

She started at the tall chest of drawers next to the door. Folded neatly on top was a black sash, stitched in long channels from end to end and secured with a band. Embroidered on the top end in neat capital letters was his name, first and last. His black belt in taekwondo.

Next to it lay a pair of gold pins—rank insignia for his uniform, he told her from the bed where he watched. In a small chipped bowl at the back were numerous others, some gold, the rest black, some identical, the others minus a stripe or two. Propped against the bowl was an embroidered patch, gray, green, gold and black, with the words "U.S. Army Special Forces" stitched around the center crest. In front of that rested a heavy silver pin of a parachute with wings curving out from the bottom on each side and topped with a laurel encircling a five-point star. Jump wings.

On the wall above the bureau was a framed certificate, the writing in both English and Korean proclaiming that Rory Hawkes had achieved the rank of fourth-degree black belt in taekwondo. Beside it hung a plaque made of wood that bore a molded crest in the center: a sword, blade pointed up, overlaid with a triangle—a delta—formed by a lightning bolt. Across the bottom was the slogan, "Oppressors beware," and beneath that was a brass plate engraved with Rory's name and rank and dated two months ago. The Army equivalent of a gold watch at retirement, she thought with a smile.

She moved on to a shadow box displaying rows of brightly colored uniform ribbons on one side and the corresponding medals on the other, to two framed commendations, both dating back to Vietnam, awarding the Silver Star and the Bronze Star from the President of the United States and a grateful country to Private First Class Rory Hawkes for heroism in combat.

Finally she stopped beside the bed and studied the four photographs hung together there. The first showed a half dozen dirty, weary men armed to the teeth. Rory, years younger and looking harder, colder, was on the right. Beside him she recognized a twenty-years-younger Zeke Monroe. The background, what little there was, revealed lush undergrowth, cool shadows, little sunlight. Vietnam.

The second photo was much more recent and included Rory, flanked by two other men. They were clean shaven and wore dress uniforms. They stared, stern and handsome, straight into the camera.

The third was black-and-white and wrinkled from too much handling: Mary Kay and Joe Hawkes. Young Joe stood erect, shoulders back, his eyes bright and alert. There was no sign of the illness that had eaten away at his mind, leaving him helpless and confused and incapable of per-

forming the slightest task. He'd been a handsome man—
Rory more than faintly resembled him—and lucky in spite
of his illness, because his wife and son had loved him dearly.

The last photo had been taken at a picnic and included a
large group of men, their wives and girlfriends and children. In this one she recognized Dr. Holloway and Rory, of
course. She wondered about the pretty blonde who sat on
the grass in front of him, leaning back against his chest, her
hand resting possessively on his thigh. Melanie. The woman
he'd lived with for five years, she thought with a fierce
frown.

She'd seen Melanie, Rory realized. The woman he had
lived with and fought with and made love with but had never
wanted to marry for the simple reason that she wasn't *this*
woman.

He added her pillow to the one beneath his head, then
smoothed the sheet that covered him. The movement sent
the faint, elusive scent of her fragrance drifting into the air.
"Now you've seen it all," he said, grabbing a handful of her
blanket and tugging. She was forced to come along or lose
her only covering in the chill morning air. He didn't stop
pulling until she was sprawled half across the bed, half
across him. "Impressed?" he teased.

"You bet. You're a *hero*."

Shaking his head, he tenderly brushed her hair from her
face. "I just did what I had to to survive."

"You risked your life to save someone else's."

"One of them died anyway."

"But you *tried*. That's more than most people would have
done." She smiled smugly. "And you *are* a hero. The
President of the United States said so—twice."

"And you believe him, huh?" He pulled her higher so he
could kiss her. "I don't want to be anyone's hero, princess." But that was a lie. He wanted to be *her* hero. He
wanted her to look at him and be proud. He wanted her to
know that he'd had courage and respect and honor.

"God, you've accomplished *so* much," she said, sounding just as proud as he could have asked for. "Everything you've done has been outstanding. You make me feel inadequate. I've done nothing except be Daddy's little girl and play at being a lawyer, and you—you've excelled at everything."

"You're a good lawyer, and you'll be even better once you start handling the kind of cases you want, the kind of cases you care about. Then you'll be exceptional."

"Do you really believe that?" she asked doubtfully.

"Yes."

"You have faith in me?"

"You can do anything you want, Shanna. You're bright, talented and willing to work. Those three things will get you anything you want."

"Even if what I want is you?"

Feeling sick deep inside, he stared at her for a long time, then shrugged and forced a weak smile and said, "I'm here. Have your way with me."

She didn't smile at his miserable teasing, but stared right back. "I'm not talking about now or tomorrow or the next day. I mean in another week. Another month. Another year."

He couldn't hold her gaze any longer. He looked down at the soft curves of her breasts barely covered by the blanket after he'd pulled her across him.

"Well . . . I guess that answer's clear enough." Her voice sounded choked and thick with unshed tears. She wriggled away to the edge of the bed, stood up and readjusted the blanket around her, then began looking for her clothes before remembering that she'd left them in the bathroom after last night's shower. She'd made it almost to the door before he spoke.

"I don't want an affair for another week or another month or another year," he said harshly. "I don't want to be someone you can walk away from when the novelty wears off or when you get tired of your friends' reactions to me or when you finally realize that your father was right all along, that I'm not good enough for you!''

"My father was *wrong!*"

He rose from the bed, clumsily pulling on his jeans before he started toward her. "I'm a Hawkes, damn it! You know what that means in this town!''

"It means everyone gets to hate you. Everyone gets to put you down and feel superior to you. It means *you* get to put yourself down." She sighed tearfully. "You told me a few days ago that you wanted me in spite of my name, not because of it. Well, Rory, I love you *regardless* of your name. I don't care who you are. I love the *man* you are—the soldier, the hero, the buddy, the friend. I love you because you're good and kind and brave and strong. Because you have honor and courage. Because you're gentle and sweet and proud. Because you loved and respected your parents and you risked your life for somebody else and you made love to me so tenderly when you should have hated me."

He felt a panicky feeling spreading through his chest. He wanted desperately to believe her, but he was just as desperately afraid to. "You're confusing gratitude with—with other emotions," he said, trying to sound calm but failing. "You're grateful that I helped you catch Channing, that this whole thing is over, that—"

"Stop it, Rory." She spoke in a quiet, firm voice. "If you don't love me, have the courage and the decency to say so. But don't tell me what *I* feel. Don't insult me by presuming to know more about me than I do."

She waited, her eyes never wavering from his, but he said nothing. He tried, but the words wouldn't come. The *lies* wouldn't come.

Shanna waited a moment longer, then went into the bathroom behind her and closed the door. She sank to the floor, the blanket puddling around her, hugged her knees to her chest and squeezed her eyes shut on the pain. She breathed in great, shuddering gasps, trying to hold the tears at bay, trying to hold herself together.

She had never taken a chance before, never in her entire life. She had never risked anything, had never lost anything. Until now. So much for getting what she wanted. So much for Rory's faith in her. He didn't even have enough faith to believe that she loved him.

Gratitude. That was all he would let himself accept from her. It wasn't all he wanted—she knew that much—but it was all he would take. So, she decided, getting to her feet, that was all she would offer.

She brushed her teeth with the extra brush he'd given her, washed her face, combed her hair, then dressed quickly. Picking up the blanket, she opened the door and walked out into the empty bedroom. She assumed he was in one of the other rooms, avoiding her, but a glance out the window as she began making the bed showed she was wrong. He stood out there next to a pile of splintered wood, cement blocks and tattered pieces of tar paper. His back was to the house, his head down, and he was aimlessly poking through the rubble with one booted foot. He looked forlorn, alone, and she couldn't go to him.

She made the bed, then with nothing else to do, she took a seat at the rickety kitchen table, her hands folded in her lap. She sat there, the Cassidy composure drawn close around her, and waited.

That was where Rory found her when he returned nearly an hour later. Abruptly he stopped in the doorway, letting the screen door bang behind him, then slowly he entered the room, stopping a few feet in front of her.

When he spoke, his voice was hard, challenging, defiant. "You said your grandmother was a product of her environment. She couldn't help being smug and snooty and superior because that was the way she'd been taught. Well, *I* was taught that I was inferior. That I wasn't good enough to be around you. That I would defile you—your father's word, not mine. I believed him. I believed all of them." He slowly shook his head in dismay. "I'm as much a product of my environment as your grandmother was. I *know* I've done a lot to be proud of. I *know* I've achieved more than many people ever will. But as long as I live here, I'll never be more than that worthless, no-good Hawkes kid. I'll lose my pride and my self-respect. But more importantly, I'll lose *you*. You can't be proud of a man who isn't proud of himself. You can't respect a man who doesn't respect himself."

Shanna sat silently, breathlessly, as he came closer and knelt in front of her, reaching for her cold hands.

"Come away with me, Shanna," he said hoarsely. "Marry me and have my children and teach me what it's like to be loved by a princess."

The tears welled in her eyes again, but she didn't speak.

She was waiting, Rory realized, to hear the most important words of all. The words he'd never said to another woman. The words he would never say to another woman. "I love you, Shanna—not for a week or a month or a year, but for always. Forever."

That was all it took—just those three words—and she was on her knees, too, her arms around his neck, her tears wetting his cheeks as she kissed him. "I do love you, Rory," she whispered.

She would always be a Cassidy, he thought as he held her close, and he would always be a Hawkes, but that didn't mean they had to be bound by the same foolish prejudices that had dogged generations of Cassidys and Hawkeses before them. As she'd told him a few days ago in the hospital...

Things change, you know.

The small radio station just south of Sandy Spring rarely had any real news to report. Market prices and weather—those were the only matters of any real importance for its listeners. But at noon Thursday the owner, general manager and full-time DJ skipped the market report and went straight into the news. "Local businessman Lawrence Channing was arrested by FBI agents last evening at his home. Channing, who has widespread business interests in Sandy Spring and West Texas, is a suspect in the recent bombing murder of District Attorney Joseph Cassidy. Channing is also believed to be involved in the disappearance and suspected murder of Wayne Singleton, a local accountant who was employed by Channing.''

He paused briefly for effect, then returned to his routine announcements. ''The weather for today...''

FOUR UNIQUE SERIES
FOR EVERY WOMAN YOU ARE...

Silhouette Romance®

Tender, delightful, provocative—stories that capture the laughter, the tears, the *joy* of falling in love. Pure romance...straight from the heart!

SILHOUETTE *Desire*®

Go wild with Desire! Passionate, emotional, sensuous stories of fiery romance. With heroines you'll like and heroes you'll *love*, Silhouette Desire never fails to deliver.

Silhouette Special Edition®

Stories of love and life, these powerful novels are tales that you can identify with—romances with "something special" added in! Silhouette Special Edition is entertainment for the heart.

SILHOUETTE·INTIMATE·MOMENTS™

Enter a world where passions run hot and excitement is the rule. Dramatic, larger-than-life and always compelling—Silhouette Intimate Moments will never let you down.